J.M. Productions info@JacinthMediaProductions.com
www.JacinthMediaProductions.com

Paperback ISBN: 978-1-960594-18-1

Hardback ISBN: 978-1-960594-17-4

Digital Online ISBN: 978-1-960594-20-4

Library of Congress Control Number: 2023942928

Book printed in the United States

Editor Acknowledgment

Big shout out to my editor DML Editing and Writing (Dominique Lambright) for molding and perfecting my story. You have truly captured my vision, captured my voice and made it better. I appreciate the effort and time you took on my project. It takes a person with a clear vision and a general love for fantasy stories, to understand the writer's point of view and transform it into the beautiful work of art it was meant to be. Thank you!

RETURN OF THE OWL

BY

MAURICE M. MCCALLUM

In "Return of the Owl" by author Maurice M. McCallum, readers are transported to the town of Belle Isle, where a seemingly peaceful community hides a sinister secret. Haunted by the piercing cries of her baby brother in the dark of night, seventeen-year-old Analisa Kelly embarks on a perilous quest to uncover the malevolent presence that threatens their town. Through McCallum's skillful storytelling, readers will be captivated by the unfolding secrets, unexpected challenges, and difficult choices that shape Analisa's transformative journey. Themes of friendship and sacrifice are woven throughout this enthralling story and will leave readers on the edge of their seats, eagerly turning pages to uncover the secrets that lie within Belle Isle.

CONTENTS

CHAPTER ONE
THE STRANGE ILLNESS

The thick air pierced my lungs as I ran through the bushy hill. Its hideous screech echoed. I turned to its dark red eyes glaring at me. Its wings flapped like a hurricane in the night. I hid behind the tallest tree and waited. My heart raced like a V8 engine, and my eyes darted everywhere. Suddenly, there was a loud thud and another. My eyes met with a pair of red ones. It opened its beak….

Ring!! Ring!! Ring!!!

"Ugh!!"

I looked over at the clock and banged it to make it stop. These dreams were giving me constant migraines.

"ANALISA! WAKE UP. IT'S TIME FOR BREAKFAST!" shouted my mother from the kitchen. "COME NOW, OR I'LL EAT YOUR SHARE."

My mother had a weird sense of humor. A dark humor. If there's one thing you never do, it is play with someone's food. I loved food. I stretched so long that I didn't realize I rolled off the bed, landing right on my face. It hurt so much, but I just wanted to lie face down on the floor without getting up. My grandmother always said a person who slept too much or slept too late always woke up a fool. I never understood what that meant or if it even made sense. Old people have always been hard to figure out with their weird proverbs. I tried my best not to understand them either; I didn't have the time or patience. My grandmother lived a couple of distances from us, but she wasn't here. She was staying in Negril for a month with one of her cousins before she came back.

I was born Analisa Margaret Kelly. Named after my grandaunt Annalise. A second-year sixth-form student at the Mount Tech High School in Belle Isle District, an old but peaceful town. In May of this year, I turned 17. It was a milestone in my life I wasn't fully prepared for.

I lived with my mother, Margaret, and my baby brother Romaine, eight months old. He was a cute little rascal, annoying when he cried, but I loved him very much.

"ANALISA MARGARET KELLY!!! I WILL NOT CALL YOU AGAIN!" She sounded more annoyed and used my full name, which was never a good sign. I'm pretty sure she would send me to school without food this morning if I didn't come out immediately.

"Alright, alright, Mommy, I'm coming. You don't need to yell."

When my parents moved here, we lived in a one-bedroom house. Angus Kelly, my late father, thought it was time to make additions and graced me with a room and a bathroom of my own.

As a 7-year-old, I hoped for a bedroom, and now that I'm 17, it's become my retreat, a place that is mine. A heart-shaped mirror is what my dad made for me and I loved it very much. My grandmother sewed a rag doll out of cotton fabric for my eighth birthday, and I've kept it on my dresser for quite some time without ever shifting it.

Eventually, I gave away most of my toys and all the childish things. So instead of toys, I had posters on my wall of reggae artists I admired, from Vybz Kartel to Spice, to Tessanne Chin, Queen Ifrica, and others. I've experimented with a variety of alternative rock music, hip-hop, and pop.

My mother didn't fancy my choice of music at all, and she always scolded me if I listened to them in the house.

After washing my face and brushing my teeth, I dashed toward the kitchen. The old floorboards creaked with each step. I entered, and my mother was at the stove fixing the last batch of pancakes and eggs, my absolute favorite.

Romaine sat in his chair, making a mess of himself with his mashed potatoes and making the sweetest cooing sounds ever. I moved over to play with him, and he stared at me, reached for my face, and gnawed at it with his toothless mouth.

"No time to waste, Analisa; hurry and eat so you can get ready for school."

"I can't rush the food like that, Mommy; you want me to get sick?"

She turned and looked at me with the sternest expression but said nothing. She walked over and slammed the plate and the cup of cocoa on the table. The smell took hold of me and slapped me senseless with its tantalizing aroma. I took the syrup off the table and smothered the pancakes with so much of it that some dripped off the plate. I used my fingers to scoop up the rest of the heavenly sweetness off the edge of the plate and greeted it with my lips. I dug in.

"Oh, Mommy, Mr. Francis wants you to come by school this afternoon," I said with my mouth covered in syrup and pastry.

"For what reason?"

"Today is a consultation. I told you last week. Since you missed the last one, he's urging you to come to this one today."

"You told me?" She asked, astonished. "First off, you and I seem to communicate differently because I don't recall you telling me anything about any consultation. I don't know if I can make it this afternoon. Tell him next time I have a lot of errands to run."

I rolled my eyes.

"Whatever," I muttered under my breath.

"WHAT WAS THAT?"

"Nothing, Mommy," I answered.

She walked up to me with the wooden spatula in her hand, waving it in my face. I leaned back to avoid being slapped.

"You're not too old to get a spanking. So, you better push back your eyes in the back of your head. I gave you them, and I can take them back from you."

I ate to avoid any more tension. She gave me the death stare to ensure I finished in time. After drinking my last drop of cocoa, I left the table, ran to my room, took off my clothes, and hopped right into the shower.

I always took pride in looking pristine as I got ready for school. I leapt towards the kitchen, grabbed an apple from out of the fridge, and headed to the front door, but my mother blocked my path.

"Mommy! You tell me to hurry and get ready, and now you are blocking me."

"I wanted to make sure you're all set for school," she said, looking at me like I was going to get lost or something. She had that same expression when I started primary school.

"You realize I'm a grown woman now. This is not my first time getting ready," I said proudly.

"Child, shut up. You live in my house, and you're still a child."

She fixed my uniform and admired my prefect badge.

"Sixth former or not, grown woman or not, you're still my baby, and I will always protect you. I love you." She whispered, hugging me tight like I was about to leave home and never come back. I gave in and hugged her back.

"Alright, now go on," she said lovingly.

A familiar face came strolling down the road. A tall, scraggy, young boy named Dean Walters, a sixth former like myself, a bookworm, bright, a true gentleman. But there was something that I always found infuriating about him. His clumsiness. He was the clumsiest person in all of Belle Isle, but as he grew, it lessened — somewhat. He came down the road with his books, then one of them flung open and out flew what seemed to be a million sets of papers.

"No, no, no, no, oh, COME ON!!" He screamed out.

As the papers flew, so did Dean as he flung his arms about. My mother and I stood there watching him, trying to jump and catch them. We guffawed. They fell on the ground, and he took his time trying to pick them up. My mother and I had fun at his expense, but then she stopped. She needed the laugh. She hadn't laughed like that in years, and seeing her happy was a personal joy for me.

"Poor boy, haha. Alright, go help him, and the two of you get on the bus now."

"Yes, Mommy, I love you."

I blew her a kiss and waved to Romaine, who had no clue what was going on.

"I love you too."

"Good morning, Mrs. Kelly!" shouted Dean, waving to my mother furiously.

I shook my head. My mother felt sorry for him and waved back, then went inside.

I didn't want him to feel any more embarrassed, so I walked towards Dean to lend a hand.

"You can't help being clumsy for one day, can you?"

He looked up at me and frowned.

"Make fun. It seems like only when I come around you, bad things happen."

"I'm going to pretend I never heard that," I said, picking up his papers.

"I worked very hard on this English assignment. 4000-word essays are nothing to joke about. I barely got any sleep."

My mouth puffed up, trying to hold in the laughter. Dean glared at me and walked faster because he thought I was making fun of him, which I was a bit. I caught up with him and tried to cheer him up.

"Look, stop taking it to heart, okay? Don't make a big deal out of it. You're smart, and you always ace anything you put your mind to."

As we got closer to the bus stop, we saw other children there as well. Lower school students who had backpacks the size of inflatable parachutes. First-form students were always the most enthusiastic bunch, eager to attain knowledge. One sat reading a rather thick book. A psychology text judging by the size.

I remember when I was that studious, eager to read anything I could get my hands on, to learn about the mysteries of the universe.

Education was important in my family since I was the only one to complete high school. I was thankful, however; the pressure was too much to handle, though they provided me with the best, giving me whatever they could, so I could reach this milestone in my life.

We saw a bus coming down the road. The students steadied themselves and tightened their bags firmly on their backs, waiting. Dean and I stood a couple of feet away from them — then…. I heard a strange sound.

Caw!!! Caw!!!

I looked up and glimpsed two strange birds — two big black crows, to be exact — hovering above in the trees, looking down at us with their dark hollow blue eyes, twitching their heads back and forth. They made me uneasy. Dean looked up and saw them, too. He shivered.

"I hate crows."

I tried to be the courageous one for both of us. The birds seemed like they were taunting us, which was very unusual. The bus stopped, and I had never been so happy. We all took turns going up the steps. The bus was full, but I spotted two empty seats at the back.

"Dean, I found two seats. Come on," I said, pulling him as quickly as I could.

We sat down, and I peeked out the window. I looked up at the tree. The two birds were gone. There was one thing Dean and I had in common: we hated blackbirds. Whenever we saw one, we turned in the opposite direction. They scared the living hell out of us, and there was always a myth tied around black birds or anything considered black, deaths, omens, that sort of thing.

The bus drove off, and the journey was quiet — with slight chatter from the excited young first formers. The sun outside was radiant, and you could see the lush trees and grass illuminated by its brightness. Dean and I always took the bus together, even when we were younger. Our parents used to take us on rides to go up the hill on weekends and look at the beautiful trees, pick fresh mangoes, big ones too, and Breadfruit.

Dean loved climbing the trees. He would always get excited when his father took him up to the hill with him on his shoulder. He would let Dean climb and show him how far he could go. But even at a young age, Dean was still a klutz. He would always go home with another bruise, each time on different sections of his body.

My father always took me to get ice cream. He bought the chocolate-flavored one because he knew that was my favorite, and we would walk hand in hand down the road, just walk, a special father-daughter moment. We sat on the rocks, looking up at the sky, watched the stars twinkle, and he would sit me in his lap, and we would count them together. But the greatest memory I will always cherish of my father was when we would paint my grandmother's house every weekend. He would take the paint and put some on my nose. When he did that, he knew he always started a paint war; and at that young age, I was very energetic, so he couldn't keep up, but it was fun. Those were the times I missed with him. He never knew his parents growing up, so he did his best to give me the love I needed.

As we neared the school gate, we looked outside, and students walked into the compound. It was almost 7:00, so Dean and I made sure that we were at the gate before 7:15, which was when the gate was to be closed.

Dean and I headed inside through the first gate with the rest of the students, and we made it past the palm trees, then the second gate. They stopped some students because they were in lower form, and because we were sixth formers, we had more privileges. Last year, starting sixth form was nerve-wracking — the work we had to put in was stressful. However, it proved beneficial because later, it would push us further to see what colleges we would attend and what jobs we would attain. I didn't think that far ahead yet.

The classes were fewer, not many students, which meant a better working environment. You were a kind of substitute teacher, and you had a certain power over the lower school students; if they disrespected you, you had all rights to punish them or send them to the principal. But sometimes, a little abuse of power was warranted.

Principal Stewart, a pudgy man with thick glasses, waddled towards us, always walking with his hands interlocked behind his back.

"Miss Kelly, Mr. Walters," he said, standing upright, his belly protruding like a big blimp.

"Good morning, Principal Stewart."

"I hope you two are ready for the community outreach programme end of this semester. All sixth formers are required to complete it before leaving their final year, but you already know that."

A fake smile crept up. But I tried to cooperate without looking disinterested.

"Sir, since we're six formers, shouldn't we have some of the privileges of choosing where to go? Last year, I wasn't too fond of the children's home. Down there was very funky, and I was very uncomfortable. The boys down there are also 'too' friendly."

"Miss Kelly, the children who occupy those homes have nowhere else to go, and while I understand your frustration with their…. sanitary conditions and behaviour, it is our duty to make sure that they receive the proper care as much as possible. You two are some of the finest students on this campus. So, I'm sure you will set such an example hmmm? Besides…. we choose where the students go, sixth form or otherwise."

"We will do our best, sir. You can count on us," Dean said.

I frowned at Dean. Principal Stewart beamed with delight.

"Excellent, Dean; now off to devotion, you two."

"Yes, sir."

"Very good," he quipped.

He walked off, still with his hands behind him, until he spotted two-second formers running on the compound. He shook his finger at them, but they paid him no mind. Instead, he tried to do the unthinkable and ran after them. Dean and I looked on and laughed, then I punched him on the arm.

"Ow! What's that for?"

"Are you daft? Why did you volunteer for us to go back to that place? Was I the only one that felt like they wanted to throw up? You know I hate that place. Anywhere else would have been good."

"You need to calm down, man. It's the only place we are familiar with. It's also an easy credit to get."

I didn't like that he was right. That was one of his many qualities, so I agreed.

"Fine, but you are feeding them this time. I'm going to sweep the rooms. Let them get handsy with you for a change," I said, walking off.

Dean's expression changed as if he had realized the grave mistake he made.

"Wah… what you mean, handsy?"

We arrived at the hall and looked inside. One of the lower form classes was conducting devotion. I opened my bag, took out my timetable and skimmed through it.

"What class do you have after this?"

Dean took out his timetable as well.

"I have Science, YES!" he said with great excitement.

"I've never seen a boy this excited about class before. Anyway, I have Comm Studies. After third period, we have free time, so we can practice some math then."

"Okay," he said, shoving the timetable back in his bag.

After devotion, I opened my locker and took out my Communication Studies text and notebook and placed my bag inside. By the time I closed it, another familiar face popped up at my locker and I almost had a heart attack. My other friend, Hanna Greenwood, quirky and mischievous, had a habit of appearing at places that I never knew when she was coming.

"Are you wearing silent shoes or something?"

She looked at me and smiled.

"Good morning to you too, friend. Tell me, what do you call a friend who tries to call another friend, but the other friend failed to pick up her phone? You know how phones work, right? When someone calls, there is a red button and a blue button. Guess which one you press?" She asked jokingly.

"The red one." I closed my locker and walked off. She followed me.

"I'm serious. You forgot about that thing again," Hanna said. "You promised you would have met with the girls. "

"I know I promised you, but I was just busy, okay? You know I have to help around the house, plus I have lots a studying to do."

"Analisa, we all have lots of studying to do. You need to come with a better excuse. So, can we try again next weekend?"

"Hanna, I can try. Just let me think about it."

She looked at me disappointed, but nodded in agreement.

We entered class and sat in our seats. The sixth form classes were empty, so we just took seats anywhere, but today, there was an actual full class. Our Comm Studies teacher walked in and slammed her books down on the table, looking at us — a familiar face that made me smile. Her name was Miss Wynters, a beautiful woman, short dark hair with nice fitted glasses. I have always admired her. She has been teaching me since second form — a brilliant teacher who always had an interest in her students' well-being.

"Good morning, all."

"Good morning, Miss Wynters."

"It's nice to see you all bright and early. I hope you had a pleasant weekend and are now ready to work. Now, turn your books to page 97 and let's pick up where we left off last week… Awareness." She turned to the board and started writing while the rest of us took out our books.

Later, after school, I visited Mr. Murray's Meat shop — a small dwelling near my house. I ate nothing at school today because the cafeteria food alone was cause for deliberate starvation. Many students I remember got food poisoning from eating whatever tasteless concoction they were making. Plus…. Mr. Murray's Fry chicken and oxtail were some of the best meals you ever tasted in the entire district. Fried Chicken was one of my favourites. He pulled a lot of customers just by the aroma alone.

I walked up, and he looked over at me and smiled. I was his favourite customer — so he always looked forward to seeing me.

"If it isn't my Miss Kell Kell, how you been? Haven't seen you in a while… wondering when you were going to pass by," he said, wiping his hands on a cloth after seasoning meat.

"I know, I know, I'm starving. You already know what I want."

"You insult me Analisa, you don't think I know that?" He asked. "I will hook you up real nice."

He took the foil off the big round pan he had on the table. Steam spewed from the pot. The heat and the smell greeted me with such delight.

Ten minutes later, I walked out with the heaviest box of food I had ever eaten. Fried Chicken, with curried gravy, macaroni pasta, rice and peas, the works. Grease flowed everywhere. The food smelled so good I wanted to devour it right there. But I wanted to wait until I got home, so I could sit down and enjoy the succulent taste of the best-fried chicken in Belle Isle district.

Suddenly, I felt a chill, like the hair on the back of my neck stiffened. I turned around, as I had the strangest feeling that someone was following me. The trees swayed from side to side and the breeze moaned. I opened my bag and took out my phone; it made this static sound. I swiped it, and pressed the home button. Nothing came up, just loud static. It was strange.

I tightened the grip on my bag and continued walking. My house was just a couple feet away, but I still felt a strange presence. It was getting bleak, and I felt uneasy. Then — CAW!!! CAW!!!

I jumped at the horrific sound and looked up…. the same two crows I saw in the trees earlier. They were here again, looking down at me. Each time I moved, their heads would follow; and I could swear I saw one of them frowning at me. I trembled; I could barely move.

"Le… leave me alone."

The crows turned their heads to the side. What were they looking at? I turned in the direction they were staring, across the road in the bushes — what I saw made me flinch. I froze. There, in the bushes, stood a very grotesque-looking figure — an old woman with shriveled hair, pale skin, red eyes, and crooked sharp teeth. She was holding on to a stick and had an old torn up shawl over her head. I looked back up in the tree; the crows disappeared. I turned to the bushes; the woman was no longer there…

…. she was now in front of me.

She pointed at me with her long-crooked fingers and let out a high pitch shriek. Her jaws extended.

I screamed so loud that I dropped the box of food, held on to my bag and ran as fast as I could. I kept looking back, thinking she was chasing me.

Reached my house and bolted through the door, not seeing my mother in the chair playing with Romaine.

"Ana…," she called out, but I was already long past her.

Ran into my room and slammed the door, breathing as hard as ever. I turned and collapsed onto my bed right away, staring at the ceiling. What was that? Who was that? I heard many weird things happened in this town, but I was never one for superstition. Whoever I saw did not look human, and if I told anyone, I don't think they would ever believe me.

My mother knocked on my door. I was too frightened to move. My body was so stiff that it felt like I was having a seizure and my heart was running on pure adrenaline. My mother kept pounding on the door harder and harder.

"Analisa, why did you come storming in the house like that? You lose you manners?" She asked, hammering away at the door.

"I'm okay, Mommy, just a little tired, sorry."

I was born asthmatic, so I was prone to panic attacks when I was excited or when I ran too fast.

The pounding stopped, and I could hear her walking off. My heartbeat slowed, but I could still glimpse that thing I saw in the bushes. How did she get in front of me so fast? I couldn't get it out of my head now, but I had to, because I had a lot of homework to do.

Nighttime came, and I was tired. I had books laid out on my bed doing math equations. My eyes felt very heavy, like two duffle bags pulling down on my face.

"ANALISA! Dinner is ready!"

"Coming!"

I felt bad for letting Mr. Murray's food go to waste. My stomach was growling, and I needed to eat. So, I got up and went to the bathroom. I turned on the light and looked at myself in the mirror; lack of sleep was clear, as my eyes were droopy. I turned on the pipe and splashed water on my face to rejuvenate. Few splashes more and I felt a little better.

I wiped my face on the towel hanging on the rack, then stood there looking at myself. Relaxation came over me…. until I heard a sound.

CREAK!

The slow creak got my attention. I peeked into my room and looked around. I thought I was losing my mind, because there was nothing in my room that made that creaking sound. So, I played it off as just my brain being tired from all the studying.

CREAK! CREAK!

It got louder this time. My heart pounded again, and I turned off the light in the bathroom. I walked out and approached my bed. The sound stopped. I didn't move for a while, as I believed it was all in my head.

CREAK!

The sound came from outside of my room. I walked to the door and opened it. The house was too quiet, and the lights were flickering. I didn't hear my mother shouting at the top of her voice with her friend over the phone, which was a regular thing during dinner, or Romaine making baby noises and banging something with his toy. I walked gingerly into the kitchen; the pot was still lit under the stove, and my mother and brother were nowhere to be found.

"Mommy, where are you?" I asked in a panicked tone.

I walked towards the stove and turned off the fire under the pot. I looked up at the cupboard glass, glaring at my reflection, but I saw something else — a dark shadow floating by outside the kitchen. My eyes widened as I turned around. I thought it was my imagination playing tricks on me again, but it felt real.

CREAK! CREAK!

The sound came again from the living room. I walked out of the kitchen towards where the sound got louder. I heard it again, like a rocking chair.

The lights flickered more in the living room. I looked around and saw this old, battered rocking chair in the middle. All the furniture had disappeared, and it was just the one rocking chair in the centre.

I approached the chair as it continued to rock. As I got closer, the rocking stopped. I walked around and looked…. no one was there, except for a portrait of a baby and baby laughter echoing throughout the living room, then it stopped. For a second, I thought it was Romaine.

The creaking started yet again, but now…. it had rhythm and it was closer. My heart was pounding as I heard footsteps behind me. I could hear heavy breathing, like someone had mucus on their chest. I wanted to turn, but a rush of warm air washed over the back of my neck, sending chills up my spine. The footsteps stopped — and I could feel the hot foul breath breathing on me…. my breathing became erratic. I cringed as I felt my hair being tugged and twirled as if it was being played with. My whole body trembled, not knowing who was behind me. I clenched my fist and closed my eyes.

"You're not real — you're not real — you're not real."

I spun around, but nothing was there…. nothing but the breeze from the window and the curtain swaying towards me.

The chair rocked again.

I turned slowly and there it was… sitting, the old woman, grotesque and ugly, sitting in the chair with the portrait in her hand, her red eyes piercing through my skull.

She lashed out at me, shrieking something awful. The portrait fell on the floor and her hands were outstretched towards me. I closed my eyes…. screaming my lungs out. Then, I felt hands grabbing and shaking me.

"Analisa! Analisa!!"

I opened my eyes and saw my mother. I looked around the living room and everything was back to normal. Romaine was on the ground, playing with his squeaky toy. My mother continued to hold on to me, looking at me like I was going mad…. which, to be honest, I was.

"What happened to you? You walk out of your room like you were sleepwalking. I called to you, you wouldn't answer, then you started screaming, are you okay?"

"I don't know, Mommy."

"You want me to carry you to the doctor? Don't want your asthma to act up again."

"No! I just want to sleep. I have school tomorrow."

I walked away from her and went to my room.

Next morning, I woke up realizing that I hadn't finished my homework. Exhaustion was killing me and I thought I was losing my mind. I didn't care. I hated math, and it didn't matter to me if I failed it. Had barely scraped through CSEC Math and I wasn't planning on doing it over. I was too occupied with all the strange things I had been seeing. Math equations were the least of my problems.

My head was pounding, and I just wanted to lie in bed the whole day and do nothing. I took up my phone and scrolled through. There were 19 messages from Dean and Hanna. I read through a couple of Dean's messages and most of his messages were conversations about schoolwork.

"Ann, remember we have a history test this week. When you wanna meet up to study? Or you want me to come by your place, either way, is fine."

His texts went on and on about the Haitian revolution and how he found the whole topic fascinating, and we had to talk about it.

I smiled and shook my head. I loved him, but sometimes he could be a bit of a nerd.... too much.

His last text read:

"Ann, this is the last message I am sending, and even though you're not replying, I'm going to send it, anyway. Principal Andrews wants us to sign off on the children's home trip before the week's finished. Just giving you heads up. See you tomorrow and please answer you bloody texts. Bye."

I rolled my eyes in annoyance. I forgot about the children's home visit. Not that I was thinking about it, I just didn't want to go. I didn't bother to read Hanna's texts because I knew what those were about. It was the same thing, about coming to her girl group meeting. I told her I would not make any promises, that I would try, but still having second thoughts. I wasn't one to break promises, but I wasn't going to go to see a bunch of her snotty friends. She wanted me to go so badly.

I walked out into the living room and sat around the table. I looked over at Romaine in his highchair, smiling. I couldn't help but smile back. He made me feel better. He was so innocent, not knowing about the ugliness of the world.

"How you feeling now?" My mother asked, concerned.

"My head still hurts."

My mother finished frying the egg and sausage, took out two slices of bread, and slapped the egg in between. Poured me a cup of cocoa and brought it to me. Then she massaged my face and my hair. I looked up at her.

"Anything bothering you? You know you can come to me, right?" She asked.

"Yes, Mommy, I know."

"So, are you going to tell me what had you screaming so loud last night?"

I wanted to tell her what I saw. I wanted to tell her how I saw some strange woman who was following me, but I didn't want her to think I was crazy and send me to Bellevue strapped to a gurney.

"I was just having a bad dream."

My mother picked Romaine up and started nibbling at his cheeks. He laughed and grabbed at her face.

"Well, when people have nightmares, they're in bed, not walking around the house, and you kept saying, baby."

"Baby?" I asked, puzzled.

"Yes, you kept repeating the same word, 'baby'. I don't know what it means. Anyway, get ready for school," she said, walking out of the kitchen with Romaine.

I sat there eating my breakfast and stared into space, trying to figure out what was happening to me and what it all meant. My mother said I said baby more than once and whatever happened, whether it was a hallucination, I saw a portrait of a baby, but whose baby was it? I was clueless, but I knew it had to mean something. I ate like a horse because of not having any dinner last night. Even though it was hot, I got up and gulped down my cocoa.

An hour and a half later, I was on the bus by myself; it was half empty. I was sure the school gate was off limits because it was now 7:20 and Dean had already left early. I sat in the back, looking out, clinging to my thoughts about what happened to me. As I mentioned before, I had seen lots of strange things.... not sure I would classify them as strange, but more… peculiar. I mean peculiar like Dean trying to fit into jeans that couldn't fit him, or Maya Ainsworth who tried to do a Michael Jackson moonwalk, which went horribly…wrong…. or when the principal tried to do the split at a barbecue in front of the entire school and ripped his pants until everybody started calling him *Ripley's* — but never anything like this. I've encountered nothing like this before.

The two crows and that old woman were connected somehow. Why were they always following me? All these thoughts plagued my brain so much, I couldn't concentrate on anything else.

The bus stopped near the school gate and I stepped out. The security guard was at the gate sitting down, or for better term, slumped over with his cap down over his face, snoring like a wild pig. As the bus drove off, I tiptoed past the security, so he didn't hear me. I pushed the gate and looked over at the snoring beauty. The gate was rather noisy, so I did my best not to wake him.

I finally got in and rushed to my first class. It was sociology, and it was only for one session, so I had to make every minute count. I ran towards the classroom door and stormed in. Everyone stopped writing and looked at me. I didn't pay attention to all the wandering eyes. I just brushed past them.

The teacher, Mr. Planket, a very short man with stubby fingers, looked me up and down.

"This is not like you to be late, Miss Kelly. Please hurry and sit."

"Yes, sir," I said, almost out of breath.

I dashed to my seat and sat next to Dean. While Mr. Planket continued writing on the board, Dean leaned over to me.

"Hey, what happened last night?"

"What do you mean?"

"You know what I mean, I texted you, and you never replied."

"I was asleep alright. I was tired from practicing math all night," I said, very agitated.

"What's going on with you?"

"Can we not do this now? Later after class we can talk."

"Miss Kelly," said Mr. Planket.

I looked up as he was watching me.

"Yes, sir."

"Miss Kelly, you're already late, so I expect you to either start working or keep quiet."

"Sir, I wasn't doing anything." I exclaimed.

"ENOUGH!"

The entire class jumped. You could hear a pin drop because of the deafening silence.

I felt embarrassed and didn't know what to do or say. I was always taught never to disrespect an adult, especially a teacher. Still, I was also taught never to take disrespect, either. They always knew me to be very feisty, but I had to learn to control myself, so I bit my tongue and said nothing. Dean held his head down.

Mr. Planket stood by the blackboard, looking down at me, twiddling the marker between his fingers.

"I was going to provide this question for the entire class. But since you insisted on interrupting, I will provide you the opportunity to answer this, Miss Kelly."

He finished writing the question and then turned to me.

"Now.... we know that sociology is the study of social behaviour or society, including its origins, development, organization, networks, and institutions. It is a social science that uses various methods of empirical investigation and critical analysis to develop a body of knowledge about social order, disorder, and change. Dehumanization and super-humanization are two sides of the same coin serving a racist agenda. Tell me, Miss Kelly, what is dehumanization?"

Everyone turned to me, looking for the answer. The blank look on their faces was a clear sign they had no clue themselves or were too afraid to answer. I didn't enjoy being put on the spot, but it didn't matter… I answered, anyway.

"Dehumanization is the process by which conscious and unconscious bias leads people to see a racial minority as less human–less worthy of respect, dignity, love, peace, and protection," I answered.

The class murmured in approval and Mr. Planket looked disappointed by the sullen look on his face, as he expected me not to get the answer correctly. But to remain professional, he formed a fake smile.

"Well done, Miss Kelly."

After class, I walked out with my books gripped under my arm. Dean followed me and seemed elated.

"Yow, that was amazing. You saw the look on his face? Nobody ever showed him up likethat before. You know he's going to give you a hard time now."

"I don't care."

Dean stopped. I turned to him.

"Alright, you going to tell me what's going on with you?"

I couldn't bother with Dean asking too many questions, but he was my best friend, and I never kept things from him.

"Alright fine. Meet me under the tree at lunchtime."

During lunch, I sat under the tree waiting for Dean. I had my tablet on the Google web search looking for anything that could tell me about spirits and supernatural occurrences. I was never a believer of the supernatural, but I've heard my grandparents and even my father telling me duppy stories over the years that had me scared of sleeping in the dark. I played it off as just stories, figments of my imagination.

 I was hoping not to find anything, but I wanted to see something, as it would further prove to my theory that what I saw was real. I scrolled through the images section and saw various depictions of monsters, evil spirits, and witches, but nothing resembling what I saw. When I looked up, I saw Dean walking towards me. Hanna followed after.

I didn't want her involved in this, but she was my friend too, and whatever happened, I wanted people around who I could trust and who wouldn't think I was crazy.

Dean and Hanna sat down opposite me.

"Hey, Ann, what's up?" She asked cheerfully.

"You look happy today."

"She's always like that," Dean chimed in.

"I sent you 100 messages last night, and no reply. I think you're ignoring me. Why?"

"I'm sorry, just wasn't in the chatting mood,"

"Offer still open, you know."

"Give the girl a break," Dean retorted.

Hanna and Dean both gave each other mean looks like they were about to tear each other's head off.

"Next time, mind your own business. I was talking to Analisa."

"Look, Hanna, we'll talk about that some other time, okay? Not in the right frame of mind right now."

"What's wrong?"

I closed my tablet and leaned back, thinking about what to say without sounding positively mad.

"I've been seeing things. Things I can't explain, or comprehend, but some weird things have been happening. You remember those crows we saw at the bus stop?"

"Yeah," Dean said after he blanked them out of his mind.

"Well, I was coming home from school right…. and I stopped by Mr. Murray to buy some food. When I left, I saw the birds again… it seemed like they were following me, but I wish that was the only problem."

"What was the other problem? Asked Hanna, curious yet excited, as if I was telling a fairy tale.

"I saw a woman, a very… ugly old woman, and I know that sounds harsh, but…. guys, this woman did not look human at all… she had red eyes and rotten teeth. She was so scary, and I saw her… again, at my house."

Dean and Hanna looked as if they didn't want to hear anymore but were ripe with curiosity.

"So… she knows you? Where did she come from?"

"I don't know her, never saw her before in my life, that's the thing. That's not all, though. When I saw her again, she was in this rocking chair, holding an ancient portrait of a baby."

"A baby?" Asked Hanna.

I tried to understand what it meant. It was all too puzzling.

"Yeah, I told you, it was strange. But I'm telling you guys, once was enough, but twice. Something is going on."

Dean and Hanna looked at each other, and I knew they thought I was crazy.

"Guys, I sound crazy, I know, but you know me. I don't make stuff up and I don't lie unless I need to. If you see me looking stressed, you know something is wrong."

"I believe you," said Hanna quickly.

"You know I believe anything. So, you think you will see her again?" asked Dean.

"I hope not. But I want to know why I saw that baby portrait."

"Maybe you were dreaming. You know dreams never normally make sense," Hanna replied.

"I know, but the thing is…. I wasn't dreaming… at least I don't think I was."

*****

Later, at home, I was in the kitchen feeding Romaine.

He didn't enjoy the mashed potatoes, which is what my mother always gave him; but I imitated eating it to see if that would make him want it. It didn't work. But I still tried. Every time I fed him, he would bang the table, spit out the food, then smile at me. I guess eating mashed potatoes every day was nothing fun. Even he knew that.

My mother walked in with groceries and placed them on the counter. She had on boots and brown overalls, which meant she just came from the farm. It impressed her when she looked into the sink and saw that I had washed the plates.

"Imagine that, and I didn't even have to knock you upside the head." She said, smiling.

"Hilarious Mommy. I am mature, you know."

Romaine looked up and was excited when he saw her jumping up and down in his highchair.

"Yes, baby, Mommy is here. You eating up your potatoes? Yesssssssss, give Mommy a kiss," she said, kissing him all over.

She took him out of his chair and danced with him.

"You finished all your homework?"

"Got two and finished them already," I answered.

"Okay, good… I'm going to sit with Romaine for a little. Dinner will be ready soon."

"Ahm, Mommy, don't you think you need to like freshen up first?" I asked, covering my nose.

She inspected herself, then looked at me. She smiled.

"This is what hard work does to you, get you dirty. Alright, I'm going to bathe. I'm going to put him in his crib, monitor him till I come out." She said, walking out of the kitchen.

"Okay, Mommy." I took Romaine's plate, threw away the rest of the mashed potatoes, and washed out the plate.

Later that night, I was pretty much half asleep. Nothing to bother me or break my peace. But again, I spoke too soon… something did wake me. I hoped I wasn't hallucinating again. I heard a scream, an ear-splitting howl of pain. This time it wasn't a hallucination, this one was very much real. I opened my room door and crying was coming from my mother's room. I rushed in and saw my mother cradling Romaine and pacing back and forth. He was screaming bloody murder. Veins started popping from his neck. I never heard him cry like this before. It was terrifying.

"Mommy, what's wrong with him?"

"I… I don't know. He just started crying…. I don't know," she sobbed.

She placed her hands under his neck.

"He feels hot."

I went to feel his neck, and he was boiling, like boiling water hot. Then I looked under his neck and I saw a big black mark.

"Mommy, what's that?"

She looked under his neck and shook her head.

"We have to get him to the doctor."

"Yes, yes…. go put on something and grab some stuff," she blurted. "And find the number for the taxi, please."

"Yes, Mommy."

I stormed into my room, grabbed my bag, opened my drawer and took out two sheets, an extra shirt, and I was ready to go. Then I heard my mother shout out.

"ROMAINE!! ROMAINE!!"

I dashed towards her. My mother stood there, transfixed, holding Romaine. He stopped crying. He wasn't moving at all.

CHAPTER TWO
THE OMINOUS WARNING

W e arrived at the hospital, and we had been here about an hour, which to us felt like an eternity.

My mother and I sat outside the waiting room, frantic with worry; sheets covering us from the cold AC. I leaned on her shoulder with both feet up on the bench while she rested her head against the wall. It was 11:30, and I was still tired. I couldn't sleep because Romaine's sudden illness took a toll. Earlier, he was fine, and then his whole body heated with this strange mark under his neck. It was like a bad dream that I couldn't wake up from.

This was the one that had to be real. I got up and walked over to the snack machine to get two sandwiches. I've always heard about hospital food and how disgusting they were; but they couldn't be that bad, besides no one has ever tasted the junk they served at school — so I tried it. I got the two sandwiches and walked back over to the bench. They were tuna sandwiches which my mother and I loved a lot, especially with mayonnaise, lettuce, and tomato.

My mother was not in the best shape. She was fidgeting and sweating like she was about to have a seizure. Even with my best efforts trying to calm her down, it didn't seem to work in the least.

"He's going to be okay, Mommy. Do you want me to get you some tea?" I asked.

She looked over at me, smiled, and kissed my hand.

"No baby, I'm alright, just want to be here for Romaine."

I felt bad at how hard she worked being a single mother, balancing work, home, and taking care of two kids. It has been hard on all of us since my father passed. I tried to be the backbone of the family, but my mother always told me I was the daughter and she should take care of me. I know she meant well, but deep down, I could see it in her eyes that she was struggling, and I just wanted to be there for her.

As we continued to sit and wait, the Doctor stepped out. My mother and I both got up, eager to hear what the news was. He looked at us with his hands gripped on his waist and a look of despair across his face. The last time I saw that look was when they told us that my father took his last breath. My eyes welled up at the thought that I would lose my baby brother too, who had not yet had time to live his full life, to experience the world in all its glory…. and ugliness.

The doctor exhaled and looked at us.

"Miss Kelly, your son is breathing, but we believe he may have a high fever. I am, however concerned about the mark on his neck… It's nothing I have ever come across."

My mother and I tried not to get too emotional and listened to the doctor as he tried to explain.

"I checked him thoroughly, his blood level is normal, and I found nothing out of the ordinary. And you say he felt hot since this evening?" He asked.

"Yes doctor, earlier he was fine, laughing, playing, and I put him to sleep, and then a couple hours later, I woke up and he just started crying. I don't know what caused it.

"Sir, please tell us, is my brother going to be okay?" I asked, hoping to hear some good news.

"I don't know what's causing his sickness. It could be a mild fever. We could run some more test to be sure. What I can tell you to do is to make sure that he drinks lots of fluids. Keep him away from anything dirty he may want to grab, and he should be fine. I can keep him here for a couple of days and monitor him. If he's better before that, he can go home. In the meantime, Mrs. Kelly, I'm going to recommend two medications for him."

He took out a prescription pad from his jacket pocket and the pen from his top, and he scribbled on it.

"I'm going to prescribe acetaminophen and ibuprofen, which are safe and effective medicines for a baby. Give these to him two times a day before meals and it should decrease the discomfort and lower his body heat."

He hands her the prescription, she takes it.

"O… okay doctor, but… I'm going to stay here with him," said my mother.

"No problem. So far, I see nothing else wrong with him apart from the mild fever symptoms, he is fine, but just to be safe, we will watch him for the next couple of days then you can take him home if he improves… if not, you bring him right back, but just fill out the prescription, and we'll see from there. He should be happy having you here."

"Thank you so much, doctor, thank you, and what's your name, please?"

"Doctor Hinds," he said, smiling. He took out a card from his jacket pocket and handed it to my mother.

"Here is my number should you need to call."

"Thank you," my mother said, putting the card in her bag.

He turned and walked back into the room where Romaine was. We sat back down and breathed a sigh of relief, but Romaine was still sick, and he had to be monitored all the time now. How could I study? How could I go to school and do any form of class activity knowing he was sick and in pain?

I missed his laugh; I missed his baby noises, but we would not hear those for a couple of days, or even months. My mother looked confused when I looked at her. She closed her eyes and mumbled to herself, like she was praying.

I held on to her hand and she just looked at me and smiled. She leaned over and kissed me on my forehead.

"Thank you for being the strong one, baby girl. I'm going to stay here for a while with Romaine. You need to get some sleep; you have school in the next couple hours."

"I'm not going to school."

My mother stared at me, thinking that I lost my head.

"What you mean, you not going to school?"

"If I go to school, I will not concentrate, and you know I worry a lot. I'm going to be here thinking about Romaine and thinking about you. I want to be here with you."

"I know you do. But you have school, you have your future, and I don't want to interrupt that. I'm the mother, remember that, not the other way around."

I didn't bother to argue. She was the daughter of Mabel McCallum, strong headed just like her. Guess I was like her too.

My mother went into her purse, took some money, and handed it to me.

"Call a taxi and go straight home. Get some sleep. I will be here. I won't let your brother out of my sight."

I took out my phone and made the call. After telling the taxi where I was, he told me he would be there in fifteen minutes. I grabbed the towel from off the bench and shoved it into my bag.

I entered the room to check on Romaine. He cooed softly. He looked up at me with his wide eyes. I placed my fingers between his cute, stubby fingers, and he grabbed it. It was an emotional moment. Tears flowed down my cheeks, but I had to go.

"Love you, Romaine, please get better," I whispered. I then leaned over and kissed him on the forehead. I kissed my mother on the cheek and told her I was leaving. My mother looked at me and brushed my hair back.

"Get some sleep," she said.

"Don't think I will, but I'll try."

I hurried down the narrow corridor, through the sliding doors, and waited outside for the taxi to come. A taxi drove up to the hospital gate, blew his horn, and I walked over.

The taxi dropped me off at my gate. I paid him and got out. I opened the door and dragged myself in. There was no one else with me. My mother was at the hospital staying with Romaine.

The bags under my eyes were heavy as I observed myself through the mirror. I thought how awful I looked. I had school in a couple of hours and I needed at least eight hours of sleep. Dean and I had a history test to study for.

After putting on my pyjamas, I slipped under the covers and closed my eyes. Part of me wanted to stay awake and just wait for daylight to come, but even I couldn't fight sleep. I needed to find out who that old lady was and why she was following me.

Why no one else could see her was a mystery to me. I had no clue where to start.

The next day, I was sitting in Miss Wynter's class taking notes off the board. The topic was *"Types of Awareness."* Miss Wynters stopped writing on the board and turned to us.

"Lau Tzu said, *'The key to growth is the introduction of higher dimensions of consciousness into our awareness.'* Before you can improve anything, you must have an awareness of where you are." Miss Wynters explained. "Awareness is a relative concept. We may focus awareness on an internal state, such as a visceral feeling, or on external events through sensory perception. Awareness provides the raw material from which animals develop early, or subjective ideas about their experience. Insects have awareness that you are trying to swat them or chase after them. But insects do not have consciousness in the usual sense because they lack the brain capacity for thought and understanding. Now can anyone tell me what Self Awareness is and what it means?" asked Miss Wynters.

About three to four hands went up, and Miss Wynters found it daunting to keep calling on the same people over and over. I felt a swift breeze brush past my head. I looked around and there was Hanna, flinging her arms all over the place just to get noticed. She had been doing that all day and begged to be called on that Miss Wynters rolled her eyes and pointed at Hanna.

"Yes, Hanna, go ahead," Miss Wynters said. "But…. for the future, please allow others to answer. You're not the only one in the class," she pleaded.

Hanna nodded and answered. The other students chuckled.

"Having a clear perception of your personality, including strengths, weaknesses, thoughts, beliefs, motivation, and emotions. Self-Awareness allows you to understand other people, how they perceive you, your attitude and your responses to them at the moment," Hanna said. "This means that awareness of your own being, actions, and thoughts with a good understanding of how we relate to others, we can adjust our behaviour so that we deal with them positively. By understanding what upsets us, we can improve our self-control. And by understanding our weaknesses, we can learn how to manage them, and reach our goals despite them."

Miss Wynters didn't seem all too surprised, so she thanked her and told her to sit. The bell rang out and all the students who slept throughout the entire session had supersonic hearing. Some of them dashed out the door before anyone else could.

I packed up my books and was getting ready to leave, then Hanna came up to me.

"Hey… are you okay? Sorry to hear about your brother. My grandmother told me. How is he?"

I was hoping not to have this conversation about Romaine. I was worried about him enough as it is, and I didn't want to bring him up in any conversation. Then I looked over Hanna's shoulders. Miss Wynters waved at me, signaling. "I need to see you when you're through," she whispered. I looked back at Hanna.

"The doctor said he might have a high fever, but they're keeping him a couple days just to do some more tests. If he is okay, they will send him home."

"I hope he gets better and if you need anything, let me know."

"Thanks, Hanna, I appreciate it."

"Okay, see you at lunch. I'm going to the library for a bit."

I approached Miss Wynter's table while she was marking papers. "You wanted to see me, Miss?"

She looked up at me and smiled. "Yes Ann, please — sit," she insisted.

I sat in the chair. She crossed her fingers and stared at me. I stared back, but my eyes kept darting around the classroom because I was very uncomfortable.

"How are you, Analisa?" She asked.

"I'm…. fine Miss. Why do you ask?"

"Well, Ann, I know the past few days have been very difficult for you. This is your second year of sixth form, and it must seem quite daunting with the extra hard work, the responsibilities, less sleep I imagine."

It's like she was reading my mind, because I felt drained, like I wasn't achieving anything.

"I just want you to know, Analisa. If there is anything at all you want from me — I'm here for you," she said. "I've seen you grow up into the wonderful, mature young woman you've become, and I know…. that since your father passed, things have been difficult for you."

My father was the last thing I wanted to discuss, especially with any teacher.

"Is everything okay at hom—?"

"Miss, do we have to do this now?" I interrupted.

She looked at me for a minute, then smiled.

"You know…. I was a house rat. My father would never let me go anywhere, not to hang out with friends, or sit on the beach…. not even go to the movies. Even sitting outside on the porch was an issue with him. One thing he loved most of all was going to the Zoo and he always took me with him and we would always look at these amazing exotic birds."

It felt weird hearing her tell me about her life story. I always thought of her as this perfect, beautiful demigoddess.

"Do you miss him?" I asked. "Your father?".

"Every day. Not a day goes by that I don't, just like you."

"You still have your mother, I'm guessing," I said.

Miss Wynters went into her handbag and took out a picture frame of a woman. I looked at the picture and she was exquisite; she was light brown and had long beautiful hair.

"She died many years ago."

I felt bad for bringing it up and wished I could take it back.

"I'm so sorry, miss; I didn't know."

"We all have our problems, Analisa. It's a matter of how to deal with them. But we shouldn't allow that to stop us from living."

The bell rang at the perfect time.

"Ahm, miss, I kinda have a class after this? Can I go?"

"It's fine Annalisa… we'll talk next time, go," she replied.

As I got up, I glimpsed her right arm. There was a burnt spot. For a second, I thought it was a tattoo.

She saw me looking; she pulled it up further and showed me.

"Made the mistake of using my wet hands while frying fish. Hot oil splash is not pretty," she said. "Off you go now."

"Okay miss."

Miss Wynters had already taken up my time telling me her life story. I had enough on my plate to be having a one-on-one session with any teacher at this point. My brother was sick in hospital with no way of knowing what caused his illness and I'm seeing things I'm not supposed to see. I had a test tomorrow that I wasn't ready for. I wish I had stayed home.

"Analisa!"

I turned around, and it was Dean running towards me with books in hand as usual, and he looked way too happy.

"Ready for the test tomorrow?" He asked excitedly.

"No Dean, but it seems like you are."

"Of course, questions on the Haitian Revolution are what I have been studying all night."

"Well, I didn't get to study anything. It's like everything is happening all at one time and I just can't cope." I said, frustrated.

I opened my locker, shoved my books in, and slammed it shut. The weight of frustration came down on me as I leaned my head against the locker door.

"Are you okay?"

I turned and looked at him and saw the worried look on his face. I didn't want to take out my problems with him. "You heard Romaine's in the hospital?" I asked.

"Oh yeah, right…. you mother called the house and told my mom. How is he?"

"Well, we'll know in a couple of days. Mommy's staying with him. She might take him home tomorrow or weekend."

"So, he got sick just like that?"

"Yeah. He was fine earlier and then later his skin felt like it was on fire, and he has this strange mark on his neck."

"What kind of mark?" Dean asked.

"A black mark, like a big black round mark on his neck. It's never been there before. Going to call Mommy."

The phone kept ringing and ringing with no answer. I hung up.

"She's not answering."

"Maybe she turned it off," Dean said. "You want to get some studying done or you want some time alone?"

"No, let's go study. I need to get my mind off this."

We arrived, and Dean went ahead of me to find comfortable seats for the two of us to sit. I walked over to the counter and asked for a card. The librarian looked at me with a mean streak, like I had stolen something from her. She took out a card and handed it to me.

"Thank you."

I moved off and looked for Dean. He waved his arm in the air to signal where he was. He stood out like a severe case of the flu. Everyone else in here was too busy texting and chatting rather than doing schoolwork, but who came in the library to do schoolwork anymore?

He had already chosen three history books on the Haitian Revolution. I barely had one. But I stopped complaining and got to it, so I could pass the test tomorrow. Dean opened one book, and I took out my notebook.

"Alright, let's start with the basics. I have often described the Haitian Revolution as the largest and most successful slave rebellion in the Western Hemisphere. Slaves started the rebellion in 1791 and by 1803 they had ended not just slavery but French control over the colony." said Dean as he read.

I started jotting notes and making some from the previous readings I did. It seemed like the study sessions were going well to the point the Librarian kept telling us to shush each time. As I kept writing, I turned to Dean but something dashed cross my vision in between the bookshelves. I turned around and stared for a good couple of minutes.

Dean stopped reading, he looked at me, "What's wrong?" he asked.

I frowned, trying to make sense of it. "Thought I saw something."

Dean looked around, then back to his books. My instincts told me to go look what was behind there. Maybe it was someone searching for a book, so I left it alone and concentrated on my studying.

Hours later, I arrived home, exhausted from all that brutal cramming and swatting that I just wanted to lie in bed. As I approached the living room, I heard noises. I looked in, I saw my mother dancing with Romaine. He wasn't making any noise, but him being here made me happy.

My mother pointed at me and showed him who it was.

"Who is that? It's your big sister," she said kissing him.

He looked at me and gave a little smile. I went over to hug and kiss him. Mommy handed him to me, and I held him in my arms. His tiny hands kept beating my chest, and he just stared with his wide eyes. I was having such a bad day today that it felt so good coming home to see his cute chubby face. I placed my hand under his neck. He was still warm, but not as bad as before.

"Mommy, he's still hot."

"I gave him the medication Dr. Hinds prescribed for him and he responded to it. He started acting like himself again, but his fever is still a little high. He said within a day or two the fever would drop, but he still doesn't know what caused it. I don't know if I should carry him back. I just hope it will pass and he's still going to find an ointment for the mark on his neck."

He pulled my hair while I looked at him. I felt so helpless. Hearing him scream last night terrified me. I've never heard Romaine scream like that before. He always cried, but never like what I heard last night — like someone was hurting him.

"How are you doing?" my mother asked, concerned.

"Mommy, I'm stressed. I feel like a lot is coming down on me. It's more work, more assignments, plus I have to be helping you with everything around here and I'm not sleeping. I'm having nightmares."

My mother walked up to me and hugged me. She kissed me on my head.

"You're expecting too much of yourself. You're still a young girl. This should not be your burden to bear. Remember what I told you? I'm the mother, that's my job. Your father dying wasn't part of the pla…"

My mother paused whenever she spoke about my father. She didn't enjoy talking about him because she knew it would hurt each time.

The tears were welling up inside her.

"I miss your father a lot, and he was a good man. Always remember that." She stroked my face. "All his strength and all his courage, even his stubborn nature, is inside you and that is enough for me," she said. "So, I don't need you to carry the burden of the world on your shoulders. You help whenever you can. At least I know I raised you, right."

"Yes, Mommy."

Romaine laughed, then Mommy and I smiled after him.

"Yes, baby smiling, aww."

She took Romaine from me. "Analisa, sleep. You were reading enough. Tomorrow you will be fresh."

She was always telling me to go to sleep, so it made little sense to argue. I told her I wasn't hungry, then I kissed her and my brother goodnight. As I opened my bedroom door, there was a dark figure standing by the window, the moonlight illuminated its shadow.

I froze — it was her, the old woman, in my room. She turned around with her hideous face, red eyes, and rotted teeth staring at me. She shrieked and floated towards me so fast, I screamed and pulled the door. I fell to the floor and started crying. My mother rushed to me.

"Ana, what happened?"

I was shaking. I pointed towards the door. She turned, then looked back at me.

"What?" she asked.

"S… something… inside my room," I said, too petrified to form words.

My mother got up and walked towards the door. I grabbed on to her arm as tight as I could. She clutched the doorknob, turned it and it opened with a long creak. We stepped in slowly. She looked around but saw nothing, then she looked at me.

"Ana, there's nothing in here," she assured me.

"Mommy, I saw her in here. She was right there by the window!!"

"Alright, alright, who is it, baby? Who is she?" She asked, trying to calm me down.

"I don't know who she is. She keeps showing up everywhere I go. I saw her when I was coming from Mr. Murray, I saw her one night when I was sleeping, and you found me in the living room and just now. I wish she would LEAVE ME ALONE!!"

My mother stared at me and didn't know what to say. She saw the fear in my eyes. My legs were quivering.

"I don't think you can do this test tomorrow."

I felt lightheaded. My feet wobbled, and my vision got blurry. My chest tightened, and I felt faint-ish, but my mother caught me and helped me get into bed.

She went into the bathroom, took up one of my dry face rags, and dipped it with warm water. She walked over to me and sat down on the edge of the bed, placing the rag on my head.

"I'll call Mr. Francis tomorrow, ask him if he can give you another sit down to do the test."

"No, Mommy!" I exclaimed. "I can't miss the test."

"Well, you going to miss this one. I'm going to make Dr. Hinds check on you tomorrow."

"No, Mommy, I'm okay."

She got up and pulled the sheet over me and kissed me goodnight.

"Mommy! Can you turn on the lamp, please?"

She switched it on, then walked out, leaving the room door ajar.

As the fan spun, I lay on my back and looked up. I didn't want to sleep; I was too afraid, and since she was going to call Mr. Francis, I could take the time and rest and do the test some other time — little by little. My eyes shut. I couldn't fight it anymore. I looked over at the window where I saw her. I couldn't shut my eyes, fearing that she would appear and grab me.

The next morning, I felt a little better, a little shaken up, but I was determined to find out who this old woman was and understand what she wanted. My mother heard me mention a woman in my room, and I knew she was going to question me about it, but I wasn't ready to say anything to her further…. not just yet.

I figured by now that my mother had called Mr. Francis, telling him I wouldn't be coming in today and that I would have to sit the test next Monday. That was good news, if I ever heard any because it gave me enough time to study and be better prepared.

My mother and Romaine weren't home, but everything looked normal, so I wasn't seeing things again. I took out an apple from the fridge and sat around the table with my phone to see if I got any messages. Dean texted me, saying that when the test was over, he would email some notes on what came on the paper. Hanna, as always, texted me again for the 100th time about her meeting with her book club sisters. My mother called me.

"Yes, Mommy," I answered.

All I heard was sniffling and moaning.

"Mommy…. Mommy, what happened? Is it Romaine again?"

"Romaine got worse," she said.

The news was becoming too much to bear. How could he have gotten worse?

"Didn't Doctor what's his face say he would have gotten better? How is he getting worse?" I asked, frustrated.

"I don't know, Ann… he didn't expect it to get worse, but —"

 "But what, Mommy?"

"Seem like it's spreading," she said.

"What are you talking about?"

"Ann, nine other babies got sick — the same thing that happened with Romaine is happening with them too, even Ann Marie's baby. All the parents are here," she said.

"You sure? The same thing?" I asked, confused.

The doctors couldn't identify what caused the sickness, and the same black mark was visible on all of them. All of them show the same symptoms, high fever symptoms.

"I Don't know if I can handle this… I'll call you later," she said, devastated, and hung up.

My heart sank even further. This wasn't a normal sickness, and I didn't know how to explain it. I left the phone on the kitchen table and walked out into the living room. Then…. something caught my attention, and I covered my mouth. High on the wall was an ominous message splashed across it.

No one ii iafe. Thii town ihall pay, and every child will die.

CHAPTER THREE
FATAL DEATHS

The message was a clear warning that something terrible was happening, and now nine babies were sick. I went to the kitchen, took up my phone, and returned to the living room to take a picture of the message. I looked at the photo to make sure it was very real.

The front door opened. My mother rushed in, looked up at the wall, and covered her mouth in horror. She saw it too. Now I know I wasn't seeing things.

"Analisa…. what is this? Who wrote this?" She asked. She turned to me for answers, looking at me with a kind of stare like I was guilty of something.

"Mommy, why are you asking me that? I don't know," I answered back.

My mother looked back at the writings and tried to maintain her sanity.

"Mommy, something strange is going on."

"All I want to know is how it got up there?"

"You wouldn't believe me if I told you," I said, looking away.

It was already stressful to carry Romaine to the doctor again, but how would she react if I told her who I thought did this? It couldn't have been a coincidence that I was seeing this strange old woman out of nowhere, those strange crows, my brother gets sick, and now other babies are sick as well—I wanted to tell her the suspicions I had, but she might think I was making stuff up and she would get even more upset.

"You say the other babies had the same symptoms just like Romaine?"

"Yes, Ann Marie, who lives down the road. She told me her son woke up crying like crazy and how she tried getting him to stop. She said he never cried like that before, not until last night, and she saw the strange mark on his neck." My mother explained.

She told me that Romaine had started crying again, but not as loud as before, so she didn't want to wake me. She left and took Romaine to the hospital.

When she arrived, she said the hospital was full of people from the neighbourhood…. all their children were sick, same high fever and no explanation of how it happened; it was a situation that left many of them confused.

"I've never seen anything like this before."

My mother told me she was going back to the hospital, but she came to pick up a towel for Romaine. She said that I could come whenever I was ready. I said I would — even though I didn't think I could manage seeing the look on those parents' faces wondering what was causing their children to be sick. I hated my brother was back there when I thought he would have improved. She looked up at the message on the wall.

"And that needs to come off," she said.

She picked up the towel and left to go back to the hospital. I called Dean and Hanna to come over after school.

Later, they arrived. Dean handed me some notes he made before the test, and I rushed to my room and placed the notes on my bed. I dashed back out into the living room, and Dean and Hanna looked at the wall, lost for words.

"I've seen ugly mangy dogs and giant rats…. but this…. I never seen before," said Dean with a slight panic in his voice.

"*No one is safe. This town shall be cleansed, and every child will die?*" Repeated Hanna. "What does that even mean?"

Dean and Hanna looked just as puzzled as I was, but unknown to them. I had a theory, but I had no way of proving it.

"Maybe it's because of that woman I saw."

Dean and Hanna looked at each other.

"You mean the woman in the bushes?" asked Hanna. "Don't you think you were just frustrated and seeing things?"

"Yeah — I thought so too, but how do you explain that?" I pointed at the wall. "Because obviously you guys can see it too, and I'm not this idle, nor can I reach THAT high."

Judging by the look on both their faces, they realized it was strange after all. Hanna suggested we go to the library and find some answers.

Later in the day, we perused through various books on childhood illnesses. We've been searching and searching for hours, but nothing new or anything out of the ordinary has popped up.

Dean was also doing some searches, but he, too, came up empty. Every bit of information he searched on Google gave him the same recycled nonsense he saw on previous links. He got so frustrated he knocked on the keyboard, which drew the attention of the Librarian, who already didn't like us…. or liked people.

"SHHHH!!!!!" she said coarsely.

Dean turned back around and faced the computer.

"Ann, let me tell you right now, google is the worst. I don't think we're going to find anything this way."

I was disappointed to think we came down here, only to find nothing. Hanna was still combing through the other books, trying to find something on her own. She, too, became distressed. A page hung loose after she threw down the book. She reached over to fix it…. but then she realized it wasn't a loose page but an old newspaper clipping. Her eyes widened when she saw what it was.

"Guys, look at this," she said, calling us.

Dean and I went over to her and sat down around the table.

"What is that?" I asked.

"Looks like an old newspaper clipping," Dean said.

You could tell the paper was old because of how crumpled and bleached out it was. It outlined the year… 1990, and the title was:

COMATOSE INFANTS DIE IN SLEEP:

Doctors unable to specify a cause of illness
Dated: October 10, 1990

The Royale Medical Clinic & Hospital reported late last night that the 10 infants who fell sick two weeks ago succumbed to their illness. Reports are that doctors ran many tests but failed to find out what triggered the sickness. According to the doctors, none of the treatments seemed to work effectively. Dr. Edward Michaelson, the lead physician assigned to treat the infants, said the babies had very severe fevers and rashes on their skin. He stated it was the first time he had ever witnessed a severe case of fever at this rate and that he did not know what could have caused it.

Dr. Michaelson said that the children all got sick at the same time. The parents brought them in, and Dr. Michaelson provided temporary treatment for the babies and sent them home. He insisted that the fever should lessen and that 'we have given them plenty of fluids.' But…. a day later, they all came back worse than before, and a couple of days following, they were comatose, and then another two weeks later… they died.

The Ministry of Health deemed the infants' death unfortunate and negligent. As a result, Dr. Michaelson lost his license and was banned from further practice. The Ministry, however, is still trying to determine the cause of deaths, and they want this incident to be kept under wraps.

The three of us stood there, frozen and horrified at what we just read. So, this has happened before. Why didn't we know about this? Why hasn't anyone found out what caused this sickness? I was so shocked that I couldn't think straight. Then I looked back on the date of the article.

"October 10th, that's Mommy's birthday," I said. "She would have been about eight."

"Are you going to ask her about it?" asked Hanna.

I don't know if I wanted to or if my mother remembered anything about that day. Who would remember anything at eight years old? I told Hanna to take the paper with her and put it in her pocket.

"We need to find out how those babies got sick before."

"How are we going to find that out?" asked Dean.

I pointed at the name on the old newspaper.

"We're going to visit the Doctor who tried to treat them, Dr. Michaelson. If anybody knows the answers, it will be him."

"But how are we going to find him? We don't know where he lives," said Hanna.

"We go to the hospital where he used to work. All hospitals have records of their employees; home address, phone numbers, everything."

"But he doesn't work there anymore," said Dean.

"It doesn't matter," I said. "They would still have a record of him even if he isn't there."

"So, we're going to the hospital. Seem so exciting. This feels like an adventure," said Hanna happily.

"If we're going to do this, you know we're sacrificing a lot for this?" said Dean, concerned. "Our schoolwork is going to be affected."

"Can you forget school for one day?" I said, agitated.

We packed up the books. Hanna folded the article and placed it in her pocket, and we left. As we went outside, Dean stopped. I turned to look at him and he looked uneasy, like he didn't like what we were doing.

"Guys, you want to do this?

I was becoming livid and wanted him to stop whining.

"Dean, if you don't want to come, you can go home," said Hanna.

"SHUT UP Hanna!" barked Dean.

"You SHUT UP!" shouted Hanna.

They started cussing at each other, and I just got fed up.

"BOTH OF YOU SHUT UP!!!" I shouted. "If you two can't get along with this, I'll just do it on my own," I said.

"Ann, I just want to know why we have to do it, why the police can't handle it," Dean said.

"Dean…. we didn't know that this had happened before until now and that this clipping ever existed. Why?" I asked, "You think the police, the Ministry, or the council are going to say or do anything?"

Dean didn't say another word after that.

"School is not on my list of priorities right now. I will do the test on Monday, but I'm seeing this through. I will not lose my brother or any of those children. So, if schoolwork suffers, then that's the risk I will take," I said sternly.

Dean and Hanna both looked at me.

"Did you notice, nobody in Belle Isle has said anything about this. It's like it never happened," I said. "We can't let history repeat itself."

Dean paced. Trying to make a decisive choice if he should join us or not. He stops and looks at me.

"So…. after we meet the Doctor then what?" Asked Dean.

I smiled.

"We're not letting you do this alone. We want to find out what's happening, too. You're not getting rid of us so easily," Hanna said.

"Okay, first… we go to the hospital where Dr. Michaelson worked and ask for his address, then we find out where he lives."

"But how do we know he's still alive?"

I had not thought about that. I was so fixated on finding out about the dead babies that I didn't think about if he was alive. If he was dead, then searching for him wouldn't have made much sense; but he was the first genuine lead we had on this sickness. So, we had to know for sure and understand what started the deaths before.

We left from the library and hopped on a bus right on time to the Royale Medical Clinic.

The building looked a little different, except for a few additions up top. It was 4:30 pm, and it was probably when most of the staff would pack up to leave. So, we wanted to make this quick and get the information we needed.

As we opened the door, we were greeted by the blistering cold of the AC. Inside, the building was spacious and beautifully decorated. There were many posters on each side of the walls and a long hallway ending with a flat-screen TV on the wall. We walked down the hallway and we saw many people there sitting and waiting impatiently, judging by their fidgeting. Patients were called by number on the intercom; some of them looked and cussed under their breaths.

We approached the receptionist's desk. It was a woman who looked like she was in her early thirties.

She was chewing gum and typing away on her computer without batting an eye our way. She eventually gave us a quick glance over and handed us a form to fill out our names, then continued typing.

"Ahm, excuse me, we're not here to see a doctor. We came to ask some questions."

"Okay," she said dryly, barely looking at us.

"We know a Dr. Michaelson used to work here. We're students of Mount Techa High School and we're doing a research project about his life and the work that he did, and we were wondering if you know where we could find him."

"Or if he's still ali—" Dean slipped out.

Hanna elbowed him in the side, and I turned and rolled my eyes at him. The receptionist looked at us suspiciously.

"Why do you want to see him?" She asked. "He hasn't worked here in 26 years."

"How come?" Hanna asked curiously.

We could clearly see the receptionist's look of disgust because we were asking too many questions and weren't supposed to ask.

"They fired him," she said hotly.

"Why?" Hanna asked, still pressing.

"Look, that's not important. Miss, he's still alive, right?" I asked.

I observed her expression and crossed my fingers, hoping to get a positive answer.

"As far as I know. Yes, he is," she answered.

"Do you have an address for him?" I asked.

Her stares got more suspicious, and she looked like she was about to call the police on us. But she rolled her eyes, then started typing away on her computer.

"They could fire me for this — David Edward Michaelson, he lives at 33 Arnold Street, Belle Isle."

I took out my phone and typed in the address and saved it.

"Thank you," I said, as we walked out of the hospital.

So, he was still alive and has lived in Belle Isle all these years. Why hadn't anyone seen him in all this time? Everything that happened in 1990 happened right in the centre of Belle Isle.

"We got the information we needed, so all we have to do is visit his house and ask him some questions. But we can do that tomorrow."

"We're not going now?" Dean asked.

"I want to go to the hospital, need to see Romaine.

"Want us to come with you?" Hanna asked.

"Are you sure you want to come?"

"Yes, we want to," Dean said, "and if we're going to find out more about what happened, we need to be there. Plus, I still think you need to prepare for the test on Monday."

Once again, Dean never missed an opportunity to remind me about the History test, but…. he was right. I needed to study. My mother already got Mr. Francis to give me the day off, so I couldn't give any excuses after this, why I couldn't do it.

So, we left the Royale Medical Clinic and waited for a bus to take us to Belle Isle Hospital to look for my brother and the other babies. Seconds later, a bus came.

We thought about the questions we would ask Dr. Michaelson about the babies that came to his ward and what he noticed about their symptoms.

If there was anything he witnessed, something he missed or overlooked, would he remember anything from twenty-odd years ago? Would those questions help us find out what was happening now? I heavily crammed all these questions in my mind like a sardine tin.

We were about twenty minutes away from the Belle Isle hospital. We drove past the Belle Isle town square, where the community council normally held their meetings.

They haven't had a meeting in years, why I didn't know. Dean's parents were a part of the council, so were my parents. My mother left after my father's death, and Hanna's parents as well (when they were alive).

Hanna might seem happy and go lucky most of the times, but she lost her parents five years ago in a horrible car accident. She had been living with her grandmother ever since. Everyone, including those at school, knew about it but never approached her. She always kept her emotions intact and channeled them elsewhere, being helpful to others, always being there, and annoying me. But I wouldn't have anyone else by my side than her.

We turned into the hospital's entrance gate and exited the bus. We walked inside, and I saw my mother standing with the other parents in the lobby. My mother turned and walked towards me.

"Mommy, how's Romaine? I asked.

"Still not feeling well," she said sadly. "Hi Dean, Hanna, how are y'all doing?"

"We're fine Miss Kelly," answered Hanna.

I was hoping by now we would have heard some good news. I looked over and saw the other parents… lost, upset, and confused.

"What about the other babies?" Dean asked.

"They have them hooked up to machines, screening them for any unknown chemicals in their bodies,".

The babies were all placed in separate machines, looking like stiff corpses. That wasn't the best way to describe them, but that's how they looked.

The parents who were there, some of whom I have known for years and some who were new to the district, looked distraught. I could just imagine how they felt, watching their children helpless and sick, not knowing what to do or how to help them.

I looked over at my brother and I was immediately grief stricken. Romaine's breathing was slow, and he was barely moving. I hated seeing him like this, and it hurt me to know I could do nothing except find answers.

I walked up to my mother, who was sitting by herself, waiting for the news. I wanted to tell her what we were planning to do—but how was I going to put that into a conversation? To ask her if she knew about the babies that died 26 years ago. But I left it alone…. for now.

"Mommy, I'm going to go home. Can you call me if anything changes?" I asked.

"You leaving? You can stay for a whi—"

BEEP!! BEEP!!

The blaring noise came from inside the room where the babies were. The swarm of doctors then came rushing in and closed the doors behind them. Worried parents got up and ran towards the window to see what was happening. My heart raced with fear, as I feared I might lose my baby brother. My mother wasn't fearing any better. She didn't get up; she sat down rocking back and forth.

"We need to intubate NOW!!!" Shouted Dr. Hinds from inside. Each doctor positioned themselves to a machine. They each placed tubes into the babies' airways to help with breathing. "Let's also give them some epinephrine to stimulate the heart and blood flow."

"Won't that be harmful? I don't think their bodies can handle the drug's effect," one doctor asked, concerned.

"Just do it! We need to do a CPAP and get air into the lungs and clear the passage. The fever is causing them to relapse."

The doctors all worked mercilessly, trying to save the babies. I looked around at the parents who were holding hands and praying, Dean and Hanna stood in the corner, unable to stomach the tragedy that was happening before them. I stood there wondering how we would stop something we couldn't understand. Belle Isle had some of the best, well-trained doctors, and if they couldn't stop this…. what hope did we have?

People considered Dr. Michaelson the Usain Bolt of Medicine for his quick and timely results. I prayed that there was some ray of hope left. That these babies would be saved.

Then we heard it —

"BEEEEEEPPPPPPP" the long beeps came from all the machines in the room. The doctors were all huddled around the machines, muttering to themselves. It looked bad, and the machines got louder. The doctors again tried to save them.

I was losing my mind… Dean and Hanna came over to hold me because I didn't know how to control myself…. it was happening again; I could feel it.

Then… the beeping stopped, and it was just — flatline sounds from each machine. The doctors all stared at each other with sullen looks on their faces. They looked outside at us. Dr. Hinds held his head down. After walking to the door, he opened it. He approached the parents slowly. He talked calmly and all I could hear were blood-curdling screams…. two babies had died. Then we heard the others died right after that.

"Noooooooooo!!!!!" Bellowed one mother who collapsed in her husband's arms.

"Oh, God! Oh, Jesus!!" cried another.

I was not prepared to hear that my brother had died. I turned to my mother. Her face, lost in grief. She froze. This was the same pain I saw when my father died. I couldn't forget it. It was the same expression that I would have to face yet again.

She just stood there, with her hand covering her mouth, tears flowing. I couldn't take it, I just couldn't. I didn't want to face the horrible nightmare that was going to be with me for the rest of my life. So, I walked off, brushed past Dean, Hanna and my mother and ran outside and knelt crying.

I buried my face in my lap and I felt empty, like I had nothing left to live for.

"Ann."

I looked around. It was my mother, and she was smiling. She told me to come inside. I walked back inside, and Dr. Hinds was standing with Dean and Hanna. They both ran to me and hugged me.

"You alright?" Hanna asked.

"Why did you run off like that?" asked Dean.

"What's going on?"

Dr. Hinds and my mother walked up to us.

"Dr. Hinds wants to tell us something in private. We don't want to cause an uproar." Whispered my mother.

"What are you talking about?" I asked, curious.

"We did a CT scan on the babies. It's what is called computed tomography. What we used was a special x-ray equipment to help detect a variety of diseases and conditions in babies, even adults. We've been doing this for hours, trying to detect what caused the babies to get sick."

"Did you find anything?" I asked.

"No, nothing…. no traces of any diseases, no hormone defect, nothing affecting the bloodstream. There was nothing there."

"But two died," said Dean. "Right?"

Dr. Hinds looked around and turned back to us.

"It's more than that now," he said gravely.

"How much?"

"Nine…. all nine babies died."

"Jesus!!" Said my mother, throwing her hands up.

"Wait….9? Doctor… is my brother….?" I was afraid to ask.

"Don't worry, Romaine is alive." whispered the Doctor.

Hearing that news made us happy. We didn't jump for joy because we knew it would upset the neighbours, and Romaine was not yet out of it.

"Right now, Romaine is in a comatose state. I don't know how he's still alive, but something is holding on to him," said Dr. Hinds, looking at us. "It's best we keep him another night."

"NO!!" said my mother, "he's coming home with us. I don't want him in here any longer. Doctor, if you want to monitor him, you can monitor him from home — but I'm taking my son," she said sternly.

"You got to do it quietly because the other parents might not like it," Dean said cautiously.

Dr. Hinds couldn't say anything else except agree to continue to treat Romaine from home and to watch his progress. What we wanted to prevent happened anyway…. nine babies died, but my brother lived, or barely. I knew now that we needed to find answers.

"Mommy… ahm, me and the guys have something we need to do. I'll see you at home, okay?"

"Alright," she said disappointed. "Be careful."

I went up to her and hugged her tight. She hugged me and kissed me on my head.

"My beautiful girl."

She held onto my face and wiped the tears from my cheeks.

"Your brother's coming home… don't worry."

"Okay, Mommy," I answered.

Dean and Hanna waved goodbye to Dr. Hinds and my mother, and we all left the hospital building. I saw the look on Dean and Hanna's faces, and they were equally upset as I was…. the other babies did not deserve to die… not like this. They had no sickness or were exposed to anything contagious…. yet they had high fever out of nowhere and now they were dead.

Parents lost their children, and they needed answers. I said I was going to stop what was happening. Maybe I was being brave or just being incredibly stupid, but my brother meant the world to me, and I wasn't going to lose him.

We failed today — but we knew what needed to be done, and that was now our priority — to find Dr. Michaelson.

CHAPTER FOUR
DR. MICHAELSON

Saturday mornings were always the busiest. This one was no exception. I woke up to loud chatter and footsteps coming from the living room. I opened the bedroom door and saw white coats brush past me, invading the hallway and walking towards my mother's room. They were setting up a mobile CT scan machine where Romaine's crib was. They moved it and placed it in the room's corner. They placed Romaine inside and hooked him up to it. A nurse was sitting at the side of the machine in front of a computer, examining Romaine's body.

I walked out into the living room and saw my mother talking to Dr. Hinds. She looked over at me and smiled. Dr. Hinds also waved at me, and I waved back. I looked up at the wall behind her and noticed the writing was gone. My mother looked behind as well and turned to look at me with a nervous smile.

"I got somebody to clean off the walls."

It surprised me. My mother looked at me, concerned.

"Analisa… what's wrong?" She asked.

"Nothing, Mommy, just hungry," I said. "Good morning, Dr. Hinds."

"Good morning, Analisa," he answered.

"Dr. Hinds was telling me about the machine he put in my room. You saw it?"

I nodded.

"Yes, it's called CereTom, and a company named NeuroLogica Corp. built it. It's a very handy radiological device. We flew it down from New York and its system is the world's first cordless and wireless head and neck mobile CT," he said.

"That's fine and all, doctor, but will it help my son?"

"We have a nurse stationed in your room monitoring him. So, if anything is wrong, we will know. Okay."

"How much is this going to cost?" I asked sternly.

My mother looked around at me with her eyes widened. Dr. Hinds opened his mouth, but he didn't know how to answer.

"We would like to know, Doctor," my mother said.

"We can talk about a payment plan later on. For now, let us help your boy."

I went to the kitchen and opened the fridge to get some Orange Juice and a muffin, then went back into my room and shut the door.

I turned on my laptop and attached the USB cord from my phone to the laptop. The files booted up, and came up on the screen. I scrolled down. I clicked on the photo I had taken of the newspaper clippings. The babies' sickness, the message on the wall and then later we found this clipping about the babies who died in 1990. The way my brain worked is that when I think something has a pattern, it does.

No one spoke about it, no one questioned it. I logged into the Google search and typed in,

"Babies dying mysteriously,"

Numerous links popped up about babies dying from cholera, babies dying from high fever, asthma, and all these sicknesses had major symptoms. These babies had no symptoms, according to Dr. Hinds, and they just died. I kept scrolling until I stopped at a link. When I looked closer, it had Dr. Michaelson's name attached to it. There was a picture of Dr. Michaelson posing with an interviewer of a small local paper called the View. It said he gave a private interview making claims about the babies' deaths, but the report never made it to print.

Living in the country had its privileges, but strong Wi-Fi access was apparently not one of them. I tried clicking on more links, but then the computer got stuck, or probably the net was failing. I grew frustrated, plugged out the USB cord, and shut down the laptop.

I didn't know what else to look for. I was hitting a dead end. We should have much better luck when we meet with Dr. Michaelson.

I was bored, so I took out my phone and scrolled through it and looked at previous messages from Hanna that I didn't read. When I read the first three messages, I felt funny in the pit of my stomach. I was a fool…. I paid little attention to her and she must have felt bad or had a feeling that I didn't read her messages. She said she had made up everything about the book club meetings. She just wanted some company, someone to talk to because no one spoke to her at school, only a couple of people who just wanted to get things from her.

Last year, she invited those who she deemed her closest friends to her birthday party. She sent out many invitations. She spent money on food, party assortments, invitations, hired a DJ for the party, and other stuff…. no one was there. They made promises to her and kept her hopes up. Her grandmother felt bad for her, that she kept her company and ate cake with her. Hanna cried all night. She was so sad that she never bothered coming to school the next day. I was so angry that I wanted to fight everybody.

I always tried my best to make my friends happy. Dean was away on a trip and I was sick with the Flu, so I wouldn't have been there. I needed to make it up to her; so, I called her. Her phone rang, and she answered.

"Hey, Ann, what's up? She asked.

I wanted to apologize to her for being such an awful friend, but I didn't want to bring that up.

"I'm gonna take a shower. Meet me by the park… let's hang out."

I heard silence on the other line, like she was contemplating what to say next.

"Really… so…. I guess you read it then," she said.

"Yeah, I know there's no book club. I know I've been a jerk lately, and I'm sorry. You're my friend and I should have treated you better. So, I'm taking the time out to come hang with you today."

"Wow… ahm… I don't know what to say," she said.

"Just get ready, will be there in about an hour time,"

"Okay, I'll be there, bye…," she said and hung up.

After showering, I told my mother I was meeting Hanna at the park. I left and walked down the road. The park was just a couple of distances away from where I lived, so it was easier to just walk. I looked up in the trees to see if I would see those crows again, but I never saw them this time. In fact, I haven't seen them at all. It seemed like they weren't genuinely trying to scare me.

Hanna was already there waiting for me. She bought ice cream for both of us. I sat down beside her, and we both started eating.

"I'm sorry I lied… I guess you would have found out if you had come. Don't know what I was thinking of coming up with that," she said. "I had a feeling you didn't read the texts I sent you because you didn't mention it, but that call told me otherwise."

"Why didn't you just call me?" I asked.

"I didn't want to bother you. I always am a nuisance to people. I just block it out of my mind and just pretend it doesn't bother me. Most times I would stay in my room, just lock myself away and cry. Nobody cares, I'm alive anyway, so…. ha ha I'm sorry… just me ranting," she said eating her ice cream.

I looked at her and I felt completely awful. I ate my ice-cream, but I wasn't feeling it. I put it down, and I turned to her.

"Listen… I don't think you're a bother. You can be clingy, but it doesn't make you a bad person. A lot of persons don't seem to remember what happened to you, everything you lost. I know what you are going through. I've been there. I'm sorry if I wasn't such a good friend," I said apologetically.

Hanna smiled. "I don't blame you, Ann—the world is evil. I learn to accept it, it won't change who I am. I'm still going to be me, help people even when they don't want it. It is what it is," she said confidently.

The breeze was refreshing. Hours had passed, and Hanna and I sat there sharing memories of our school days and how we met in first form. At first, I couldn't stand her because I thought she was weird. Over time, we had grown to know and respect each other, and I got to understand her weird personality and where it came from. I looked at the time; it was 4:30 pm.

"I think it's time we get Dean," I said.

"Are we going to the house now?"

"Yeah, we are going to tell him to meet us there."

I texted Dean, telling him we were about to leave to go to the house. My phone pinged seconds after and he texted back.

"Okay cool, will meet you there."

"I wonder what Dr. Michaelson looks like now," Hanna wondered.

"Hopefully friendly. Do you have the clipping with you?"

She took out the old newspaper and showed it to me.

"Brought it just in case," she said.

"Good…. we need to get over there now before nighttime comes. You ready?"

"I'm ready," she said.

We left the park and walked towards the bus stop. I looked up into the trees as I always did. I don't know why I did it all the time; it was a like a reflex action now. I've seen the crows everywhere I went and now they have just stopped showing up and I found it strange; not that I wanted to see them; but I just wondered why they had stopped. Hanna and I saw a pair of bright lights coming around the corner.

"It's coming now," she said.

Fifteen minutes later, the bus dropped us off at 33 Arnold Street, a silent place. We saw Dean, who was already at the gate waiting for us. The number 33 was practically invisible from the lack of paint. I pushed open the gate, and we walked inside. It looked abandoned, old, and worn out, covered with lots of grass…. like he hadn't mowed the lawn in ages.

We stepped onto the creaking steps that looked like they would give way any minute. As we approached the doorstep, an overwhelming sense of fear and anticipation ran over me. Hanna and Dean also felt scared. I pressed the doorbell, and it chimed loudly. It went on for a good while before it died down, but nothing happened.

"Maybe he's not here," Dean said.

That would have been disappointing if he wasn't — so I pressed the doorbell again. This time, we heard footsteps coming from inside. Chains began unhinging, and the door opened. An old man peeped out from behind it. He was short, frail, with a mean look about him. He looked like he had a bad temper, judging by the unpleasant look he gave us.

"Yes… what do you want?" He asked in a harsh tone.

Dean hid behind Hanna, and she pushed him off.

"Yes sir, my name is Anali—"

"I don't care if you're the bloody Queen of England… I don't want to talk to anybody today," he snapped.

As he was about to shut the door on us, I wedged my foot in the doorway.

"Sir, please. My name is Analisa Kelly, and these are…."

"Wait…. you said Kelly?" he asked, astonished. He opened the door a little.

"Yes… you know that name?" I asked.

"Is your mother Margaret Kelly… Mabel's daughter?"

"Yes… yes, she is," I answered, surprised.

Then I saw him crack a smile, probably the first smile he has given in years.

"Well, imagine that. I knew your mother when she was a little girl. Sweet girl, gave a lot of trouble," he laughed.

"I know you must have stories to tell,"

"She sent you here?" He asked curiously.

"No sir," I said. "May we come inside for a bit, if it's okay with you?"

His smile faded, and then he just stared at us. He opened the door fully and turned his back. There was a walking stick in his hand. He limped over to his chair and sat down. We looked at each other and walked inside.

"Close the door behind you…. with the latch."

Hanna closed the door and hooked the chain back on it. We sat down on the couch opposite each other and looked around the place in silence. His house was quite small, unkempt and smelled of cigarettes and beer. There weren't many pictures of himself or any family members. Judging by how guarded he was from society, always in the dark…. he seemed alone.

He looked at us, then took out a cigarette and lighter from out his pocket, then lit it.

"Smoking's bad for you, you know," Dean interrupted.

Hanna and I turned to Dean, and Dr. Michaelson gave him a smug look.

"Is that right?" He asked, purposefully inhaling the cigarette and blowing massive smoke in the air. Dean inhaled and looked as if he was about to pass out, but he maintained composure.

"Yes. It is said that 99.9% of persons who smoke often develop lung cancer. In fact, Scien—"

I elbowed him, signaling him to be quiet. Dr. Michaelson laughed.

"You need to get him a girlfriend," he said.

Dean frowned.

"Anyway… Dr. Michaelson…"

"Don't call me that. I'm not a doctor anymore," he said firmly.

"Okay…. Mr. Michaelson…. the reason we're here is because of this." I said, turning to Hanna and nodding at her.

Hanna reached into her pocket and fished out the newspaper article and showed it to him. When he looked at it, his eyes widened as if all the terrible memories came flooding back.

"Where did you get this?"

"We found it in one of the library books," Hanna said.

"Why? Why do you have it?" He asked.

"We wanted to ask you if you knew anything else about the babies that died in 1990?" Dean asked.

Dr. Michaelson had an uneasy feeling and put out his cigarette. He tried to get up, but he couldn't. I held on to his hands. He stopped fidgeting and looked at me.

"Dr. Michaelson, please help us. My baby brother is sick, and he is in a coma. Nine other babies died last night, and more could die if we don't know what we're up against."

He was aghast. He leaned forward.

"Dead?" He asked.

We all nodded.

"And your brother is still alive? It's happening again. Can't believe it's happening again."

"You need to get him out of here, out of Belle Isle as soon as possible," he said, panicking.

"Why? Do you know how it happened? We need to know," I asked.

He got up and then turned to us.

"Follow me."

We followed him down a dark, narrow corridor and stopped at a door. He took out a key from his pocket and opened it; he then turned on the light. We entered a small room where we saw lots of clippings on the wall. Several newspaper article clippings about the dead babies. In 1990, they called it '*Belle Isle Mishap: A Royal Medical Tragedy.*' We walked over to the wall and looked at each article closely. Each of them classified Michaelson as a disgrace to his profession. Others were asking for his license to be revoked — all old articles. He limped over to the wall and stared at them as if it was the first time he had seen them.

"This has haunted me for years. I felt so embarrassed. Everyone came to see Dr. Michaelson, the best physician in Belle Isle. They referred everyone to me. I was the best at what I did. There was no disease I couldn't cure."

"Until this happened," I said.

Dr. Michaelson was crestfallen.

"It was a tragedy that day. It was a shame that I couldn't save those babies, but they also ruined my life."

"Do you know what caused their sickness?" I asked.

"No one knew…. we did every test possible, took blood samples, looked at the family history for any hereditary illnesses…. nothing. It's like the sickness came out of thin air. Everyone tried, but no one could understand why they got sick…. but your grandmother knew — she seemed to know exactly what was happening. I didn't believe her initially, but it made sense when I saw it myself."

We became intrigued. We felt as if we were getting somewhere now.

"So, you're saying my grandmother knew about this? Knew about what?" I asked.

He studied us carefully.

"You sure you want to know?"

"Yes," we all said.

"This was no ordinary sickness. 1990 was tragic… very tragic, but it was not the first case of the sickness either — so I understand. This… 'sickness' has been around for ages. Each day a baby gets sick, next day, two or three, next day 100 babies, nobody knew why. "And all of this…. happened in Belle Isle."

We tried our best to process every bit of information we could get, but I felt like he was holding back on us, like he didn't want to tell us the full story.

"Yes, but we still want to know what's causing the babies to die," said Hanna.

"I think it's best you talk to your grandmother." He said looking at me. "When I told the Medical Board and the Health Ministry, the same thing she told me — they fired me and ordered me never to mention this to anyone, like I was insane, trying to cover my own failures… their words," he said touching the paper clippings.

"We don't think you're insane," Dean said.

Dr. Michaelson smiled, "That's nice of you to say, son, but it won't change anything. Nobody can stop it, nobody ever even tried. Your grandmother and I brought it to the previous council, and they shunned it, saying we had no proof and were spreading lies."

"You were a part of the council?"

He nodded. "They were afraid. You ever noticed why those yellow bellies stopped having meetings? It's because they know people are going to bring it up, ask a lot of questions.   They never want to start a panic. Belle Isle has been a ghost town for years. Parents barely come out, only work at home, and children hardly play on the streets these days…. because they know. That's why I don't leave from here. I appoint someone from time to time to buy my groceries and bring it here. I thought the nightmare was over with, but I guess not. That thing will keep killing babies and no one will do a damn thing about it."

It felt as if lightning had struck me. Did he just admit to what I was thinking?

"What did you say?" I asked.

"What?" He asked.

"You said thing — you said that thing will keep killing. So, you think something was killing these babies?"

"Yes, I do. Unexplainable things have happened in this town you wouldn't even imagine. Many people have gone insane; some have left the district, and never returned. I haven't left this house in 27 years, and for good reason," he said. "Lots of people called your grandmother '*weird*', '*mad woman,*' '*the town clown*', because of what she believed in. But the thing is…. she wasn't. She was the smartest one out of all these idiots who were on the council. Mabel had enough balls to speak the truth and confront any problem head-on. A wise woman she is."

He paused and gazed into the distance. A perturbed look on his face.

"Some nights, I would wake up and hear strange noises."

"What noises?" I asked, curious.

"Sometimes, I would hear giant wings flapping up on the rooftops."

We exchanged looks. Hanna looked at him, confused and a bit frightened.

"Giant wings?"

Dr. Michaelson nodded.

"I've often hid in the corner because I knew I would hear it again. Wings flapped like a hurricane. But then, one night, I was in the living room, reading. I felt a chill. When I looked up, I saw its eyes glaring at me through the window. They… were…. terrifying." He recalled.

"What eyes?" I asked.

He turned to me slowly and looked at me.

"A pair of red, sharp eyes. Big ones."

"What was it?" Dean asked.

"I don't know. But it was massive."

I felt a giant lump in my throat. It paralyzed Hanna and Dean with fear. Giant wings, glowing red eyes. That sounded like a giant bird, but it made no sense. He probably made it up to scare us. Though I felt happy knowing he admired my grandmother, that she was fearless and didn't care what others thought of her. What he said about what people called her was not new to me. I have heard people talk things about her many times, things that have gotten me upset to the point I had gotten into trouble for punching someone older than me… an adult at that. But it didn't stop there because my mother took a swing at him too. All I knew, despite what a few people have said about her, I knew there were some who loved and respected her for the courageous woman that she was, and she was my last link in the chain to find out what's happening, so we could stop it.

I took out my phone and showed him the picture of the message that was left on the wall. His eyes widened when he saw it.

"Oh, dear," he said.

"What do you think it means?"

"You need to go to your grandmother. After what happened to your uncle, it must be hard for her to go through this again."

Dean and Hanna froze, they turned to me. I looked at him but I didn't know what to say or how to respond.

"What are you talking about?" I asked, confused. "I don't have an uncle."

The look on his face suggested he knew something I didn't know, and he regretted saying it.

"She hasn't told you."

"What Uncle???" I asked agitated. "What are you talking about?"

"I think you need to leave now."

"Let's go Ana, we have enough," Dean said. "Thank you,"

I stormed out of the room and out of the house. Dean and Hanna followed behind. I paced up and down, trying to remain calm. Was he speaking the truth? Did I have an uncle? Why would my mother keep that from me? And if I had an uncle, how come I've never met him? Did he die? I turned and looked at the house; he was standing in the doorway, and then he slammed it shut.

It was 6 pm. We were in there for about an hour and we got as much information as we needed. I needed to confront my grandmother for her to tell us the rest of the story, and about who my uncle was or if what Dr. Michaelson said was true, or maybe my mother knew and never told me. She knew all of what happened around here, so she was the next person to visit; and if my suspicions were correct, that old woman, whoever she was, had something to do with it before and now—I couldn't prove it, but I could feel it.

The bus stopped near the town square. We walked down the road and noticed many people walking inside the town hall and the lights were on.

The hall was full when we walked in; it had been empty for a long time. Up on the podium were the five council members, including the mayor, who sat in the middle. They were trying but failing miserably to quell the disorder among the crowd.

We stood at the back just to hear what was happening. I saw more people walking in and some tried to find seats but ended up crumpled in the corner.

"Seems like the news is out," Dean said.

"They couldn't keep something like this secret for long," said Hanna.

The towns' people were upset and shouting at the top of their voices. We recognized some as the parents of the babies that died.

I also saw my mother and Dean's parents up at the front. But why was my mother here and who was looking after Romaine? I didn't want to dwell on that right now because too many thoughts were running through my mind and I wanted to focus. Besides… I wanted to know what this was about, and I just had to be confident that he was fine.

The Mayor of Belle Isle… Adolphus Burton banged his gavel to calm the crowd down. "Ladies and gentlemen, please let us have order," he pleaded.

But they continued to voice their anger and frustration.

"Our babies are *dead*!!!" shouted one man.

"How are we supposed to keep our babies safe if we don't know what's making them sick?" shouted another.

The mayor banged his gavel again, multiple times… this time they calmed down, but just a little.

"Citizens, I understand your frustration, but this is not the way to handle your problems," said Mayor Burton.

"You can say anything. You don't have children," said an angry male resident.

The rest of the residents cheered his remarks. The mayor banged his gavel again.

"You have lost your daughter, Mr. Greenwall, and you are in a moment of grief. So, I will allow your insolent remark to slide just this once. However, I promise each of you, we will investigate this fully," he assured them.

"You guys always say that yet nothing is done. There are a lot of problems happening here in the Belle Isle District that need addressing. But all we hear is promises all over again," said another angry resident. "Y'all are just like the politicians, all bark, and no bite."

The residents cheered and approved of his discontent with the council.

"We have been smelling gas or something up here. We don't know where it is coming from or if it's poisonous. We have children here… small children Mr. Mayor and you and the board are not doing anything for us, so we basically must help ourselves," an angry female resident chimed in.

"Nine babies have died, and it must be the foul smell we been smelling in the community these past days that's killed them."

The crowd agreed with her. I didn't recall smelling any smoke or fumes. Did this happen during the day or in the night?

The crowd grew restless again and the mayor again banged his gavel, anymore knocks from that thing and it would split in half.

"Ladies and gentlemen, you need to understand, these things have to be looked at informally. There must be an investigation which most times takes even long —"

The residents were no longer listening and ordered the mayor to try harder or step down. Dr. Michaelson was right. The council was hiding something they didn't want to tell the residents about. It sickened me; children have died while they cowered behind their comfy chairs. I couldn't stand it anymore, so I spoke up.

"Is that why you shunned Dr. Michaelson?" I shouted from the back.

Everyone stopped and turned to me as I walked up. Dean and Hanna looked on, shocked, and tried to pull me back.

"Analisa!! What are you doing here?" My mother asked. "The council is for —"

"Adults only, yeah, I know, but I'm technically an adult, right?"

I walked up to the stage and faced the mayor; he looked right at me and then at my mother.

"Mrs. Kelly, is this your child?"

My mother looked on embarrassingly and answered.

"Yes, she is."

I didn't care if she was upset with me. She owed me an explanation.

"This council has done nothing but hide in its shell, keeping the truth from the people while babies are dying. So, is this council going to repeat the same mistake they did in 1990 when ten babies died?"

The residents murmured in surprise. The mayor looked at me with disdain and leaned over his table.

"Yeah, that's right, a news article came out on October 10th, 1990. Ten babies died, and no one knew about it. The paper didn't even go public, and so I did my research, and the Ministry, along with this Council, kept secret meetings about this and ordered the news reports destroyed because they didn't want to start — a panic," I said, annoyed. "I guess you paid off the parents to leave and never speak of it again."

"You will mind your manners, little girl. What we do and how we handle policies regarding the safety of this district is none of your business."

"IT IS MY BUSINESS WHEN MY BABY BROTHER MIGHT BE THE NEXT VICTIM!" I shouted.

The hall got silent.

"I'm sorry to hear about your broth—"

"I don't need your sorry, you just need to bloody grow a pair. My brother is not dead…. he's alive — barely. He's in a coma, but he will die if the council doesn't act soon.

The residents acted up again. This time, their fury landed on me. *"Why is your brother so important?" "Why is he alive and our babies dead?"* were some of the irate questions thrown at me. My mother held her head down. Dean and Hanna came and pulled me away. They walked me out of the hall meeting while the crowd continued to spew their hateful remarks. I looked over at my mother again… she didn't look at me.

We left the hall and continued walking down the road up to my house. Minutes later, we arrived.

I pushed the door open and Dean and Hanna followed me straight into the living room. I slumped on the couch.

"I don't think angering the council was such a good idea," Hanna said.

"Hanna is right. We know you're upset, but the best thing to have done was to reason with them calmly and objectively," said Dean.

"I don't care… don't you guys get it? They wouldn't have done anything anyway, no matter how calmly or objectively I spoke. They would rather sweep everything under the rug and pretend nothing happened because they are afraid."

Dean and Hanna looked at me, disheartened, but they understood my frustration.

"I'm not losing my brother, and I'm going to do everything I can to save him," I said firmly.

Suddenly, the door flung open and my mother stormed into the living room like a raging bull ready to charge. Dean and Hanna moved out of the way, but I didn't flinch. I sat in the chair and stared at her.

"Who the HELL do you think you are storming into the council meeting like that, embarrassing me???" She barked.

I crossed my legs and folded my arms. I was practically signing my death warrant crossing my mother the way I was, and I know the temper she had, but she owed me an explanation. I think I deserved that much. Suddenly, the nurse entered the living room with her bag around her shoulder. We all turned and looked at her.

"Miss Lee, you can go. I'll take it from here the rest of the evening."

Nurse Lee nodded and headed towards the door. My mother turned to me.

"Little girl, you better uncross your legs if you know what's good for you."

"Analisa, just let it go\ please," Hanna pleaded.

"Let what go, Hanna? I think I have a right to know, right Mommy?"

"Child, what are you talking about?" Mommy asked.

I got up and walked up to her. "Why didn't you tell me I had an uncle?".

My mother gaped at me as if I had finally lost my mind. She glared at Dean and Hanna.

"If I find out the three of you smoking something fishy, you see, I whip all three —"

"MOMMY, ANSWER ME!" I barked at her.

I heard myself when I said it. After it came out, I felt a lump in my throat. I knew I felt a huge backhand coming eventually, but it was a risk I was going to take, no matter how irrational it was.

"Who do you think you talking to?" She asked as she walked up to me. "Just who the hell you think you raising your voice at? YOU LOSING YOUR PLACE?" She barked, draping me by my shirt collar. She raised her hand to hit me, but Dean and Hanna held on to her just in time and pulled her off me.

"Mrs. Kelly, calm down, please," Dean pleaded.

"Ann, Stop this!"

My mother shrugged them off and looked at me…. her eyes welled up with tears.

"I don't owe you a damn explanation, you hear me? I work too DAMN hard to put food on the table for you and send you to school when I had little to nothing, for YOU to come and disrespect me. The day that happens, little girl, is the day you LEAVE this house."

She stormed off to her room, and I jumped when she slammed the door. Dean and Hanna were speechless and didn't know what to say. But they looked at me and realized that I was wrong for what I did, and I was hurting too. The tension was so thick you could literally cut it with a knife.

"Guys…. I think I want to be left alone tonight," I said sadly.

"You sure?" Hanna asked.

"Give her some time. She'll come around, but you need to calm down."

"Dean don—"

"Going off on her like that will not help. You need to sit down and talk to her. Maybe she had a reason… just…. listen."

Dean, again, the voice of reason, but he was right. I was way out of line. Dean leaned over and kissed me on the cheek, and I smiled.

They both said their goodbyes and sauntered out the door. I turned and walked towards my room door, but I stopped. I turned and looked at my mother's bedroom.

I walked to her door and raised my hand to knock…. but I heard something. I pressed my ears against the door, and I could hear her crying. I felt bad and then I broke down. What I had done was unforgivable, and I felt like a jackass talking to her like that.

I went into my room and closed the door. I didn't even bother taking off my clothes, I just took off my shoes and laid in bed, curled up and started crying. I couldn't help it. I let my emotions get the best of me and I hurt my mother. I wanted to talk to her, to tell her I was sorry, that I shouldn't have raised my voice.

Woke up the next morning with a splitting headache. The house was silent, and the only thing I could hear were the birds chirping outside. I didn't have any visions, any weird visits from the old woman or those two crows. I found it strange, but that didn't stop me from wanting to know what was going on, which meant, making peace with my mother and learning more about my uncle and why I was never told about him.

I was so busy thinking about everything else that I did not even think to pay my respects to the parents who lost their babies. I know I was the last person they wanted to hear from right now because I could hear them repeatedly saying, why is she so lucky? Why does her brother live and ours die? I couldn't forget those questions lingering in my mind. Everything was happening so fast that I didn't know how to process it and I had a history test to do tomorrow, and I wasn't even ready.

I opened my door and walked towards my mother's room. It cracked open a bit, so I pushed it and went inside. As I walked in, I saw Romaine hooked up to the machine. The nurse was there monitoring him on the computer. They changed Nurses from time to time. I went over to his crib and said my good morning. The Nurse turned to me and smiled.

"I'll give you a minute," she said.

"No, you can stay. I just want to look at him," I answered.

He was still quiet…. nothing was coming from him.

I wanted to hear his laughter, his incoherent babble. I laughed every time I remember him grabbing my eyelids, trying to open them and laughing each time I closed them. He just wanted to say something. I caressed his face and held on to his little hands.

"I won't let anything happen to you, I promise," I said smiling.

Pot covers were banging in the kitchen. I walked out of the room and closed the door. Then I headed slowly to the kitchen and peeped. It was my mother cooking breakfast, and I could smell the aroma that was brewing in the pot; Ackee and Saltfish with Breadfruit and plantain, one of my favourite meals. I didn't think I deserved it after how I behaved towards her last night.

I walked into the kitchen; she turned and saw me. We both stood there, staring at each other without saying a word. She turned back to the stove and continued cooking. I went to the fridge and took out the bottle of Orange Juice, took out a glass from out the cupboard and poured myself a cup.

I took the glass and walked out… but I stopped. I turned back, put the glass on the counter, ran and hugged her tight from behind. Tears flowed, and I couldn't control it. I said nothing, but I was sorry, and I knew she felt it because she caressed my hands. I let her go and hurried out of the kitchen. I peeked from behind the wall, and she just stood by the stove…. frozen. I had to make peace with her; I had to let her in on what was happening.

Next day, it was back to my regular life at school. I sat in the classroom, fidgeting, my palms were sweaty. You would think I haven't done this before, after five years in high school, which was torture and finishing one year of sixth form, this should have been a walk in the park for me by now. Apparently, it wasn't, with all the work, I had to do back-to-back.

Each year, more work piled up, and each time, it got harder. I stayed up last night doing nothing but beating the books. Ate a light snack and slept for about four hours, got up, beat the books again, then took a break, showered now I was here.

Mr. Francis walked inside the room with the other papers and set them down on the table. He then walked over to me and handed me the question paper. I took it from him and it felt thick, like five to six pages long thick. Mr. Francis looked at the clock above the board. It was 9:00 am. He turned to me.

"This paper is two hours long, Miss Kelly; you are required to answer all questions. If you finish before the gained time, you may take 15 minutes of which you will revise your work. You know the drill, so I don't need to ask if you understand," he said sternly.

"Yes, sir," I said, feeling my throat swell up.

He walked off and sat behind his desk. He took out his pen and started marking what I assumed to be the rest of the test papers. As I was about to start, I heard a strange sound.

"Psst." I looked up and Dean and Hanna were outside the door giving me a thumbs up. I couldn't concentrate with them there and even though I wanted to laugh, I fanned them away. Mr. Francis looked up instantly.

"Is there a problem Miss Kelly?" He asked.

"No sir." .

He held his head back down, and when I looked outside, Dean and Hanna were already gone. I took up the paper and looked it over through and through. I was happy that most of the questions that came were the very things I studied for. What a relief. What Dean gave me was very much helpful as well. So, there was no way I was going to fail this test or else I wouldn't hear the end from him. Thirty multiple-choice questions for Section A and five short-answer questions for Section B.

SECTION B:
Please read and attempt all Five (5) questions carefully.

1.   Who was the first post-revolutionary leader of Haiti?
2.   What was the name of the fortress built in the north of Haiti to repel invaders?
3.   What large slave uprising in the United States was inspired by the Haiti Revolution?
4.   How many plantations were in Haiti in 1754?
5.   What is the slogan of the Haitian Revolution.

I looked up at the clock and it was 9:20. So I got started.

I was already halfway through the multiple choice and it was easy because of Dean's notes.

An hour later, I was on the third short answer question, and I had to consider my answers before I wrote. I looked up at the board, then I realized Mr. Francis was gone. So were his papers.

Suddenly — the board made an annoying scraping sound, but no one was at the board, then — words formed out right across. My eyes widened. I tried to get up, but it seemed like I was stuck in the chair…. again. Then I heard faint whispers, very soft at first, then the whispers gradually got louder.

I looked all around me like I was going crazy, then I looked up on the board and letters formed. It wrote;

"Your… brother…."

I wanted to scream, but it seemed like someone had pressed together my lips with super glue.

"Is…. mine!!"

The message then flamed up, and I heard loud, rapid drum noises outside the window. The drumming continued for a couple of seconds… then it stopped. I turned to look; nothing was there. I turned back around…. there she was — standing in front of me…. the hideous old woman, her red eyes and teeth. She moved closer to my face and grabbed on to the desk.

"MINE!!" she shouted.

The whole classroom shook, and I started screaming. Then, out of nowhere, I heard.

CAW! CAW!

I turned to the window again and the two crows were there…. they let out a giant shriek, shattering the glass. The old woman screamed and disappeared in a puff of smoke out the door. Then — I woke up from a tap on my desk.

I looked up and Mr. Francis was standing over me with the sternest expression.

"You're finished. I hope Miss Kelly."

Right on time, I looked up at the wall. I looked down at my paper and I had completed all questions.

"Yes sir, I'm finished," I said, looking around the classroom. I handed the paper to Mr. Francis, took up my bag and walked towards the door. As I exited, I bumped into Miss Wynters knocking her books out of her hand.

"Oh!" she exclaimed.

"Oh, miss, I'm sorry, mis…"

"It's alright Analisa," she laughed. "Accidents happen."

She bent down to help me pick up the books. She looked at me. "Are you Okay?"

"Yes Miss, I'm fine… just had a test to finish."

"Well, I will have to take your word for it then," she said.

We finished packing up all her books, then she got up.

"See you next class, Analisa." she smiled and walked off. She then turned back around. "Oh, Principal Stewart wants to see you right away."

"Okay, Miss, thank you."

Just what I needed, another lecture about why I needed to go to the boys' home again this year. Why was it always mandatory for you to go to the children's home?

I needed to do something different.

I went to the principal's office and I knocked on his door.

"Come in."

I opened the door, walked in, and closed it. I sat down and waited till he was off the phone. The last time I was here, the office looked different. I've heard from many of my classmates and students in lower forms, mostly boys who got in trouble for fighting or fraternizing with girls, that he decorated his office almost every two weeks and counting weekends. Most of the pictures I see here were not there before. I guess he liked to redecorate.

He finally hung up the phone and turned to me.

"You wanted to see me, sir?" I asked.

"Yes, Miss Kelly, it's about the boys' home trip. I distinctly remember telling you and Mr. Walters to come and see me last week," he said.

"Yes sir, but things are complicated," I said without explaining too much.

"Yes…. I heard about your brother and I'm so sorry… how is he?"

"He's in a coma, sir."

"Oh dear, if you need anything, please let me know," he said.

"Just want him to wake up sir…. that's all."

"Yes, yes," he said, shuffling through papers on his table. "Ah," he said as he found what he was looking for. It was the forms we had to sign to go to the homes to complete our community service.

"Here are the forms, one for you and one for Mr. Walters. You can give him his copy to sign and bring it back to me," he said, handing me the forms. "I'm going to hand out the rest of the forms to the other sixth formers later today."

I looked at the forms, but I didn't take them. Suddenly an idea came to me, that I thought would be better for both me and Dean, but I needed the principal's permission.

"Sir, I have a request to make, but I hope it's not too late," I said.

He raised his eyebrows and leaned back.

"What sort of request?" He asked curiously. "I hope you're not trying to weasel your way out of this community service. It is going to happen."

"No sir, I'm not. It is for community service, but I think… with your help, we can improve it. We can combine it." I said, "Just give me a few days to sort out some stuff, please," I pleaded.

He rocked his chair back and forth, knitting his brow in thought.

"Very well, a week!" He said.

"Thank you, sir," I smiled, and I got up, then walked out of the office.

 Later, I arrived home and walked into the living room, and I saw my mother sitting reading her bible. I stood there watching her.

"Hi Mommy," I said.

She took off her glasses and looked at me.

"Hi," she replied, putting her bible down on the couch.

I dropped my bag on the floor, walked over, and knelt at her feet. I looked into her eyes. She investigated mine.

"Mommy, I'm so sorry," I said.

"Analisa, I don't want to do this now."

"But I want to," I answered.

"You already said sorry… that hug was enough. You've been through a lot too and I understand," she said.

 I took her hand and held on it.

"You remember what you told me when I was five?" I asked.

She laughed. "I told you many things when you were five."

"You said I was your shining star, your reason for living, and no matter what, you will always be there for me, and that there is nothing in this world you would keep from me."

Her smile faded, and she moved her hand right away as she picked up what I was trying to do.

"Ana, let me get back to my reading."

She picked up the bible, but I took it from her.

"Mommy, I'm trying to talk to you," I said.

"About what Analisa."

"Do I have an uncle?

My mother shifted her eyes. She wanted to avoid it. Her mouth agape. Words failed to come out.

"Mommy…. do I have an uncle?" I asked again.

She let out a deep sigh and looked down at me. "Yes…. you had an uncle," she said.

I already knew the answer. But hearing it from her made it more alarming that I didn't know.

"Why didn't you tell me, and what happened to him?"

My mother got up and walked over to the window.

"His name was Marcel. I was 8 years old when he died," she drawled, looking at me.

I got up slowly and walked towards her.

"1990… what hospital did he die in, Mommy?"

She smiled. "Analisa, you're a smart girl. I think you already know."

"When I heard you coming into the hall meeting and you mentioned Dr. Michaelson's name, I knew it was a matter of time before you found out," she said.

"So…. he was one of the babies who died at Royal Medical?" I asked.

She nodded.

Things were starting to come together. That I had an uncle that I never knew I had and that he was one of the babies that died mysteriously at Royal Medical. It was racking my brain. If that's true, then she also knew what caused it.

"Mommy…. you know what caused this sickness, don't you?" I asked.

As she was about to answer me, the doorbell rang. My mother went to open the door. I didn't realize the rain was pouring so heavily outside. When she opened it, a surprise greeted us as a medium built woman with short greyish hair and beautiful hazel nut-coloured eyes, holding a bag and an umbrella in hand…. it was my grandmother Mabel.

"Mama!" my mother said surprisingly."

My grandmother looked at her and smiled.

"So, you going to let your old lady stay out here in the cold or you going to let her in?" she asked.

"Mama, you know you don't need an invitation to come in."

My grandmother walked in and hugged my mother tight, then studied her.

"My lord Margaret, you look pale. You, okay?"

"Mama, can you stop?" she asked, looking around at me, embarrassed.

It was weird seeing how my mother acted around my grandmother, the same way I acted around her.

"Grandma," I said excitedly as I ran to her and hugged her.

"Look at you, girl, you getting too big. I know you eating good food, at least someone is," she said, looking at my mother. My mother rolled her eyes and walked off. I closed the door and took my grandmother's bag. I walked her into the living room and I placed her bag on the couch.

"You want to sit, grandma?" I asked.

"No, grandma is fine, dear," she said. "How is your brother?"

"Still in a coma," I said.

She walked over to me.

"How you doing? It hasn't been easy for you."

"I'm trying to cope, Grandma, but it's difficult."

My grandmother walked over to the window and looked out. This was the opportunity I waited for. If there was a time to ask all the questions, I wanted to ask… it was now.

"Grandma, there is something I need to ask you."

"I know you do, sweetheart, and I know what you want to ask," she said, smiling at me.

My mother came into the living room with two cups of tea, one for my grandmother and for herself. My grandmother always used to mix the tea bag even when it was already mixed. Take it out and put it on the side of the saucer. She took a sip and smiled.

"Just like old times. Your mother used to beg me every night to make tea bag for her. She loved it," she said to me.

Embarrassment was shown on her face. I could tell. My mother did that to me often. Told people stories about me when I was younger. It seemed like such a mother thing to do. I always said I would never do that to my child if I had one, but…. who knows, as you get older, your mindset changes.

"Did you tell her?" she asked my mother.

"She kind of found out from Michaelson."

"That old hog is still alive?" she asked, sipping her tea.

"Mama, do we need to tell her? It already messed up my childhood enough as it is. I don't want to burden her with this."

"You need to stop sheltering her. She is a grown woman."

"She's my child, Mama," my mother replied.

As they were exchanging words, I had to stop them from chewing each other's heads off.

"Guys!" I shouted.

They both looked at me.

"Analisa, just let me say this to you now, yes… you had an uncle and not a day goes by that I don't think about Marcel. I miss him and it's sad that he never got to live. I told your mother not to tell you because I didn't want to involve you in what's happening now," she said. "But know this…. it's not an airborne sickness or a virus of any kind…. the supernatural caused this sickness."

My mother turned her back. I sat down, focusing. Whatever I heard would change how I viewed the world altogether. I leaned forward.

"Grandma…. I've been seeing things… things that no normal person should see. I've seen creepy crows with blue eyes, but… what crept me out the most was this woman…. an old woman. I kept seeing her everywhere I went. I saw her here, at school, on the road. She left messages on the wall and at school…. I don't know what to think. Sometimes I'm afraid of sleeping at night because I think she might kill me. Also, Michaelson told us he heard giant wings on his rooftop, and red glowing eyes."

My grandmother stared at my mother. She was terrified.

"She's back….," my mother said. "Mama, please tell me it's not her again?"

"Who is she?"

My grandmother came over to me and sat down. She held onto my hand and looked at me.

"You're not seeing things…. she is real," she said with all seriousness.

All the fear I felt built up again. Now I knew who was making the babies sick. But how was she doing it, and why?

"In order to understand what's happening Analisa, you need to know how it all started."

CHAPTER FIVE
GRANDMA'S TALE

Growing up in the country was like living in paradise. We would wake up to the peaceful melody of the mockingbirds, breathe the fresh morning air and listen to the roosters crow. We would walk past neighbours who knew how to show respect, who always looked out for each other; always said *'good morning'*, *'good afternoon'* and the kids would all run and play with each other and have a good time… that sort a thing.

When I was a little girl, I used to run up the hills and fly kites with my brothers and sisters. I was the fastest out of all of them. My father would let me ride on the donkey's back in the mornings, so I could follow him to work. He was a farmer and he would let me pick the provisions from out of the ground and pick green bananas from off the trees to carry back home to have for breakfast.

I grew up in the beautiful Belle Isle District, a few houses down from where my daughter Margaret lives. Born in 1948, I was the third child of 6 children to Clifford and Bethel McCallum.

I am Mabel or 'likkle' as they so fondly called me because I was very skinny and short. I was the favorite of the family, and everybody loved having me around. They always had treats to give me, and no matter what, I always accepted. But as sweet as I was, I was prone to trouble. My siblings and I would often get scolded by our father for disobeying his orders. My mother was stern too, but she was naturally the calm one, the one who would scare us with the, *'you wait till your father gets home.'* threat. None of us liked to hear that because it was the fathers who gave the punishments.

We loved climbing the hills. That was our favourite pastime. My parents were lenient when they should be or when it mattered, but they always set ground rules for their children to follow and if we didn't obey, we would all sleep outside and let the cold air freeze us to death. My father would always say that to scare us, but he made good on his promise with my eldest brother, Elrond… he was the black sheep of the family who constantly got into trouble.

My father bought a bicycle with the little shillings he made from the ground provisions he grew. He needed the bicycle, so he could get to the market faster. He told us not to touch the bicycle, or we were punished.

We obeyed his orders because we were afraid of him, but Elrond, he was the daring one. He was the big troublemaker, and he thought he could ride the bicycle without being noticed or caught…. he was very slick.

"Don't want nobody to tell Papa what I'm doing," said Elrond. "Just going down the road and coming back."

"Papa said you mustn't ride the bicycle Elrond," I said, "He said if anybody rides it, I must tell him."

Elrond frowned at me. "You do that, and I don't buy you no more ice cream," he threatened.

He knew I loved ice cream. I would disobey even the harshest of orders just for ice cream, even when I regretted it afterwards and got in trouble.

Eventually, my father found out about it from one of the nosey neighbours and trounced him. Whipped him with his belt and sent him outside to sleep for the night; and from that time, none of us ever tried to disobey his orders ever again — well, not intentionally.

I attended Notten Hill Primary in Belle Isle. That school at the time was right next to Mount Techa before it burnt down. Most mornings, because it wasn't far from where I was, my mother allowed me to walk to and from school. I would stop at the local shop to buy sweets or Nutribun before or after school.

One day, I was coming home from school and I went to the shop to buy a Nutri bun and bag juice, what we used to call '*suck suck*'. I was low on coins, and I was very sad and hungry, but a mysterious lady was there buying stuff. Her bags were full of groceries. The lady saw me and took out shillings from out of her purse and handed it to me. I looked up at the woman and was in awe. This woman was attractive, light-skinned and smelled like cocoa butter, long black beautiful hair and she had on a floral dress and one of those straw hats.

"What's your name, little one?" the woman asked.

I looked up at her and smiled.

"My name is Mabel Miss, but people call me likkle Mabel because I'm likkle bit," I said proudly.

The woman looked at me in a puzzle. "What is likkle?"

"It means I'm little," I answered proudly.

The woman laughed. "I love that name. My name is Eliza…. Eliza Gutzmer," she said and shook my hand. Her hands were very silky smooth.

"You have a funny name. Why did your parents give you that funny name?"

"It suits me. Don't you think? I live up on the hill. Have you ever been up there?"

"Yeah, but I don't go too far because my daddy would know and beat me and I don't like beaten," I said.

"Fair enough. Well, if you are good, I can talk to your father and have you visit me one day. How does that sound to you?"

I thought about it for a while, and then I smiled. "Okay, Miss, you have a deal."

"Excellent. I will see you around Likkle Mabel. Such a cute thing you are," Eliza said, smiling, then walked off.

I had lots of friends in the district, but I never felt connected to anyone as I did with Eliza Gutzmer. After just meeting her that day, I saw her a couple times, more than I expected. Eliza, at one point followed me to school and even made sure I was safe and would wait for me after school to come back home.

I never told my parents about Eliza; she was my secret friend, even though she thought I did. I had told my father that I was going to play with some friends and that I would be back, but I secretly visited Eliza up in her little house on the hill in the evenings, when I should have been home. It was a steep climb and very rocky, but I was used to climbing the hills, having three brothers to climb with.

I often saw goats and cows roaming around rummaging for food and I would just stand there and watch them eat before going to Eliza's house. Being around my father, I was used to taking care of the animals, feeding them, and making sure they were healthy.

Eliza separated herself from the rest of the town, barely spoke with anyone except for me. I didn't know why—she seemed strange, but in a good way, she was different. But a 10-year-old befriending an adult in those times was high risk because children at that age or younger were vulnerable to being kidnapped or worse.

But I had nothing to fear from Eliza because she was genuinely nice. She lived in a rustic cottage with a thatched roof and her home was very welcoming, although small, very decorated with flowers neatly planted and had a very lemony smell. Everything was in order; nothing was out of place. I looked at everything in the cottage, but the one that intrigued me was Eliza's black owl. I loved birds, but I had a particular interest in Owls, they were very mysterious looking.

"This is a Black-barn owl, a very rare breed, very difficult to find," Eliza said, opening the cage to feed her. The owl flapped its wings and opened its beak as Eliza extended her arm. It jerked its head and nibbled on what was in her hand.

The owl's eyes were dark and hollow. Eliza caressed it, then closed the cage.

"Owls are sensible creatures; they can sense fear or when danger is near… but they can be friendly…. depending on how you treat them," she said.

Then I heard a noise coming from a room, the sound of a baby crying.

"Oh, someone is awake," Eliza said, walking to the bedroom.

The baby continued to cry, and then the crying stopped. Eliza walked out of the room with a beautiful baby girl.

"Mabel, meet my beautiful daughter, Constance," she said happily.

Constance was the most beautiful little thing I had ever seen. If she was a dove, she would be the most beautiful dove in Belle Isle, with wings of an angel and who would bring joy to all who saw her. She looked up at me with cute little eyes and gave the most joyous smile ever. I grabbed her fingers, and she gripped mine.

I was in such awe of Eliza and Constance that I often skipped school just to go up the hill to visit her and the baby to play.

One night, I went up the hill by myself with no one knowing, not my father, or my mother, or any of my siblings. I just wanted to see Eliza.

When I arrived near the cottage, I saw Eliza with a man, a man I recognized as a friend of my father, Victor Johnson. I hid behind the tall tree and watched as Victor kissed Eliza passionately on the lips. I was shocked because I knew Victor… he was a married man and I even went to this skunk's wedding. Why was he kissing Eliza? I walked closer and hid behind a bush, close enough to hear them speak, but they went inside the house, and Eliza closed the door behind her.

I crept further towards the cottage, ensuring I didn't make a sound. I tiptoed around the back and looked through the window, which was half visible. The two of them were getting intimate with each other. Then I heard Constance crying. Eliza held him off and went to the bedroom for Constance. Mr. Johnson looked upset because he couldn't kiss Eliza. I was sick to my stomach to think he had a loving wife at home with two children and he was here having an affair with someone who I considered a friend.

When Eliza came back, she had Constance in her hand, wide awake… what she said next left me dumbstruck..

"Look…. there's Daddy, say hi Daddy," she said, smiling.

I couldn't believe what I was hearing. I didn't know what to think of Eliza then. She was a home wrecker and had a baby with a married man. Did she know he was married and if she did, would she still have seen him? I looked up and Eliza and Mr. Johnson started kissed again… so I got up and left.

A couple of days passed, and I was upset and hurt. My father always taught me that a man should respect his relationship and honour his wife and children. What I saw was the direct opposite of that and as someone who admired Eliza, I was wrong. I have been avoiding her lately, taking shortcuts to go to school and coming back in the afternoons. Growing up in this town, you learn all the different ways to get somewhere.

On Sunday, church had just ended. My mother always overdressed and loved to show off and my father, as usual, wore casual gray suspenders, nothing fancy.

He was always one to leave as soon as church service was over. First one in, first one out, but my mother loved to stay back and chat with the church members.

As we got ready to leave the churchyard----there she was, right in front of us. She looked upset. Everyone around us gasped and started pointing fingers and trading nasty looks at her. Did they all not like her? Why were they looking at her like that?

"Hello, Mabel," she said, looking at me intensely.

"Likkle… How did this woman know your name?" My mother asked curiously.

Eliza looked at me, shocked, then chuckled.

"You didn't tell them. And here I thought I was going to get to meet them."

"We know all about you... stay away from our daughter," my father sternly guarded me.

How my parents were behaving towards Eliza was strange. They spoke as if they knew her personally. Did they know she was sleeping with Mr. Johnson? Eliza stared at my father, then looked at me, ignoring him.

"I haven't seen you these last couple of days. I missed you coming to visit me," she blurted out.

"What is she talking about, Likkle?"

I wanted her to stop talking before she told my parents that I visited her at her cottage way up in the hills, which was forbidden.

Suddenly I turned, and I saw Mr. Johnson stepping out of the church with his wife. He was smiling, but his smile quickly faded when he spotted Eliza. Eliza directed her gaze at him and something in me just spat it out.

"I saw Mr. Johnson kissing her and they have a baby!" I shouted, pointing towards Mr. Johnson. I covered my mouth after that huge outburst.

Everyone looked at me and murmured amongst themselves. Mr. Johnson stood there dumb and stiff, unable to say anything. His wife turned to him, folded her arms, and stared angrily. I looked over at Eliza; she was boiling mad, her lips twisted, and she frowned something wicked.

"You were spying on me?"

But I saw something else… her eyes…. her eyes became bloodshot red, and then they changed back as she calmed.

"Will see you again, Mabel," she said calmly, then she walked off. While Mr. Johnson was being cussed out by his wife and being hit in the head with her handbag. I felt scared. The look Eliza gave me was the look of immense betrayal and hatred. Her relationship with Mr. Johnson was a secret, and I ruined it. But something else puzzled me. Why were her eyes red?

I felt bad for revealing that Mr. Johnson was secretly seeing Eliza. Now because of me, his wife was furious and threatened to leave him… but in all fairness, he deserved it, and I couldn't put the blame all on Eliza; maybe she loved him, maybe she didn't know he was married, but now that would not happen because now, she was mad at me too.

My parents put me on punishment for a week for disobeying them, which meant no after-school activity, no sweets, no games, just from school to home. This was the time I wished I had kept my mouth shut. Then I wouldn't have felt this bad about something that was wrong. I should have left the cottage when I had the chance and minded my own business, but it was too late.

One afternoon after school, I opened the gate and I heard screams coming from inside the house. I rushed in, pushed the door open, and froze. On the floor, in the middle of the living room, was a bloody head of a donkey… my father's donkey. The stench was foul, and flies were swarming all over the head. My mother and other siblings stood by the kitchen horrified, then my mother looked at me… the look you gave someone when they were furious beyond comprehension.

"Likkle, you brought shame into this house," she cried.

"What did I do Mama"? I asked, confused.

"You know how much that Donkey meant to you father, look what happen now. He's going to be furious if he sees this."

"But I never do it Mama."

"You never do it, but you know who did… that woman you keep seeing. You going to stay away from her, you hear me?"

"She wouldn't hurt us Mama, we never do her anything," I said.

"That woman…. is dangerous. What do you know about her, huh?"

I tried answering but couldn't come up with an answer. I knew little about Eliza, except that she had a baby and that she was very kind to me; other than that, everything else was blank.

"Maxie, Elrond… help me move this head before your father comes home, please," she pleaded.

But it was too late. My father stepped in a few minutes before Elrond and Maxie could dispose of the head. A look of shock and anger swept across my father's face. He had that donkey his entire life, the donkey was his livelihood, part of his workforce…. and he came home to find his bloody head on his carpet. He fell to his knees, almost to tears, touching its bloody head. He started breathing hard; then he looked up at my mother.

"Who did this?" He asked angrily.

My mother looked at me.

"Think we know who Cliff," my mother said.

Then my father got up and turned to me, he walked up to me. I didn't know what to do.

I didn't know what he might have done, but he just stopped and looked at me. I held my head down.

"Likkle."

I looked up in his eyes… cold and filled with hurt.

"Yes, Papa."

"Go to your room, don't come out until dinner time."

"Yes, Papa," I said unhappily. I hung my head in shame and dragged myself to my bedroom. I pulled the curtain, went inside, and sat on the edge of the bed.

I refused to believe that Eliza was this cruel, that she would put my family through this much hurt just to get back at me. I had to see her; tell her I was sorry. I knew I was breaking my parents' rules…. again, but I had to set things right.

I had to clear my conscience or else it would have haunted me for the rest of my life.

That night, I snuck out of the house through the back door. Everything in the house was quiet, everyone was asleep, except for the crickets outside singing loudly. I pulled the latch and pushed it slowly so it wouldn't creak. I tiptoed outside and closed it. Then I dashed towards the front and went off up the hill.

I realized climbing the hills at night was never a smart move if you didn't have a lantern or flashlight…. I had neither, which was fine because I knew the hills like the back of my hand. Coming here many times, you remember certain things about a place.

I crawled through grass, twigs and stepped on jagged rocks that I didn't know were there, then… I finally got to her cottage. Her light was on. I walked up to her house, but then I heard the door open and I quickly dashed behind the tree. *Why was I hiding?* Probably because I outed her as Mr. Johnson's lover and she didn't like that or the fact that I knew.

She walked around the back. Seconds later, she came around and went back inside with a live chicken which was clucking all about, flinging feathers everywhere. She closed the door, and I tiptoed across her yard and around the back of the house, where the window was visible. I peeked through and I saw Eliza putting a bowl on the table. Her owl sat in the cage twitching its head and then…. it turned its head in my direction. I ducked in time, but my heart was pounding. I heard the chicken clucking and fighting for its life. Eliza took the chicken and pressed it hard against the table. She raised a large knife in her hand and swung the knife down on the poor chicken's head, blood spattered everywhere. I looked up and the chicken's body jerked like crazy and the chicken's head was there, lifeless…. dead… just like the donkey.

Her facial expression, the look she gave as she beheaded the chicken, was terrifying… cold. What I saw next… was beyond anything I have ever seen. She drained the chicken's blood into the pan, then she put the chicken on the table. She had her hands outstretched, closed her eyes. Suddenly, the lights started flickering, and she was mumbling some strange language. Then fire blazed from the pot. I became frightened and wanted to leave.

After she finished, the lights came back on and the fire died down. She dipped her hand in the pot and took out a doll, a very well carved doll… a doll that kinda looked familiar. When she revealed it closer, I gasped… cover my mouth, and stepped back quietly until —

CRACK!!

I stepped on a twig. I looked up and Eliza gave a hostile glare in my direction. She headed towards the door. I ran off as quickly as possible and hid in the bushes. Eliza came out and looked around with the knife in her hand. I then heard a crunching sound behind me and a large hand covering my mouth telling me not to scream. I looked up, and it was Elrond. I pushed his hands off.

"Why are you out here?" I asked.

"Why are you out here? You know if Mama and Pops find out you were out here, you're going to get in more trouble."

I told him to be quiet and not say anything else. Elrond and I knelt and watched what was going on. Then we saw someone walking up to the cottage. As he stepped into the moonlight… it was Mr. Johnson and he looked pretty upset. I was thinking of me and Elrond getting closer to them, but they spoke loudly, so we heard everything.

"How did Bethel's daughter know we were seeing each other?" he asked angrily.

"I don't know, she snuck up here obviously."

Mr. Johnson paced up and down. Eliza walked up to him and caressed his face. Mr. Johnson looked down at her hand and saw the knife with the blood dripping from it. He looked up at her and frowned.

"Why do you have a bloody knife in your hand?"

She stared at him. "Does it matter?" She asked.

He continued to pace up and down.

"Why are you stressing? Everyone knows now. Besides, who cares what they think?" she said, trying to kiss him. He shrugged her off.

"I care. The council doesn't know yet and if they find out, I'm out for good, and all my funding stops." He said panicking.

Mr. Johnson, being a part of the council, shocked me. I turned to Elrond, who was equally shocked.

"I didn't know Mr. Johnson was on the council Elrond," I said.

He looked at me. "Don't think Papa knew either," he said, equally shocked.

I turned back in Eliza's direction and she looked at Mr. Johnson…. angry …hurt.

"So, all you care about is your stupid council? What about ME? What about Constance?"

"Look, we had a little fun, yeah, and we produced a beautiful daughter, but…. think about the bigger picture Eliza. How would it look for a prominent member of the council to be seeing someone outside of his marriage, much less have a baby outside of marriage…. and then if they found out I was dating you and…. knowing what you are — that could be a problem, too," he said, "I'm this close to moving up the ranks in the council."

Eliza was livid, twisted… like she wanted to explode.

"So, me being a witch is too much for the prominent councilman, is it? Wasn't such a big deal when you were SCREWING me WAS IT?"

And then something happened…. in just a split second, Mr. Johnson was grabbing on to his throat, like he was about to convulse. He floated. Eliza's hands were outstretched, controlling him somehow. If I didn't see it for myself, I wouldn't have believed… that I had befriended a witch.

"All my life, I had to deal with men like you. I didn't think I was good enough. Because I was different, people shun me, treat me like I was trash you could throw away, and that's what you're doing to me now Victor, treating me like trash."

She clenched her fist tighter. Mr. Johnson groaned in pain, grabbing on to his throat.

"You screwed me, had your fun, now you want to bail," she said, seething angrily. She closed her fingers even tighter, initially increasing the grip on Mr. Johnson's throat. His eyes bulged out and his colour was turning into an unpleasant shade of purple — we needed to leave. "They have pushed me around long enough."

Elrond and I knelt in an uncomfortable position for the past couple of minutes now, watching Eliza choke her lover to death.

"Likkle, let's go," Elrond whispered.

As we backed away, we tried to move quietly, but the rocks gave us away and got Eliza's attention. Mr. Johnson was free from her grip. Elrond then ran away, leaving me like a coward. I turned, and Eliza made eye contact with me, then I too ran.

We ran as fast as we could down the hill as I caught up with Elrond. I looked back, thinking that Eliza was following us, but she didn't. She was capable, but she didn't want to hurt me. I saw it with my own eyes.

I was afraid of her now. If I knew who she was in the beginning, I would have just gone straight home that day without the Nutri bun, then none of this would have happened.

Days went by. My parents were furious that I had disobeyed them yet again and that Elrond, who was the eldest, should have known better. They didn't know what to do with me and it annoyed my father to even look at me. I felt bad.

Elrond told them that Eliza was chasing us, which was a lie. He also told them, much to my disapproval by tugging on his shirt, that Eliza was performing magic. My father was furious.

My father and the whole town carried out a manhunt for Eliza. I wanted to tell them it wasn't true, that Elrond was too busy running like a scared little girl to know that she never chased us because of me. My father and the rest of the townsfolk marched up in the hills with stones, torches, dogs, and pitchforks in search of Eliza, but they seemed to have lost direction.

My father came to me and asked for the direction of the house. I told him that Eliza was my friend despite what she was. He barked at me and told me if I didn't tell him where she was, he would disown me and have nothing to do with me. Most times he said things to hurt my feelings, but I loved my father none the less, so I did what he said.

"She lives right up there, behind those trees."

The Townsfolk climbed higher until they approached the cottage. It was gloomy. No light was in the house. My father marched in front and called out.

"ELIZA GUTZMER! We're calling you out, you wicked witch."

The rest of the townsfolk were readily preparing for whatever happened. The door opened slowly with an eerie creak and out of the pitch blackness…. Eliza walked out calm, not saying anything. Just staring at us, then at me. I didn't look up. I kept holding my head down.

"Little Mabel… I'm disappointed," she said.

"Don't you ever speak to my daughter again! Are you going to come quietly or you going to make us come for you?"

Eliza smiled. "You're welcome to try. "But be warned, it will not end well for you."

As the men made their advances, Eliza extended her arms and all the men, their bodies pummeled against the trees, grimacing in pain. I begged her to stop, looking at my father kneeling, crying out. Eliza didn't care. Her eyes turned red. She swung her hands and men were flying all over the place, in trees, bushes… some were even flung far across the deepest, darkest part of the hill — nobody could have survived that.

My father saw what was happening, took out his cutlass, and threw it at Eliza…. but then, it froze in mid-air…. my father's eyes widened. He tried to move, but he couldn't. I looked at him and I could see the fear.

I turned to Eliza and her eyes were as red as blood… the hate and the pleasure she felt was disturbing to see. The edge of the cutlass turned towards my father; she was going to kill him. As she moved her hands to plunge the cutlass into my father's chest, I ran in front of it.

"MABEL!" My father cried out.

Eliza's cold features softened when she saw me. The cutlass fell.

"You made me do this Mabel. You caused this."

"I'm sorry, I never meant that to happen."

Suddenly…. I looked behind Eliza, and one man walked out of the house with Constance. Eliza heard the footsteps; she turned around and yelled.

"NO!"

The men got up finally and raised their weapons. Eliza, on the ground, turned to me, crying.

"You led them to my house… to get my daughter?" she asked, shaking with anger.

"No, no, I wouldn't do that. I —"

"LIAR!!!" she thundered.

The earth trembled beneath us and we could barely keep our balance. I pleaded with her, tried to get her to stop, but nothing worked. The ground then cracked with Eliza's anger increasing without thought.

Eliza was given an ultimatum; either give herself up to the council for practicing unauthorized magic or lose her child forever. When she heard this, she calmed down, and the ground stopped shaking. The men left the hill with Constance and Eliza had no choice but to stand there without risking hurting her child.

I asked my father about Constance and whatever happened to her. He told me to forget about it and that it wasn't my concern. I wondered how Eliza was doing and that she must have been going crazy without Constance.

We learned later that Constance had died. No one knew how. But Constance never deserved that. She was innocent. Eliza found out, and was consumed with rage.

A week after, 9 houses had burnt to the ground in Eliza's wake, five children got ill and later died. We were so scared of what was happening, my father moved us out to go stay with our uncle in Darliston. Then later we heard our house burned down as well. I couldn't believe what was happening and somehow, I thought I caused Eliza's pain.

I felt so guilt-ridden that I took the brave route and talked to my parents about talking to Eliza and pleading with her. That plan didn't go as well as I thought; they quickly reminded me I was still grounded and even thought about extending my punishment. Then my father decided it was time to end it all.

He went to the Council and begged them to give him permission to lead an army against Eliza, to put an end to her terror on the town. The council forbade it and told my father to leave it alone. My father, disappointed in the council's decision, cursed them off and stormed out. He didn't listen to them, though; he mounted an army of powerful men, bigger than before, to get any weapons they could find, to march up to the cottage against Eliza once and for all… one last time.

That night, the group of men along with my father went up to the hill, armed to the teeth and arrived at Eliza's cottage. Eliza apparently prepared for them. I wouldn't have believed if I hadn't witnessed it with my own two eyes. A gigantic owl replaced Eliza's small frame. She had shed her skin. It was hideous. The Owl fought them hard. The men were initially no match for her supernatural abilities and now, with her enormous transformation, many men died. Then my father had one last plan. There was a bottle with gasoline in it. He ran up to the house while the other men tried but failed miserably to subdue Eliza in her current form. He went around the back, broke the window frame and threw the bottle through it. The bottle broke as it hit the floor.

He then took out a match from out his pocket and threw it. The flames roared and spread instantly.

Eliza heard the blaze and saw the ferocious fire coming from her house and the loud shriek of her pet owl. Eliza shrank to her normal size.

She screamed and ran towards the burning cottage, possibly to save her owl; but while she was inside…. the flames spread even more.

The foundation fractured until there was nothing left to save. The whole cottage went up in smoke and crumbled; then…. there was nothing but ash, smoke, and rubble — Eliza Gutzmer was dead.

I was heartbroken when I heard she died; she was my friend, misunderstood, but she kept killing people. My family moved back to Belle Isle to rebuild our home and everything seemed normal again… somewhat.

I didn't get to tell Eliza how much I appreciated her friendship, even though I betrayed her. The guilt I felt was gnawing at me to the point I had trouble sleeping some nights. So, one afternoon, to clear my conscience, I came home from school and trudged up to where her cottage was to pay my last respects to her and her daughter. When I went further up the hill to her house…. there was no debris, no ash. The spot where Eliza's cottage was… had disappeared.

CHAPTER SIX
THE LOST CHILD

I sat in my room, going through many scenarios in my head from my grandmother's story. The clouded thoughts in my mind were hard to explain. I honestly didn't know where to begin. So many things I didn't know about my grandmother suddenly made more sense. All this started with her and Eliza Gutzmer, who was apparently a witch who could transform into an owl and she lived right here in Belle Isle.

I had two sets of assignments to complete and I couldn't find the time to do them even if I attempted to because I was too engaged with the history lesson. All I could think about was Eliza Gutzmer and how she lived.

From my grandmother's recollection, she was thoughtful, not genuinely a threat to anybody, but lived in a cruel society who thought she didn't deserve to be among them. If she and my grandmother never met, then probably none of this would have happened. She said that she blamed herself for what happened to Eliza and her daughter Constance. Maybe it was her fault, but regardless of that fact, she was a threat to society and it couldn't have gone any other way.

I went into the kitchen to set the table for dinner and while I did that; I thought about the night I saw the old woman, and the portrait of the baby on the chair.... what if that baby was Constance? What if her baby dying was the reason she went on a rampage and killed a lot of babies? Was it revenge? Was it the reason she came back?

My mother and grandmother walked with the pots of rice and peas, barbecued chicken, and potato salad and placed them on the table.

We ate in silence, which was awkward. We usually had dinner conversations about everything.

I looked over at Romaine's high chair. Even though he was here in the house, it felt as if he wasn't.

I was just hoping he would wake up now and start crying; let us know he was okay.

"Romaine is fine… he has us to protect him," my grandmother said.

I looked over at my grandmother and questioned her somehow. Maybe there was something I could know more about Eliza that could help us stop her.

"Grandma, does anybody know what happened to the cottage after it burnt down?"

"No. Just from what my father told us. I went up there and everything was clean, no house…. it's like nothing was there, just a big space."

"It couldn't just disappear."

"Something is keeping her here, but I don't know what. Everything she owned got burnt," said my grandmother.

"In my… vision, the one I was telling you about…. I saw a picture of a baby, a little baby girl in a portrait."

My grandmother looked at me instantly.

"Constance," my grandmother said as she got up from the table to go in her bag.

"You think it's her grandma?" I asked.

My grandmother took an old picture from her bag, walked back over to the table, and sat down.

"Eliza wanted me to take this picture of Constance when she was learning to sit up," Grandma said, handing me the photo. "This is the baby you saw?"

I looked at the photo and thought long and hard, and then it registered.

"Yeah, that's her. That's the picture of the baby. I saw the old woman holding it. But it's how she held it. She gripped the portrait tight. I didn't even know I noticed it because I was terrified, and she looked at me so angry," I said, recalling the horrific moment.

"It's her," my grandmother said gravely. "It's Eliza. She's seeking revenge for Constance's death and taking it out on my family. I was so hurt when I heard Constance died."

"It's not your fault, grandma, you know that," I said.

"I know that child. I couldn't stop her then, and I don't know if I have the power to now. I don't know what she has become. Last time I saw her was when she took my son away." She said, clearing her throat. My mother held her head down in silence.

"Marcel's crib was in my room, and your mother slept with me. I had gotten up to go to the bathroom and then I heard Marcel fussing… so I thought he was hungry. When I finished using the bathroom, I opened the door and there… I saw a dark figure standing over him. It moved closer like it was kissing him and Marcel started crying more. I shouted out, and it turned to me. It was like I couldn't recognize her. She was the most hideous thing I ever saw. It started gliding towards me, but I just put my hand on the light switch and turned it on. It screamed and flew out the window. I ran to the window and looked out…. it disappeared." My grandmother said.

"That's how Marcel got sick."

My grandmother tried to put on a brave face, but deep down I could feel that she was still torn up about her baby who died 26 years ago.

After we finished eating, I got up and cleared the table and washed the plates.

Later, I walked into my mother's room to check on Romaine… but my grandmother was standing over him. I smiled and closed the door. As I was about to open the door to my room, I heard laughter coming from the living room. *That's strange!* I walked towards the living room and it seemed as if my eyes were playing tricks on me… because sitting right in front of the TV were my mother and grandmother. They both looked around.

"What's wrong baby?" My mother asked, concerned.

"Grandma, were you with Romaine just now?"

They looked at each other. I sprinted towards the room and busted open the door…. no one was there, only Romaine. I held on to my head in frustration. My mother and grandmother trailed behind.

"She was here… I don't know how she was, but she was just here…." I said. "Grandma, you were here, right by Romaine."

My grandmother walked past me and looked around the room, then she sniffed and turn towards us.

"Something was here," she said.

"Oh god!" my mother said, rushing towards Romaine. "How are we going to keep him safe if she can still get to him?"

My grandmother looked towards the window and walked over to it. She noticed a trail of black substance left along the windowsill. She touched it and sniffed it and turned to us with a grave look on her face.

"Mama?"

"What is it, grandma?" I asked frantically.

"Ash," she said.

"Ash? Why is ash on the windowsill?"

"She must have come through the window," said my grandmother.

I was now confused how a restless spirit could make tracks. Spirits don't leave marks or trails…. unless she wasn't a spirit at all. I theorized.

"Mama, what spirit leave marks like this?"

"There was a story I was told as a child by my uncle, and I told your mother the same story when she was younger. I didn't think nothing of it before until now," my grandmother said.

Then my mother looked at her strangely.

"Mama, you not talking about that Ol'Hige duppy story?" My mother asked.

"I'm sorry, the ol' what now?" I asked, confused.

"Ol'Hige," my grandmother said.

"What's an Ol'Hige?" I asked.

"The Ol'Hige is an ancient powerful spirit going back biblical times. This spirit takes the shape of anything or anyone. A spirit that feeds on young children, steals their essence, making them young while the children wither and die."

I remember my grandmother telling me that a witch caused why the babies were sick, but then she was telling us about some Ol 'Hige spirit. I looked at my mother, who was lost in her own thoughts, remembering the stories told to her as a child.

"I used to have sleepless nights over those stories," my mother said.

"Grandma, I don't understand. How is it that the witch and this spirit have the same abilities? Where did this Ol 'Hige come from?"

"Legend has it that 100 years ago, obeah practitioners messed around some powerful dark magic calling on any spirit they could find to get rid of their enemies," my grandmother said.

"Why??"

"Because they wanted to scare townsfolk. People who made fun of them and classified them as animals. So, one night, a group of obeah practitioners sat in a circle and they had a book with them, a dark book filled with black magic and many creatures. They searched the book for the perfect creature, so evil, so scary that even the boogeymen wouldn't mess with one…. and they found a very specific one… the Ol'Hige… otherwise called 'The Omen of death' or 'destroyer of youth'," my grandmother said. "Ol'Higes are powerful spirits who can inhabit a living being, allowing them to shed their skin when their bodies are dying. They could transform into anything, a bright fireball that flies across the sky in search of its victims, or a wolf who draws her victims by using a mother's voice to call to the child and the wolf would lash out and feed on them or whichever. They prey on the young, and they feed to gain power. Once they have fed, they transform again into their new form."

"So, what happens after the Ol'Hige is summoned?" I asked.

"Many babies were sick, lots of them died. Parents would leave their homes, take all their belongings and go far away to make their children safe. But the Ol'Hige follows them wherever they go, no matter how far. Those were the stories we were told to scare us, but…. it's not just a fairytale," my grandmother said.

The more I heard the more frightened I got. I second guess if I wanted to continue this journey of saving the town. Dealing with something so old and powerful was not what I had bargained for… this Ol'Hige or whatever, if what my grandmother said was true, then we would need a lot of help and I know I would have to fill Dean and Hanna in on it tomorrow.

"Do you think Eliza was the Ol 'Hige or became the Ol 'Hige?" I asked.

"I don't know. If she was — then she was old. Maybe I didn't know her to begin with. If she is indeed the Ol 'Hige, this entire district is in trouble. We are dealing with a powerful entity."

This was the first time I had ever seen my grandmother this worried. Her eyes darted everywhere, and her legs were shaking. She was genuinely afraid, so was my mother and so was I. This was an old ghost story come to life and we did not know how to stop it.

I told my mother that Dean, Hanna, and I would find some time at school to go to the library to dig up some more information on Eliza Gutzmer. We needed to know more about her past, her likes, weaknesses, what she ate, what she was allergic to… anything that would help us defeat her.

We now had enough to know what we were dealing with…. Ol'Hige, an ancient evil. The thought of it made me want to jump out of my skin.

While my grandmother was explaining to me about the Ol'Hige and how it transforms, I was thinking about how the crows fit in all of this. Then I forgot during my…. supposed hallucination in the History test; I saw the Ol'Hige, and the crows came and scared her away. *What did it mean?* Were the crows trying to help me or just scare her away?

There was a lot to process, so I would not get this done tonight. I went to bed early because there was so much to do, and I needed to be sharp and ready.

Dean and Hanna met me at the bus stop the next day and I told them that my grandmother came over and she had lots of information that we could use.

While on the bus, I filled them in on how my grandmother and Eliza Gutzmer knew each other and were close friends, but Eliza lived with a dark secret and had a daughter with a council member, which was strictly forbidden. When I told them the rest, they too couldn't process everything at once. Dean looked as if he was in an episode of the twilight zone.

We came off the bus, walked through the school gate and continued our conversation.

"So, wait… you telling me that your grandmother actually told on a witch and lived to talk about it?" Dean asked. "Wow, she was brave, not so smart — but admire her courage."

I punched Dean very hard on the shoulder.

"Ow! Jeez alright, sorry," he said, rubbing his shoulders.

"If this Eliza is the Ol' Hige witch, you think she's gonna strike again? We haven't heard of any attacks lately," said Hanna.

"She'll be after my brother. I think she knows he's still alive and is waiting for the right time to finish him; and I will not let that happen. So, before we let anything like that come to pass… we need to find out everything we can about her. We meet up at the library after school, okay?"

"Okay," they both said, and we went to our separate classes.

During the second period, I walked over to my locker to take out my text for geography class. I closed it and I turned to see Mr. Francis walking towards me. He had a paper folded in his hand. I felt my heart beating like crazy and he had a very smug look on his face. He just stood there looking at me, saying nothing, and then he smiled.

"Miss Kelly…. I must admit, I didn't think you would have scraped through this test given your…. current situation with your brother and such, but I'm here to say I'm pleased with your paper," he said.

He handed it to me, and I unfolded it. My eyes lit up like I had received the best Christmas present ever.

"An A+, well done, Miss Kelly," he said, smiling.

"Thank you, sir."

He walked off, and I squealed like a little girl. This lifted my spirits a lot, and I needed some good news despite everything that was happening.

In Geography class, I sat down with my book opened, smiling from ear to ear, and then…. I heard it…. a strange whisper. It started off slow at first, then it gradually got louder.

"*I WILL KILL YOU!!!*" A raspy voice barked.

I jumped in my chair, causing my textbook to fall on the floor. The entire class stared at me, especially the Geo teacher who was writing on the board.

"Is there a problem, Miss Kelly?" she asked.

The whispers came back, and it was all around me like it was bouncing off the walls in the classroom. Then the voices trailed off outside. I grabbed my book, and I rushed towards the door.

"Miss Kelly, where are you going? Class has just started."

"I'm sorry miss, but I…. ahm am not feeling well so… yeah sorry," I said, rushing outside of the classroom.

The whispers came back stronger now, and it was coming from the direction of the third form block. I followed the voices… then I turned the corner and saw a student sitting in a male student's lap. I stopped and looked at them, forgetting for a moment that I was a prefect.

"Excuse me, you two don't have class?" I asked hotly.

They looked at me, chuckled, and went back to their routine. I was in no mood to be disrespected, so I grabbed the girl by her arm and it was a third former who I didn't particularly like.

"I don't have time for your foolishness, so you either go to you class or I take you straight to the principal!!" I snapped.

She shrugged me off.

"Do I look like a child? Don't touch me again."

I walked up to her.

"This little bad girl routine you have might work with the other preppy sixth formers. They don't work with me, you hear me…. Priscilla."

Her eyes widened.

"Yeah, never thought I knew your real name? My mother knows your mother and trust me, all she has to do is make one phone call and the way you've been behaving at school is on record. You'll be pissing yourself through graduation when you mother is done with you… and you and I both know how your mother is."

Her eyes darted from me to the boy, and then she rushed off in the other direction. I exhaled slowly and my glances were now directed at the boy sitting. He took up his books and left. Then I saw Dean and Hanna coming down the walkway.

"What was that about?" Dean asked.

"Nothing important. Guys, something just happened."

As we walked further up the third form block, I explained to them about the series of whispers I was hearing. Each time I heard the whispers, a loud raspy voice disrupted it and basically scared me out of the class.

"This happened when you sat down?" Hanna asked.

"Yeah, right as I sat down, and the whispers were bouncing off the walls in the classroom. I know it sounds stupid, but I'm telling the truth."

"We're not saying we don't believe you, but why are you hearing it and we are not?" Dean asked.

I stopped and looked at Dean.

"I don't know. Seems like it was trying to warn me or something. We need to get to the library, like right now."

"But... we still have class," Hanna chimed in.

"Yeah, this week is going to be the hardest week ever and we need to step our game up, exams coming up soon," said Dean.

"Guys, I know all that, but if we don't put a stop to all of this... studying for some test won't matter. The witch will continue to live on for years and years."

Dean and Hanna looked uncomfortable as they were never ones to skip a class, ever... neither was I, but this was way more important to me and my brother's life depended on it.

"Alright, we'll do it... need some excitement, anyway."

"We're doing this for your brother too," said Hanna.

"Thanks, guys," I said happily. "Let's go."

I knew deep down they thought I was crazy, but I knew something was wrong and we had to do something about it. We continued down the hallway and made our way to the library. We gathered as much history books as we could and Hanna borrowed the school's laptop to help with the search.

"Find anything?" I asked.

Hanna typed in the name 'Eliza Gutzmer' and about a hundred links came up with the same name. Hanna leaned back and shook her head.

"This is going to take a while. How are we going to know what to look for?"

"We just have to keep looking. Find something that fits the description. Use keywords like 'Belle Isle' or 'Cottage fire' or 'Belle Isle Cottage fire' anything. My grandmother said she kept to herself. She loved to plant, and she kept a lot of flowers in her home."

"So, she was a gardener?" Dean asked.

"Could be, or maybe she just loved flowers," I said.

"Think I found something," said Dean, placing one book in front of us. "This book outlines every aspect of Belle Isle's history."

We looked and couldn't find any connection to what Dean was showing us. We skipped a few pages, and we saw some pictures dating back as far as the 1700s during the slavery era. Pictures of slaves being shackled, tortured, pictures of slaves kneeling, tied together with their slave masters.

"Dean… what we lookin' at?" I asked.

"What do you see in these pictures?"

Hanna and I looked for the past couple minutes and we still couldn't see what Dean was looking except for pictures of slaves.

"In every one of these pictures we see…. there is a picture of a woman dressed in a floral dress. Look carefully."

We turned back a few pages and looked again…. we saw a light-skinned woman, always standing at the back with the slave masters.

"You said your grandmother remembered Eliza loved wearing floral dresses, right? What if… this is her, or was her?" Dean asked.

"That's impossible…. she couldn't be…. it can't be," said Hanna in disbelief.

I looked at the bottom of the page where the names of slaves and slave masters were. We looked carefully but didn't say Eliza's name. Maybe she went by another name.

"If that's her…. she must be hundreds of years old."

"Well…. she is a witch," Dean outlined.

"But if that's true…. she would be the thing the obeah practitioners conjured up," I said, trying to put the pieces together.

"Not necessarily," Hanna said, typing away on her laptop. "Look at this."

She turned the laptop to us and showed us a family history page. Someone who apparently did some digging up of a family wrote the article called the Bertrams.

"Who are the Bertrams?" I asked.

"Look at the picture," Hanna said, pointing to the screen.

We saw a picture of a man and woman and standing in front of them, very mean looking, and there was a clearer picture of the woman we kept seeing in the floral dress, but much younger — teenager, perhaps. The parents' names were underneath their pictures. 'Anthony and Lizzie Bertram. Their daughter's name etched at the bottom of her picture.

ELIZA BERTRAM
Born April 09, 1612–Died September 12, 1712

I looked closer at the date.

"How accurate is this?

"Only one way to find out…. read Hanna," Dean said.

"It says here that Eliza Bertram was born to a St. Lucian family who moved to Guadeloupe."

"Guadeloupe?" I asked, surprised.

"Yeah, her parents, who were career criminals, moved to Guadeloupe after police caught them stealing expensive artifacts from a wealthy crime family."

They were hunted down and almost killed. They left St. Lucia and somehow entered Guadeloupe without being seen.

"While they were there, they had no money and didn't want to earn by doing labouring work. They instead wanted to carry on what they started by stealing. Eliza wanted to earn an honest living, but her parents weren't having it and they abused her and often forced her to steal for their survival. She refused, so they beat her repeatedly and bruised her to where she blacked out."

Hanna read with a disturbed expression on her face.

"Does it say anything about her changing her name?" Dean asked.

"Well, it gets interesting."

She continued reading.

"Most nights, Eliza would go to bed hungry and wake up in the middle of the night with belly pains. She would tell her parents that she wasn't feeling well, but they would run after her and force her to watch them eat while she starved. Eliza became so broken and lost that she couldn't take anymore, and she ran away from home, disappeared without a trace. Her parents didn't want to involve the authorities because of their record. So, they went out to look for her themselves.... then eventually gave up."

Dean and I sat and listened attentively as Hanna read on. They found Eliza on the side of the road in an impoverished neighbourhood. Rats sprang across her body and often tried nibbling on her face; but they scampered off when they saw a white woman walking towards her. The white woman saw her, infuriated that people were just strolling past her without even trying to help. She took her in and nursed her back to health. A state of shock came over us when we saw what her last name was — "Gutzmer!" we all said.

"Did you grandma know about this?" Hanna asked, looking at me

"I don't think so," I said. "Continue."

"For years, Eliza has been trying to get her parents to love her, accept her, not try to change who she was or who they wanted her to become. But now.... she found acceptance, she found love and happiness in her new guardian, her adopted mother — Constance Gutzmer," Hanna stopped.

We all looked at each other with shocked expressions. So, this is where she got the name for her daughter. Eliza named her daughter after the woman who took her in... even took her last name. We were waiting to hear more, but realized Hanna wasn't reading.

"Why did you stop?"

"That's it.... there's nothing more," said Hanna, disappointed.

"Seriously.... that's it?" I asked, brushing Hanna aside and scrolling down at the rest of the page, but it blocked us from the rest of the site.

We were stuck, but we started getting bits of information about who Eliza was.

I don't think my grandmother knew Bertram was her last name and not Gutzmer. Eliza changed it to Gutzmer because her adopted mother loved and protected her, and she hated her actual family. *Whatever happened to them?* We needed to know the rest of it, how she became the Ol' Hige.

"What about the author? Did you see a name?"

Hanna scrolled up to the top of the page.

"No, no name…. anonymous."

"Then how do we know this is all true?" Dean asked.

"Well, it does kind of make sense. Everything grandma told me was her version of Eliza's identity when she met her. Eliza was already an old…. old woman when she met my grandmother, so this — this is telling us who she was as a child."

"But you think it's enough?" Hanna asked.

"No…. I don't… not nearly enough. We need to know more."

"But how are we going to do that? No one who lived through those times is alive now unless they're immortal." Dean said with a serious face.

Hanna and I looked at Dean, then we all looked at each other and laughed.

"But seriously… immortality is a possibility," Dean added.

"All right nerd, let's go," I said, pushing him to leave.

We walked out of the library, discussing more of what we read. As we were leaving the third form block, we could hardly pass because there was a massive crowd in the middle of the campus and excessive loud chatter. Teachers and students gathered around something. Students scampered all over the place. One student ran in my direction and I pulled his arm, stopping him.

"What happened?" I asked, concerned.

"Priscilla, she collapsed… look like she had a seizure," he said, panting.

"So, where are you going?"

"The principal asked me to get the nurse."

I let him go, and he ran away. We walked over to the crowd and tried to push our way through. Principal Stewart was on the intercom, trying to calm the students down.

We pushed through, and saw Priscilla on the ground…. pale as a ghost. Her eyes dilated and her whole body was stiff. The teachers and the other students looked on whispering among themselves, others looked on and were crying… most likely

Priscilla's friends. I walked up to the principal, as he was still trying to calm the students.

"Sir, what happened?" I asked.

"I don't know Miss Kelly. Priscilla was in Mrs. Warby's class. They were supposed to go on a trip this afternoon. The bus is already here — but Priscilla said she wanted to use the bathroom and when she left… she never came back until," he said, pointing at her body.

We all looked at her. I bent down, touching her hands. She still felt warm. Then I looked at them closely. They looked dark.

"What's wrong?" asked Hanna.

I looked up at her.

"Dirt," I said "There's dirt under her fingernails and on her hands."

"Maybe she touched something," added Principal Stewart.

"With black substance? What black substance would there be for her to touch and make her hands all black like this?"

Suddenly, the nurse came running with the third former trailing behind carrying a wheelchair with a bucket of warm water and a towel. She set the bucket down on the ground and urged the students to move out of the way. The principal then turned on his com.

"Students, please give the nurse some space please. Everything will be fine from here. Please return to your classes."

Hanna looked at him.

"Sir… school is over."

"It is?" he asked, looking at his watch.

"Yes, sir, didn't you hear the bell?"

"I was too busy trying to keep these children quiet. I didn't hear," he added, sounding exhausted.

He breathed in deep and let out an enormous sigh.

"All this happened on my watch," he said, embarrassed.

"Did you call her mother, sir?" Dean asked.

"She's on her way…. she didn't sound happy. Not to worry, I'll handle it. I am the principal, after all."

Dean, Hanna and I looked at each other, trying not to laugh, but nodded our heads in agreement with the principal.

The nurse had finished wiping Priscilla down.

"Alright help me get her into the wheelchair," the nurse said.

Two third form boys held on to her from both ends and hoisted her up into the wheelchair. She looked like a crash test dummy. I don't think she would have felt a thing if she had bumped her head. I know it seemed harsh for me to say, but that's how it looked.

"Will she be alright?" I asked.

The Nurse looked at me with a grim expression.

"Too soon to tell, but she is boiling. I will have to do some check-ups. There is a strange bruise or mark on her neck. Don't know where that comes from."

"Wait…. what mark?" I asked immediately.

"The black mark on her neck, you didn't see?" she asked.

The nurse turned Priscilla's head to the side…. there was a large dark mark on the left side of her neck. I stepped back, the look of shock clear on my face. I looked at Dean and Hanna. They too had the same expression. Principal Stewart didn't seem to understand any of it.

"You think it's a condition she has?"

"We won't know until I do some check-ups," she said. "Alright young men let's go."

The third former escorted Priscilla off to the Nurses' quarters, while the other boy carried the bucket with the Nurse following close behind. Dean and Hanna walked up to me.

"It's not possible — here at school?" Asked Hanna in hushed tones.

"I hate to think it, but it might be," I said, "It's the same mark on her neck like the others…. same symptoms—burning feeling like she has a fever."

"But I don't get it…. I thought the Ol'Hige only attacks babies."

"You think she's escalating?" Hanna asked.

"I don't know, but if the Ol'Hige can make her way here into Grange Hill…. the school might no longer be safe."

"But why here? What is she trying to do?"

"Need to talk to my grandmother again and we need to know where else we can get info on Eliza Gutzmer."

We left school right away and headed straight to my home. When we arrived, my mother was in the kitchen preparing food. Curry Chicken, white rice with yam, banana, mashed potatoes, and Carrot Juice. I told her Dean and Hanna were here with me and she was more than happy because she had prepared a mountain of a meal.

I don't know what flew up in her head, but somehow, she knew people were coming over. Dean and Hanna…. especially Dean, who didn't mind one bit when it came on to free food. I told my mother what happened at school today with Priscilla and how she fainted. She was so shocked that she almost dropped the pot. I also told her about the additional information we got on Eliza and how she changed her name from Bertram to Gutzmer after her adopted mother.

"We were just getting to the good parts… but the article just ended. Some parts were missing, so we know it was incomplete," I said.

"You think there is more to the story?" asked my mother, stirring up the curry chicken in the pot.

"There has to be. The person who wrote the article didn't finish it," Dean said.

"And we don't know who wrote it because it came under anonymous. So, we basically just running blind," said Hanna.

"Then how do you know it's real?"

We looked at each other.

"Well, it kinda makes sense, Mommy. Grandma said Eliza was a loner, didn't have many friends, and was the only one who ever visited her cottage. No one knew her family or where she came from. After she ran away from home, it got to the part where this stranger adopted her…. that's where it ended. So, there must be more to the story. "

I hoped to see my grandmother, but my mother told me she had gone on the road to do some stuff and would return later.

"Mommy, we're going to my room."

"Alright, I'll call when dinner is ready."

I stopped by my mother's room first. I opened the door to go check on Romaine. It felt like ages since I came to see him. I stared at him, laying peaceful with the machine beeping away. He was just a baby; he should have been in his crib jumping up and down and screaming at the top of his lungs… that's what I miss.

"I just want to hear his voice," I said, touching his fingers.

Hanna and Dean both put their hands on my shoulder.

"We're going to save him…. We'll figure it out," Dean said.

I looked at them both and smiled.

"Thanks, guys, that means a lot."

"Guys…. dinner is ready!!" My mother shouted from the kitchen.

"Let's go eat Ana, it should relax you, then we get back to our little mystery."

Dean and Hanna helped to share out the food while I set the table. Just then, the front door opened, and my grandmother walked into the kitchen with a grave expression on her face.

"What happened, Mama?" my mother asked.

My grandmother took off her hat and pulled up a chair to sit. We all looked at her with worried looks on our faces. You would think someone had died for her; then she said it — "Four more babies got sick," my grandmother said gravely.

The news struck a heavy blow. We weren't expecting any more attacks. Five attacks in one day.

"When did this happen, Grandma?"

"About two hours ago," she said. "Mrs. Willow took ill too…. but she passed."

We couldn't express shock anymore at this point because now it seemed like the whole town was being wiped out completely.

We didn't feel like eating because our appetites were gone upon hearing the news.

But my mother slaved in the kitchen all day, so wasting the food wouldn't have been fair. While we ate, I filled my grandmother in about the page we found on Eliza Gutzmer, about her early life, how she changed her name, ran away from her abusive parents, and was raised by a woman whose last name she carried until her death.

My grandmother's expression went blank after I told her, which told us she didn't know Eliza that well at all.

"So, you telling me all this time…. her last name was Bertram and this woman who found her, her name was Constance?" she asked, surprised. "I thought I knew her."

"She may have lied to you about her actual last name," Hanna said.

"And you said after you learnt who she was, it just ended like that?" my mother asked.

"Yeah, just like that," I replied. "It came from an anonymous source, so we don't know who it was or if that was the only link."

"Hold on." Having some sort of brainstorming moment judging by her expression. "The last couple of times, I was in Eliza's cottage…. each time I was there, I walked around her house. I was very nosey back then, not minding my own business. I knew every inch of her cottage from top to bottom," my grandmother said as we listened to her while munching on our delicious meal.

"She was outside. She was always outside; I didn't know what she was doing. So, I did some little snooping around the house, and I went to her room. One thing I can tell you, Eliza was a neat woman, bed always made up, floor spic and span. The room smelled like roses. Constance was sleeping in her crib, so I didn't want to disturb her. I opened one of the dresser drawers and there wasn't much in it — but I saw a portrait, a picture of a white woman in it."

"A white woman… Yes!!" said Hanna excitedly.

"Did the portrait have a name at the bottom?"

"No, it didn't," my grandmother said. "But she has a diary. I tried to open it, but I heard her come inside, so I closed the drawer quick and ran over to Constance's crib. I got no more chances after that."

"What did she say? Was she angry?" my mother asked.

"If she was angry, she calmed down when I told her I only wanted to see Constance."

"So…. the diary, what happened to it?" I asked.

"I don't know. Why?"

"Since we couldn't find any more information about how she became who she was on the website…. her diary might be the best bet."

"We could check Museums… the main library," Dean said. "The Museum is the one place you will get historical artifacts."

"But wasn't it destroyed in the cottage fire?" Hanna asked.

We never factored that in. How would anything survive that kind of fire? Eliza was burnt alive…. if she survived and is now terrorizing us, the diary might have survived too, or if she knew there was something in there, she didn't want anyone during that time to find out, she would have hidden it. So, we needed to get it to know the rest of the story.

My grandmother and my mother went into the living room. We finished eating and got up to clean the kitchen. Dean and Hanna helped to wash the plates while I wiped the stove.

"You guys think that diary still exists?" I asked.

"I don't know. I mean, it's a long stretch."

"Let's say we find it right…. will that be enough to help us stop her once and for all?" Dean asked, concerned.

"What do diaries contain, Dean?" I asked.

"Intimate information," he answered.

"Exactly. People who have diaries are those who have something to hide—important stuff."

"So, whatever she had in her diary—"

"Are things she didn't want anyone to know."

"But the person who wrote that article, on the page… if her diary was so secret, how did they know stuff about her no one else did?"

"Maybe it was someone close to her," I said. "Maybe the person died and didn't get to finish."

"We need to find out. We owe it to those the Ol'Hige hurt. Anyway… night is almost here, so as much as I would love for you guys to stay…. you gotta go," I said, smiling, "See you at school tomorrow."

After Dean and Hanna left, I prepared to start the two assignments. This week was going to be a busy week for us. We wouldn't get time to hang out as much until after this week finished; but we all agreed we would meet up to locate Eliza's diary and if we do, hope that it was enough to give us some way to stop the Ol'Hige once and for all.

CHAPTER SEVEN
MOM'S BIRTHDAY

October came, and it was that time of month my mother had her unusual mood swings. It was her birthday, so I wanted to do something special for her. To bring some happiness in her life.

My mother was sitting by herself in the living room, staring into space. Her mind drifted elsewhere, far from this existence, far from now. She knew what today was, but she didn't look like she wanted to celebrate anything. Her birthdays of late haven't been happy, especially since Romaine was in a coma. But that's not the only thing. My dad proposed to my mother on her birthday too. It was a very special time in her life. She always looked forward to it because it was a birthday and an anniversary in one. She was always ecstatic when he surprised her, but his death slowly killed that part of her.

Last year, I wanted to surprise her and take her to her favorite restaurant, *The Majestic Gardens*. It was the restaurant my father took her to propose. But I didn't have enough money to get a seat for her, so I took her out for ice cream instead. She said little, but I knew she appreciated the gesture, and she just said because she didn't want me to feel bad. *'It's the thought that counts, honey.'*

I ran up to her and jumped on her, kissing her all over. She was so frightened she almost had a heart attack.

"Jesus Christ Analisa! You crazy, you scared me half to death," she said, laughing.

"Happy birthday, Mommy; how young are you now?" I asked jokingly.

"Ha ha, get up off me, you big old pickney. You are not a baby anymore."

"I'm your baby, aren't I?" I said, still kissing her.

She acted like she was upset, but her smile told me she was feeling a little better.

"Thank you, darling. I appreciate it… but you heavy man. I remember I used to bounce you up and down on my knee. Now I can barely move one."

I went to the kitchen to make her a cup of tea with pancakes, toast, and eggs. I opened the top cupboard and took down the pancake mix and I took out the frying pan from the bottom cupboard and worked my magic.

Dean and Hanna loved birthday surprises. So, I asked for their help. One night before her birthday, Dean, Hanna, and I sat up brainstorming — wrote ideas for planning the perfect surprise, but in the end, the plan failed because my mother was spying and listening to our conversations and giggling at us behind the door.

After I finished making the most scrumptious breakfast, I set it out on the table with a nice cup of tea bag. Went to the cupboard and took out a glass and put it on the table next to the teacup, took out the box of Orange Juice from the fridge, and poured it out in the glass. Then I went to the living room, but when I got there… she was fast asleep — keeled over on the sofa. I felt disappointed. After all the work I did in the kitchen, she was sleeping. But I just smiled.

I went to her room and took out a sheet from her drawer; I looked over at Romaine…. just reminding myself that he would get better and that we would hear his voice again. I walked back to the living room and covered my mother with the sheet. She smiled. Then I leaned over and kissed her on the cheek.

"I love you, Mommy," I said, looking at her.

I left her to sleep and headed towards the kitchen. I covered her food until she was ready to eat.

This was her day, so I would not allow any distractions to ruin it. I cleaned the kitchen from top to bottom, swept, wiped, and washed all the pots, pans and plates that were left in the sink covered in grease stains from last night. When I finally finished, I went to my room to rest a bit. I slumped on my bed and looked up at the ceiling, wondering how to make her birthday special.

I turned over and looked at the clock. It was 10:00. I had time to go on the road and do what I needed to do… thank God her birthday was on a Saturday. I would have called Dean and Hanna, but they were both occupied. Dean was helping his parents out at a bake sale at their church, and Hanna and her grandmother went to visit her uncle. I didn't need them for this, even though the company would have been great. I was on my own.

As soon as I finished showering and dressed, I left the house to catch a bus. It has been a while since I have driven so far from Belle Isle. I hardly remembered that there was life outside of where I grew up. I only knew about Belle Isle and the neighbouring districts.

Shopping malls, grocery shops, supermarkets, they were all here on Paisley Avenue…. the other side. I got off the bus and walked down the sidewalk, looking for a decent pastry shop. I stopped at one and went in. The aroma was the first thing that hit me as I opened the door; it hypnotized me to where I wouldn't want to leave even if I had gotten through. I looked through the glass and they had different sizes, different shapes, and flavours. Chocolate was one of my favourites: Vanilla, Raspberry, Lemon, Coconut Lime, Red Velvet; but the one I knew my mother, and I loved the most, was Black Forrest.

The line wasn't long, so I knew I was going to get through in time. When I finally reached the top, the cashier, who looked about my age, gave me a welcoming smile.

"Good morning, welcome to Tasteys Treatz. What can I give you today?" she asked.

"Hi, I would like to order a Black Forrest cake please, and I want the name written on it."

She typed in the order.

"Okay, no problem… that will be $350."

Luckily, I had $1000 exactly in my pocket, so I gave her $400, got back my change and receipt and walked over to the window for pickup. A guy looked through and stretched his hand out for the ticket. I gave it to him, and he looked at me.

"What do you want on the cake?" he asked.

"I want it to say, 'Happy Birthday, Mommy, You are the BEST.' That's it."

He gave me the thumbs up and closed the window. I went over to the chair and sat down.

Minutes went by and I sat patiently, waiting for the cake. How long did it take to just write happy birthday? I took out my phone and started randomly scrolling through it. Neither Dean nor Hanna texted or even called. I wanted to text them, but they were probably still busy.

Just then, a man walked in, and he sat beside me. I thought nothing of it at first until his body odor hit me. As I was about to get up, he grabbed my arm firmly. I tried to drag away, but his grip was strong, and his eyes were closed.

"Ahm, can you LET ME GO?" I hissed.

Then his eyes popped open, and he turned to me. His eyes were dark blue, and he spoke to me in a deeply disturbing voice.

"You have little time… beware the child…. beware the owl," said the man.

I looked at him, confused.

"Excuse me!" I exclaimed.

"Beware the child…. beware the owl," he repeated.

"What does that mean? What are you talking about?"

"*When the moon rises, her true face is revealed*!" he chanted.

Then…. his eyes reverted to their normal form. He shook his head and looked around as if he was in a trance. He looked at me, and I shrugged him off, releasing his grip.

"How did I reach here? Who are you?"

"I should ask you. What did you mean by that?"

"Mean by what?" he asked, looking around, unsure of himself.

The window popped open.

"One Black Forrest birthday cake!" the man called out.

"Yes…. yes, that's me," I blurted.

I walked over to the window and collected the cake. When I turned around, the man was gone. I looked all over, and I couldn't find him. I left the store looking in every direction…. there was no sign of him, he just disappeared. There was something about him that made me uneasy, the colour of his eyes and what he said to me — *"beware the child…. beware the owl,"* what did he mean?

I made sure the cake box was sealed tightly and hastened towards the bus stop. I pondered what the message meant… and that man, did he come there on purpose just to warn me? I racked my brain trying to link the two together, 'child' and 'owl'. What was the connection? It made no sense. Who was the child and what did an owl have to do with it?

Was he speaking about Eliza as a child? Nothing I thought of was making any logical sense.

The message still haunted me as I tried so desperately to figure out what he meant and that last thing he said; '*When the moon rises, her true face is revealed*'.

I arrived home and quietly opened the door. I didn't want my mother to hear me coming, so I tiptoed past the living room and dashed to my bedroom. When I closed the door behind me, I opened the drawer. In it was a box of matches and some candles I kept for this moment.

My mother was now 35, but I would not take out 35 candles to put on the cake, so instead, I just took out a good number of candles and placed them around the cake. I took out the matches and lit all of them. I stepped back and admired it. It was beautiful, with the candles and the fine-tip writing on top of the cake saying, '**Happy Birthday Mommy, you are the Best**'.

I heard footsteps outside and ran towards the door and pressed my ears against it. There were bags ruffling and footsteps in the kitchen's direction. I took up the cake and opened the door slowly, looking out. I held the cake as best as I could and tried not to make it slip from my hands, because if it did…. that was $350 dollars mostly wasted.

I peeped behind the kitchen wall. My mother was packing out the bags. So, I walked in, and I started singing happy birthday. She jumped and dropped a can of peas. She spun around quickly, clutching to her chest and smiled. I kept on singing and failing miserably at it, but my mother saw me smile. I placed the cake on the table, and she looked at it with tears streaming down her face.

"Happy Birthday to you," I finished by kissing her on the cheek and clapping extra hard.

She blew out the candles quickly and I clapped again.

"Thank you, baby girl, this means a lot," said my mother softly.

"So, Mommy, anything you want to do? Daylight is still here. We can do lots of stuff?"

My mother stood at the table and stared at the cake. She was silent for a few minutes; then looked at me.

"I don't need any fancy birthdays, don't need no expensive presents," she said, walking up to me. "You and Romaine are the most important things in my life now. I just thank God that I'm able to live to see another birthday—"

"Yeah, you getting old, Mommy," I interrupted jokingly.

She gave me a serious look, but smiled.

"I'm happy to see another birthday…. thank you," she continued. "What I wish for my birthday — is for my children to be happy, to be successful in life. But right now…. I want my baby boy to wake up; that's all I want. It's been weeks…. a month now without hearing him cry, hearing him make noise, or talk gibberish. I just need him to wake up."

"Me too Mommy," I said, hugging her.

Suddenly, the door flung open. I looked around, and my grandmother and Hanna sauntered into the kitchen with enormous bags. Dean walked in struggling with a rather large box and almost dropped it.

"It's cool. I have it. It won't drop."

 My grandmother walked up to my mother and hugged her.

"Happy birthday, my daughter…. turn, big woman now."

"Mama…. stop ha ha," said my mother happily.

Dean and Hanna placed the bags on the table and took turns hugging and wishing my mother a happy birthday.

She didn't get the perfect birthday she wanted, but she kept reminding me I didn't need to do anything for her to show I loved her. She already knew. Dean and Hanna, however, went all out. Dean got his parents to pitch in and got her a new microwave. Hanna and my grandmother opened their presents;

Hanna bought her a perfume set. My mother's eyes widened as she brushed her fingers across the bottles. She always wanted a perfume set, and I felt bad that I couldn't get one for her, but I was happy to see her smile. Last, my grandmother gave her a large picture frame.

"We can take pictures together, me, you, and the kids. Hang it up in the middle of the living room," she said. She motioned to Dean and Hanna, who smiled widely.

"Alright everyone, get comfy because I'm a make you Mama's favourite food. Oxtail and beans."

Just the thought of having Oxtail opened our appetites. My mother was now loving her birthday.

"Mama, don't spoil me now," she said happily.

Throughout the evening, we sat and ate cake. My grandmother told stories upon stories about my mother we've never heard. My mother hung her head in shame and wanted to get up, but my grandmother held her down. Dean, Hanna, and I laughed so hard we could barely contain ourselves. Then my grandmother went to the kitchen and came back out with the delicious oxtail, rice and peas, mac and cheese with Guava Juice.

After dinner, my grandmother agreed to clean up the kitchen. Dean, Hanna, and I went to my room, and I briefed them on what happened today at the bakery. Their expressions told me they were just as horrified as I was.

"He just came up to you like that?" asked Dean, alarmed.

"Yeah, his eyes were blue, and he spoke in this deep voice. But then, his eyes… they weren't blue anymore and when he looked at me, he looked as if he had never seen me before. It's like he was—"

"Under some spell."

I turned to Hanna, and she wore a puzzled look on her face. "But what do you think it means? Beware the child, beware the owl?" she asked.

"That's what I been killing myself over all day trying to figure out. I have no clue. At first, I thought he was talking about Eliza, but I don't understand the owl part. That one has me baffled,. And the last part got me. When the moon rises, her true form is revealed."

"Full moon?" asked Hanna.

"Full moon… hmm, there is going to be a full moon next month," Dean added.

"But what's so special about that specific time?".

"Really wish we had that diary, then we might have an answer for everything we don't know."

"And what if there's nothing in it?" Dean asked gravely, looking at the possibilities.

"Then we would have wasted our search, and all this would have been for nothing. We need to do a wide search. Find out what happened after the Cottage fire."

I took up my laptop and turned it on. The browser came up instantly, and I started typing. Many searches came up with very little information. Nothing was on it about the Cottage fire, nothing about it burning to the ground. I put the laptop aside and got up off the bed, pacing back and forth, venting my frustration.

"Now grandma said that Eliza kept the diary hidden, right?" I asked.

"Right."

"Is it possible that she hid it for safekeeping? Somewhere she didn't want anyone looking for it?"

"Well, she would have hidden it somewhere before the cottage fire. Do you think she knew what was going to happen to her?" Dean asked.

"Grandma said when she went back up there, there was nothing there…. no debris, no trace that a fire even happened," I said. "Come to think of it, no one has said anything about it. Didn't it seem strange that there were no ashes or burnt bodies?"

We had drawn a lot of conclusions about what happened that night and if Eliza had hidden her diary, maybe she realized my grandmother was in her room snooping and hid it somewhere else only she knew where.

"Still, we need to know that it's here before we say or do anything,"

"Okay cool, we can do that after school on Monday. We must check the library to see if there were any mentions of the diary being moved before or after the fire. If we're lucky, then we will find the diary."

Two days later, at school, we got our first lunch break. Dean, Hanna, and I were in our separate classes. Miss Wynter was giving notes and interacting with the rest of my classmates on a new topic while I drifted into my imagination — locked in a continuous daydream.

"Miss Kelly," Miss Wynter called out.

I snapped out of it and looked up at her.

"Yes, Miss."

"Are you tired? You've been yawning for the past couple minutes."

"No Miss, I'm fine," I answered quickly.

RING! RING! RING!

The bell had finally rung, and I grabbed my books right away and stormed out of class. I walked up to my locker, opened it, and shoved my books inside. I took out my timetable to see what classes I had next. Afterwards, I had a free period. I wondered if I could skip the rest of my classes; they weren't doing anything that I didn't already know and with these other classes, I could easily find notes online.

I folded my timetable and shoved it back in my locker. As I closed it…. I jumped. Mr. Francis was standing right by my locker. He folded his arms and looked at me with the most disapproving look. I was uncomfortable.

"Is there something wrong, sir?" I asked.

"My office…. Now!!" he said in a disgusted tone.

I followed him to his office. Wondering what I had done wrong. As I entered, I closed the door behind me. I stood and waited for further instructions. He walked behind his desk and sat down slowly…. very animated… robotic like. Something looked off about him. There were no expressions or movements on his face.

"Sit," he said dryly, motioning me to the chair.

I sauntered over to the chair and sat down, looking at him suspiciously.

"Do you know why you're here, Miss Kelly?"

"Ahm… no sir."

He interlocked his fingers and leaned forward. "I told you I wanted to see your mother, didn't I?"

"Oh! Yes, sir, I'm sorry, I completely forgot; a lot of things have been happening, sir, with my brother and—"

"Miss Kelly… your excuses are becoming most tiresome, and I don't have time for this, so I'll get right to the point. I've been watching you…. for quite some time now and I heard that you and your friends are off…. to gain something of great importance — do you have it?"

I tried to form words, but nothing came out. If he was asking what I thought he was asking, then this whole thing was much bigger than I thought. Could he be talking about the diary? How could he have known what we were after? We just thought about looking for the diary moments ago. I had to warn Dean and Hanna. They could be in trouble. I tried to get up.

"I wouldn't try that if I were you, Miss Kelly," he said. "You can't move. There is a charm placed on that chair… there is no escaping until I want you to."

Suddenly…. the blinds behind him closed by themselves and the room got darker. Everything around me got quiet.

The only thing I could hear was my heart beating alarmingly. The darkness was so thick, I felt as if I was being stifled.

"Now, I will ask you again. Where is it? Eliza's diary?"

"S… Sir… I. don't know what you're talking about," I said trembling.

"DON'T LIE TO ME!!" He barked, banging on the table.

I jumped, my breathing spiked, and I looked around wondering how no one came bursting through the door.

"I know you're in search of the diary, Miss Kelly, and if you think your little 'plan' of getting it to save your brother or save anyone is going to work, you're not as smart as you think. We wouldn't allow it," he said, looking above my head.

I felt a chilling presence. The same one I felt during my visions. The hairs on the back of my neck stood like twigs. Suddenly, a pair of dry clammy hands held me down, grabbing me at the back of my neck. My body shivered and my screams were inaudible.

"You know who this is…. don't you, Miss Kelly?" he asked with a smug look.

"OL'… HIGE!" I said, shakenly, trying not to look behind me. The only thing I could feel was her hands gripping me tightly.

"Clever girl. You have been doing your reading. Then you know what she is capable of. Now, you tell me where the diary is, and I promise you…. no one in your family will be harmed. Don't and I can't guarantee anyone's safety in the school."

"You wouldn't?"

"This school doesn't pay me enough to care what happens to it. That fat gas ball of a principal is just as clueless as all these students here. It's even unfortunate that Priscilla was in the wrong place at the wrong time. But she was a bit too, how you kids put it 'nosey'. She never knew to mind her own business, and she will soon die because of it."

The man I saw at the bakery seemed to be under a spell. I struggled to understand how Mr. Francis got caught up in all of this. He acted of his own free will. He got up, walked over, and knelt in front of me.

"Now, Miss Kelly, the diary… where is it?" He asked silently.

I stared at him, my brow frowning, and my teeth seethed with insurmountable fury.. Tears ran down my face. "I don't know."

Mr. Francis got up, walked back over to his table, and sat behind his desk. "Then we're going to have a problem."

My vision blurred, I almost passed out. Everything around me became clouded. All I could hear next were loud shrieks and wailing. I opened my eyes barely, and I saw flashes of blue light and heard screaming — then — silence.

CHAPTER EIGHT
THE DIARY

I jumped up in shock after I was splashed with water. I looked up, and it was Dean smiling at me. Hanna was next to him. Miss Wynters was over me mouthing words which I couldn't hear. I couldn't hear anyone except for the mind-numbing ringing in my ears. Everything sounded muffled… then little by little, the ringing died down and things were getting back to normal.

I tried to get up. My neck was still sore, but Dean pulled me up. The other students looked on, wondering what was wrong with me and all the other teachers were staring at me, asking me if I was okay, if I needed water, or to go to the nurse.

Dean put me to sit on the bench. Miss Wynters knelt in front of me and snapped her fingers. Her snapping made my eyes hurt, so I pushed her fingers out of the way.

"Looks like she's sensitive to noise. Someone, please go call the nurse now," she said.

"She's coming now, Miss," said one student, pointing toward the third form block.

The nurse cáme running onto the pavement. "Alright, students, please let's give her some breathing space. Let's move it," said Miss Wynters.

The students began to disperse and go their separate ways. The nurse sat beside me and opened her bag.

"Look towards me, dear." She took out her ophthalmoscope and looked into both eyes. "You have slight redness in your right eye; I will have to prescribe some drops for you," she said.

Then she took out her stethoscope and checked my breathing, which I didn't think was necessary because I wasn't having any extreme pains except for my neck.

"Nurse, I'm fine. I don't need all of this."

"Okay then, let me call your mother."

"NO!" I shouted.

The nurse jumped, very startled by my outburst.

"Sorry, I want to go home, don't want to worry her. She worries a lot."

"Analisa be quiet."

Hanna never spoke to me like that before. I looked into her eyes, and I could see that she was scared. I looked over at Dean and he tried to play tough. I didn't know Mr. Francis was in league with the Ol'Hige and I felt everyone in the school had a right to know. They were afraid of losing me. To be honest, I thought I was going to die too.

The nurse finished checking with me. Then she gave me the drops and told me to go home and rest. School had ended anyway, and most of the students had already left. The nurse left as well, and Dean and Hanna sat with me.

"We thought she got you too," Hanna said.

"She almost did."

"What happened?" Dean asked.

"Mr. Francis knows."

Hanna and Dean looked at each other.

"What you talking about? Knows what? Hanna asked.

"He knows about the diary. He wants it too."

"What! How?" asked Dean.

"He knows that we're looking for it and he tried to get the information out of me. He's working with the witch…. She was here."

Hanna's eyes widened. "Seriously?

How do you know?"

"I could feel her hands pressed against my neck. I felt so cold," I said, recalling the tragic moment. "I called her name, and he knew it was her."

"Since when do witches have partners?" Dean asked.

"I don't know, but I don't like it."

"You think he is under her spell?" Dean asked.

"No, he was pretty much himself, darker. She didn't need to control him. If Mr. Francis is in league with her, there might be more working with her; in this school, the district, who knows. We can't trust anyone at this point."

Dean and Hanna looked at each other, then at me.

"Can we go to the principal? Dean asked.

Hanna and I gave him the '*are you an idiot*' stare.

"I just said we couldn't trust anyone. What are we going to do, go up to him and say, 'Excuse me, sir, but you know all these attacks that have been happening, an ancient blood-sucking witch who kills children caused them. That's what you want to say?"

"Was just a question," he said apologetically.

"We are nowhere near finding out where this diary is and the more we look for it, the more danger we're in. If we want to survive this, we can't do it at school."

Hanna was conflicted. She thought this would have been a good idea as well, since no one else was going to do anything about the Ol'Hige. We were the only ones brave enough or probably dumb enough to tackle her. Since we ruffled her feathers, it seemed like we were on the right track. The next course of action now was to locate that diary.

"Dean, if you don't want to do this, that's fine. I won't force you, but I'm seeing this through," I said firmly.

Dean wore an uncomfortable look on his face, like something horrible was going to happen kind of look.

"We can't abandon her Dean. There's no point in coming to school if we're all dead. We need to do something."

Dean could no longer argue a point he knew he would not win.

"Fine… I'm in, but the principal will be mad."

I tried getting up, and they both helped me.

"We can't worry about that now. The Ol'Hige is recruiting. So, the only people we can trust are the three of us right here."

"But what could she offer anybody that would make them join her?" Hanna asked.

"Immortality, power," Dean added. "But what I want to know is, where's Francis?"

"I don't know," I answered, equally upset. "None of you saw him?"

They both shook their heads.

"The janitor said she was cleaning up, and she came and knocked on Mr. Francis' door. When she never heard an answer, she opened it and that's when she found you on the floor," continued Hanna.

"No one else?"

"No."

"I need to get home. Let's go."

On the bus ride home, I filled them in on what happened before I blacked out.

I told them I saw a flash of blue light. It swam swiftly across my face and whatever it was, attacked the Ol'Hige, then disappeared. Mr. Francis must have run away as well.

Dean and Hanna theorized that someone was trying to protect us, but we did not know who it was. I told them we needed to speak to Mr. Michaelson again and find out if he knew anything about Eliza's diary. But, after our last meeting, I didn't think he wanted to speak to us again.

"Maybe those crows were there to protect us from the very beginning. They must have known what was going on."

I got up and walked up to the driver and asked him to take us up to 33 Arnold Street. The driver agreed and made a left turn to reach on the other side.

Minutes later, we arrived at Mr. Michaelson's house. We each paid the driver and stepped off the bus; then it drove off. We stood at the gate, looking up at the dark dwelling. The house looked worse than how we left it. It was naturally quiet the first time we came here, but this time — it was extra quiet. I had a funny feeling in the pit of my stomach.

"You okay Analisa?" Hanna asked.

"Yeah, I… I'm okay, but…I think something might be wrong," I said, trying to figure out what it meant.

We reached up the steps and I stopped, extending my arms, preventing Dean and Hanna from moving further.

"Look," I said, pointing at the lock.

It was jimmied open. We looked under the door and saw a black substance…. the same substance we have been seeing everywhere. I turned to them.

"Anyone want to guess what that is?"

They turned to each other and nodded in agreement. I pushed the door open, and as we entered…. we were in shock.

 The whole place was ransacked.

Everything was torn apart, but no sign of Mr. Michaelson. I walked over to his chair and looked at the ground; one of his cigarette butts was on the floor, still slightly lit by the tip, which meant he was here not too long ago, and judging by the scratch marks on the floor, he was trying to get away from someone.

"She was here. She got to him."

"You think he's…"

"I hope not," I answered.

He was reading a book on the sofa. The book was called *'The Autobiography of an Ex-Coloured Man'* by James Weldon Johnson. I turned the back of the book, and it said that Johnson drew from the lives of people he knew and from events in his life. The Ex-Coloured man spoke about the belief… that the desperate class comprised poor blacks who loathed the whites. I was impressed. All the time Mr. Michaelson was here, he was caught up in his reading, being knowledgeable about the world around him. I didn't know he was such a learned man. I put down the book and continued to search for him.

We walked down to his secret room and realized that the door was open. The moment we met him, he was never one to keep his door open. I gently pushed it and to our horror — we saw him spread out on the floor, pale, very glass eyed.

I approached his body and touched him. His cane was over in the corner. He was stiff as wood. I turned him over, and underneath his neck had the same dark colour.

"Oh No!" Hanna exclaimed.

"She knew we came to him?" Dean asked. "How?"

"Must be Mr. Francis. Somehow, he knew we spoke to him."

"Or the giant Owl. The Ol'Hige would have known we came to him with or without Francis' help," I said, touching Mr. Michaelson's hands. "It's because of us, that's why he's dead."

"Why would you say that?" Hanna asked.

"If we didn't come here and ask a bunch of questions, he would still be alive… alone, but at least he was at peace. We disturbed that. Now he's gone."

I looked over at Dr. Michaelson and placed my hands over his eyes and closed them.

"We're sorry, Dr. Michaelson, we didn't mean for this to happen…. we're so sorry."

I got up to go for his cane and put it beside him, but then I saw something clutched in his hand.

"What is it?" Dean asked.

"I don't know."

I bent down again and tried to pry his hand open. It was a piece of paper, with a series of numbers on it, '162109'.

"Is it a phone number?" Hanna asked.

"No, it's not a phone number. Phone numbers have seven digits, and these only have six."

"I don't get it." Dean said, "Who did he write this for?"

"For me, I think."

"How do you know that?" Hanna asked.

I showed them the paper with a note at the bottom that said, 'For A.'

"Analisa," Hanna said.

"It has to be. He must have left this for us to find. Which also means he knew the witch was coming for him, and he knew we would come back."

"Well, it's a clue, and we have to follow it. Let's go," I said, folding the paper and shoving it in my skirt pocket.

Later that evening, after Dean and Hanna went their separate ways. I was home in bed, staring at the paper for about an hour, trying to figure out what the numbers meant. I tried to think of everything possible, of what it could mean. A code, a room number, nothing that I came up with made any sense to me. They weren't phone numbers, and no numbers were missing. The numbers were clear and concise, so what were they? Just then, I heard a knock on my door and it opened. My mother walked in.

"Hey, how you doing?" she asked.

I sat up in the bed.

"Alright I guess…. I don't know," I said sadly.

She sat on the bed next to me.

"I heard what happened at school today. Why didn't you call me?"

"Jesus, I told them not to call you," I said, annoyed.

"What do you mean you told them not to call me? If something happened to you, who are they supposed to call, huh?"

"Alright, alright Mommy, I'm sorry. I didn't want to worry you."

"So, what happened?" she asked, giving me that stern look she always gave whenever she wanted a straight answer, and she wouldn't stop until she got it. I tried to get comfortable enough on the bed to tell her exactly what happened.

"Well, I came out of class…. I went to my locker to put my books in. After I closed it, Mr. Francis was there… something was off about him. Anyway, I was in his office, and he started asking me questions about you and…. Mommy, he knows about Eliza's diary."

Her eyes widened.

"How?" she asked, concerned.

"He's working with the Witch."

My mother looked on in disbelief. Not believing that a teacher would be involved.

"Where is he now?"

"He disappeared. No one knows where he went. Before I fainted in his office, I saw this flashing blue light…. The Ol Hige was there."

"She WAS?"

"Yeah, in his office. Something saved me, Mommy. The witch was fighting off something, and then I woke up, surrounded by students and teachers, that's all I remember," I said. "Everything we tried to do, everything that we tried to look for, something always goes wrong. We went back to Dr. Michaelson's house — he's dead."

My mother didn't seem perturbed by the news. She only hung her head down.

"I know… it came on the news," she said. "Someone passed and said she saw the door left open and she went inside and saw him."

"When we left, the door was closed. We never left it open."

"I know dear, I know," she said, trying to comfort me.

"Somebody went there after we left or waited for us after we left."

"Analisa, don't worry yourself about that. There is nothing you could have done."

"He's dead because of us," I said, holding my head down.

She held on to my chin and turned my face towards her.

"This is not your fault. This is the Ol' Hige; this is all on her, you hear me? I'm just sorry you had to take it up on yourself. After what she did to my son, I don't know what I would do if I saw her."

"How can we stop something we can't even see? You're the only one who can see her?"

I looked at my hand and unfolded the paper.

"What's that?" My mother asked.

She looked at the paper with the numbers. I was trying so desperately to find out what they meant. I told my mother that Dr. Michaelson had it in his hands and was apparently holding on to it for me to get at the time they killed him. She looked at the initials at the bottom and looked at me, very confused.

"Why would he give you this?" She asked.

"That's what I'm trying to find out…. 162109, I'm not getting it," I said, frustrated.

"Relax, just breathe… it will come to you," she said. "You need to get to bed and get ready for school in the morning."

She got up and walked to the door.

"Mommy. We can't think about school right now," I said, looking directly into her eyes. She turned to me and gave the look again.

"Analisa, I will not argue with you. You are going to school.".

"Mommy, I think I can make that decision for myself, and I said I'm not going."

"You still live in this house, and I don't care how big you think you are."

"Mommy, we can stay here and bicker, or you can let me do what I need to do."

My mother didn't pursue the matter further because she knew I was right. She stood there for a couple of minutes before she said anything. I looked at her and I wondered what was going through her head.

"We can't pretend like everything is okay. It's not."

"Analisa, you think I don't know that? You think I don't go to bed every night just praying… begging to hear my baby boy cry, make noise, do something? You think I don't want to wake up in the mornings and just see him jumping up in his crib, reaching for me to pick him up? I know you're hurting, but you don't have it rough. I've provided for you in whatever way I could. My mother had to struggle with me and Marcel, God rest his soul. My father was not there. He bailed on us. It was hard on me when I lost Marcel. He never even got the chance to grow. I never had a father; I lost my brother — I lost your father…. and now I'm afraid to lose Romaine," she said, tapping on the doorknob. "The last thing I want now is to lose you."

I couldn't say anything after that. I felt like shoving a rather large shoe into my overly enormous mouth.

"You need to go to school. Education is important and yes, bad things are happening, but at least you have life, baby girl," she said.

I looked up at her.

"Education won't matter if you're dead. This happened before, and it will continue if we don't stop it. Nobody will admit it, but I'm the one who is seeing her everywhere I go, so I have to do something about it, even if you don't like it," I said firmly.

She shook her head, disappointed. Then opened the door and walked out. I didn't know how else to convince her that going to school would not matter. I couldn't concentrate on work, exams, and class activities while the Ol'Hige was roaming around. But the thing that puzzled me was she could get to everybody else. Why couldn't she get to Romaine? She could get to me and she could have killed me. She could have taken Romaine anytime…. why didn't she? What was she waiting for?

I looked at the paper again, but I couldn't think because my head was hurting, like someone grabbed a hammer and jammed it into my skull.

I put the paper on the table and laid back down on the pillow.

School was silent the next morning. Many students didn't show up for class and parents were outside the gates chanting and raining down hell on the principal, asking him what was happening in the school because their children were complaining about feeling ill. The only thing visible were a bunch of leaves floating by and you could also hear them crackling and whizzing away in the air.

Principal Andrews was in such a panic that he was thinking of closing the school until he could figure out what to do. If he only knew what was going on, I don't think he would want to be the principal much longer. He would want to shut down the school for good.

Dean and Hanna had already been at school because they were very much determined not to leave, but they didn't go to class. In fact, for the entire week, we hadn't gone to classes because barely anyone was there. So, we stayed in the library racking our brains over the numbers that we got from Dr. Michaelson, that we had little time for anything else. This was more important to us.

We spent all day in the library most mornings, even went without food because we were so determined to see this through.

The following week, we were at it again, and we became fatigued. Skipping one week of class didn't sit right with us and it wouldn't look good on a college application. So, we decided not to do that anymore. My mother was right, education was important, and we needed education if we were going to beat the Ol'Hige. We had two tests to do that following week and if I missed it, it would have weighed heavily on my conscience, on top of what was already on my mind.

Our assignments were completed and we got through most of our class work. I had two tests to do: Sociology and Math. Dean and Hanna both had chemistry, and we all aced them — thank God.

Now that we had gotten those out of the way, the focus went back to the six mystery numbers and the search for Eliza's diary. We hit the library again and sat through various books and used Hanna's laptop to find out what we were missing, what we didn't find before.

"Do you think the numbers are scrambled?" Hanna asked.

I looked at her.

"Why do you think they're scrambled?"

"I don't know. I mean, what if we rearrange the numbers in such a way that we can pinpoint the actual numbers?"

Dean and I looked at each other, trying to figure out what she was saying.

"What if Dr. Michaelson wrote the numbers like that on purpose for us to figure it out? These numbers, as they look now, mean nothing. All Libraries have six-digit numbers right, which is basically a set of combination numbers. That's what this is. If you want to get books or if you want to purchase something, you need sets of combination numbers to access it. For a museum, it's different. You would need something of value there, something you wanted to keep safe, to have a combination number."

Hanna logged into the school's website and clicked on the search bar. She typed in the six numbers at the top of the search bar and clicked confirmation. Nothing came up, all that came up each time was *'search not found.'* Hanna scrambled the numbers a couple more times and still nothing came up.

"Try 126109," Dean said.

Hanna typed it in and the same message came back up.

"Try 169021."

She typed it in, same message. Frustration was evident on our faces. We slumped back in our chairs. Hanna and I both hung our heads down while Dean was so bored, he resorted to twirling the pen in between his fingers. We sat for hours trying to find out what the actual numbers were. The afternoon bell rang, which meant school was over and so far, we got nothing done.

"Maybe the Witch saw the paper and tried to figure it out as well but couldn't," Dean theorized.

"No, his hands were already clenched when she killed him. There's no way she would have known."

I looked at the paper again and I tried switching up the numbers in my head, then…. something happened, like a light bulb had ignited inside my head.

I sat up in a moment of excitement which alerted Hanna and Dean — Dean fell off the chair, but he got up in time.

"What happened? Something wrong?" he asked.

"I think so. I mean, it has to be," I rambled.

When I opened my notebook, I ripped out a piece of paper and wrote on it.

"162109."

I turned the paper to the guys.

"Look closely. Does it look familiar to you?" I asked.

Dean and Hanna looked at each other like I was high or sleep deprived.

"No, actually the first time we're seeing it," said Dean sarcastically.

"I'm being serious, dummy. The article we read on Eliza Bertram."

"Yeah."

"What does this number and Eliza have in common?"

They looked confused, which was understandable. I took the paper, and I wrote the numbers again, but this time I switched them around. I wrote 1-6-1-2-0-9. I underlined it with the pen and showed them once more, hoping it would make more sense.

"Look familiar now?" I asked, looking at them, waiting for their lightbulbs to switch on.

They both looked at the numbers carefully, and then their eyes widened. I smiled.

"Is that?" Hanna asked.

"That's exactly what it is — Eliza's birthday — that's the combination number," I said confidently.

"1612 the year she was born and the 9th of April, the day," said Dean.

"That can't be an accident, guys. There's no way. So, you know what that means? Dr. Michaelson knew more than he claimed and that's why he was killed. So…. if this combination number worked, we were right."

Hanna took up the book and turned to the laptop. She pulled up the school's website and typed in Eliza's birthday. We all looked at each other and Hanna pressed enter. Suddenly a link came up and a name.

"Godfrey National Museum, 45 Maberly Street," Dean said. "The number is a combination to a museum? What's in there?"

Hanna and I stared at him with the urge to slap him across the head — which Hanna rightfully did.

"For someone smart, your head thick," she said. "Dr. Michaelson held on to this paper for us to find, tried to decipher the correct formation of the numbers, hoping that we would link it to Eliza Gutzmer's birthday, which also happens to the combination number at the Museum. What you suppose we will find there?"

Dean thought for a while, then looked up at me and snapped his fingers.

"The DIARY!" he shouted.

"SHHH!"

"Sorry…. the diary," he whispered, embarassed.

"Yes, the diary you ninny, it all fits. So, if we go to the museum, that's where the diary will be."

"But how did the diary get there in the first place?" asked Hanna.

"Maybe whoever she trusted guarded it until they could find a safer place for it," Dean thought.

"Maybe, but we won't know unless we find out. Come on."

We now had to be careful not to draw too much attention to ourselves. We had to assume that it was Mr. Francis who killed Dr. Michaelson for the combination numbers under the Ol' Hige's orders. Everybody was a suspect. We didn't know who else joined forces with the witch, and we didn't have anyone else to trust but our immediate circle, Dean, Hanna, my mother, my grandmother, and I.

We hurried up to leave the library. I shoved the papers in my pocket and made sure it was safe.

"What do we do now?" Dean asked.

"You two, come to my house later on. I have to let my mother know what we're doing before we move off."

"Should we leave school, because barely anyone is here?" Hanna asked. "I don't think they will miss us."

"If we leave…. you know we won't have much time for school work? A lot of our energy is gonna go into this. Which means we can forget about graduation."

I thought Dean was about to pass out when I said that.

The look on his face was grave, like he had just lost something, or someone died.

"But…. the community service, our credits. You want to throw all that away?" He asked.

A devious smile came across my face. I chuckled at the horror on Dean's face. He frowned, holding on to his chest.

"You have a sick sense of humour," he replied.

"I just wanted to rattle your cage a bit. But, if it comes to it, that's the sacrifice I'm willing to make to save the district. Right now, this is our priority, and we are the only ones who actually want to do something about it."

Dean and Hanna looked at each other. Hanna didn't argue because she knew what was at stake, and she will be a part of it. She stretched out her arm.

"I was never a part of a team before. This is dangerous, even for us, but I'm willing to fight for our district," she stated.

I stretched my arm out as well.

"For our district," I replied.

Hanna and I looked towards Dean, who was still uncertain if he wanted to be a part.

"I couldn't live with myself if anything happened to you guys."

He threw his hand in last. I smiled. So, we settled it; we were all in this together and there was no turning back after this because we agreed.

Our next stop was the Museum to locate Eliza's diary, but first we had to make my mother and grandmother aware.

We left the library and walked down the hallway, where some students were staring at us weirdly. As we walked, we looked over at the teachers' lounge and saw some teachers looking in our direction as well. We felt uneasy, and we just wanted to leave as quickly as we could.

We each went to our lockers and took out our bags — we still had glaring eyes on us, so we hurried up, closed the lockers, then walked off.

"Why they are staring at us like that?" Hanna asked in a whisper.

"You want to stick around to find out?" I answered back.

We walked as fast as we could, finally reached the gate and walked out.

We stood there waiting patiently for the bus to arrive. Then we noticed the clouds got very bleak. Thunder rumbled, but there were no rain drops. The wind got heavy as well, and it felt strange.

"Oh, seriously, and I didn't even carry an umbrella," Dean said, looking up.

Hanna tried to cover herself because it felt chilly.

"Ahm, anyone else feeling cold?" Hanna asked, rubbing herself.

"I don't think this is normal."

Something was very wrong; I could feel it. Just then, a bus came around the corner, heading in our direction. It stopped, and the door opened for us to enter. As we were about to step in, we heard strange sounds coming from the distance.

Dean turned and walked to the back of the bus. Hanna and I moved from the steps and followed Dean. Lightening flashed across the sky, then we saw something…. or some things — little black things. They began to multiply. We couldn't figure out what it was until we heard a series of —

CAW! CAW!! CAW!!!

My body shivered when I realized a swarm of crows were coming towards us at immense speed. We could see the blinking red dots piercing through the clouds —

dark red eyes, different from the two I saw before. Dean and Hanna could not move as they fixated their gaze on the horror they were witnessing before them.

"We need to leave… NOW! I shouted."

We boarded the bus and told the driver to press the gas as hard as he could.

When he asked why, I turned his head around and showed him what was behind us.

His eyes widened, his cigarette fell from his mouth, and he punched the gas immediately.

The bus jerked so fast that Dean, Hanna, and I lost balance. I had hit my head hard on the glass window. The crows were coming down on us heavily.

"Where did they come from?" Hanna asked, trying to regain her balance.

"Three guesses who."

The driver swerved on all corners trying to avoid the birds, but they were coming like a bullet train, fierce and swift. Suddenly, we saw the birds perched on the windows of the bus and they looked at us, with the menacing red eyes, frowning at us. Then we heard a knocking sound. We turned and saw a crow knocking on the glass with its beak — then, all the other crows started doing it until the glass cracked little by little. I walked up to the driver.

"DRIVER, CAN'T YOU GO ANY FASTER?" I bellowed. "SHAKE THEM OFF OR SOMETHING!"

"Little girl, I'm not getting paid extra to be driving you up and down like this. Next time you want to bring your pets, I will charge you extra," he said, swerving out of a pothole.

"You see the sign?" He tapped on the written rules above him; *No smoking, no eating or drinking, no pets.*

I looked at him and frowned. That last rule was a kind of ridiculous and it seemed very hypocritical of him to be lecturing us about rules of the bus and yet he was breaking his first rule. The crows were making their way through the window, then we saw a swarm of them swirling around in a circle coming at raging speed and burst through the back of the glass.

We screamed and ducked out of sight, fanning away the birds as they tried to scratch us. I got a book out of my bag and I swatted them.

Dean and Hanna followed suit and got books out of their bags and started to slap the birds away. They moved away, but there were too many of them.

"AHHH! COME OFF ME ARGGH!!" The driver screamed out as he let go of the steering wheel.

The bus careened out of control and swerved on its own. We knew it was only a matter of seconds before the bus would turn over and crash, so we prepared for the worst.

"HOLD ON, GUYS!" I shouted.

We each grabbed on to a chair and hugged it tight. Then suddenly…. we couldn't react fast enough as the bus hit a tree. The impact had caused it to spin in the air, landing headfirst into a house. The first hit gave me a nasty blow to the head and as the bus was spinning, I could hear Dean and Hanna screaming. Then — we couldn't hear anything except the deafening silence and my heart beating loudly.

I opened my eyes, and I noticed I was upside down. I could barely move. We had no idea how long we were out for because we could hear fire trucks and police cars on the other side. Suddenly, I heard something trying to tear through the bus. The passenger door was being ripped open by the Jaws of Life. I've always read about them and how they were used to cut open badly damaged vehicles. I just didn't think I was going to be in one of them.

They ripped the bus door opened and the firefighters pulled me out. I cried out in pain as they were taking me out and I kept looking back to see if I saw Dean or Hanna anywhere.

"Where are my friends? Where are they?" I kept asking, looking around frantically.

I sat down with a towel over my shoulder, and I looked up…. many people gathered with their phones out snapping. The firefighters tried to keep me still, but I was already a handful. They got me out finally and walked me towards the ambulance for me to sit.

"ANALISA!" cried a familiar voice.

I looked out, and I saw my mother and my grandmother pushing through the crowd and running up to me. They hugged and kissed me all over.

"Baby girl, you okay? You look hurt, oh god."

"Mommy… I'm fine."

"Stop smothering the girl Margaret, she's a McCallum she is strong," my grandmother said proudly.

My mother shot her a nasty look and turned back to smother me, but I was pushing her away, looking at the bus to see if they had found Dean and Hanna.

"Baby, what you looking at?" My mother asked.

"Mommy, Dean and Hanna are still in there."

"WHAT!" she exclaimed.

She turned to the bus and looked out. The firefighters tried their best to get in. They used the Jaws of Life to tear open the bus further, then the firefighter looked inside.

"I see two more people in here," one of them said, turning towards one wearing a black hat and black jacket, who I assumed was the chief.

"Are they alive?"

The firefighter went in further, then turned back to his chief.

"They look so chief, but won't know till I get in," the firefighter answered.

"Alright, get them out," the chief ordered.

My breathing was laboured. I just wanted to see their faces. I wanted to know they were alright. My mother hugged me for dear life, like she was never ever going to let me go. My grandmother just stood there, not saying a word.

Her facial expressions were just blank, like she didn't know what to say.

I felt like the more we wanted to get to the truth of something, something bad always happened, and this was cutting it close to bad.

"WE'RE COMING OUT NOW!" the firefighter shouted.

Then I saw him walking out with Dean first, who looked badly bruised, but at least he was okay. Then he went back and walked out with Hanna, but he had to lift her. I looked at her and I got up. My mother tried to hold me back, but I shrugged her off and hopped over to Hanna. They placed her on a stretcher, her eyes were closed. I walked up, and I touched her face. My eyes welled up. I held on to her hand, hoping she would grab it.

"Please wake up…. please wake up Hanna."

I felt an arm around me. I looked over, and it was Dean. He was teary-eyed as well. I turned, and I hugged him tight.

Part of me wanted to just give up and stop looking, just move on with our lives, go to school and just live a normal life. It was clear today that the witch wanted us dead, and she proved she would do anything to do it.

"WE HAVE ANOTHER BODY IN HERE!" the firefighter shouted out. "IT'S THE BUS DRIVER."

"Is he okay?" asked the Chief.

"I'll check."

I had forgotten all about the bus driver. The front of the bus was badly damaged, and it was highly unlikely that anyone would have survived that impact. The firefighter went up to the front of the bus and didn't say a word. The crowd stood there anxiously waiting to see what was happening and had their phones out, taking pictures.

The firefighter walked out with a sullen look on his face. He shook his head… then the Chief held his head down. At that point, I knew the driver didn't make it. He was just driving us home; he didn't deserve this.

Hours later, we were at the hospital. I was in bed waiting for the doctor to come and check up on me. I looked over in the corner and I saw my mother in the chair sleeping while Dean, and Hanna were in separate rooms.

My grandmother was at home watching over Romaine. I was scared for him, but I knew he was safe.

I sat up slowly in the bed and held on to my head. It was throbbing like crazy. Then my mother woke up and looked over at me.

"Analisa, why you up? The doctor said you should rest.".

"Mommy, I can't sleep. I need to go see Dean and Hanna."

My mother pushed me back down when I tried to get off the bed.

"I said…. stay in the bed and I won't tell you again," my mother demanded. "Sometimes you must hear."

I wanted to argue, but I was in too much pain to do that. So, I laid back down quietly and sulked, saying nothing. She looked at me and shook her head. She held on to my hand.

"When I saw the bus…. I didn't know what to think. I thought I lost you."

I looked at her.

"You almost did," I said "The driver? He's —"

My mother nodded. My heart sank further.

"His wife and daughter are here now," she said.

"He has a wife and daughter?" I asked shocked "How old is the daughter?"

My mother hesitated for a while, then answered.

"Four… his daughter is four."

I felt a tight knot in the pit of my stomach. I shuffled and became very uncomfortable.

"There's nothing you could have done. Maybe he was driving and lost control or was probably drunk."

"NO!" I shouted. "He wasn't drunk, and he didn't lose control."

My mother looked at me, concerned.

"What you talking about?" she asked.

"We were leaving school and stood at the bus stop as usual. The clouds got dark."

"It was raining?"

"No, it just got dark, like dark, like night was coming. Anyway, the bus came, and Dean was in front of us. I looked around, and I heard some strange noises — flapping noises."

My mother looked as if she was about to panic and not expecting what I was going to say next.

"Then we went to the back of the bus, looked up and saw…. what looked like a million crows heading towards us."

"I'm sorry… what? Crows as in the birds?"

"Yes, Mommy the birds."

"Wha… why? Where did they come from?" she asked, confused.

I looked at her long and hard and soon after; she picked up right away.

"She sent those things after you?"

"It can't be a coincidence. We were at the library trying to find info — wait — where's my bag? Did they get my bag?" I asked in a panic.

"Relax, all your bags are at home. Mama is there. Now, back to what you were going to say."

I breathed easy and continued the story.

"We were at the library trying to find out where the numbers came from, and we didn't know the first place to start. So, we tried typing them in the school library archives, but nothing worked. We theorized the numbers were combination numbers because all library combination numbers have six digits. We unscrambled them, tried every different number…. nothing happened."

My mother pulled up a chair and sat down comfortably. I looked at her. "What?

Continue, baby, I couldn't stand on my feet the whole time. Continue."

"So anyway, I had a brainstorm and remembered that the article we had read online before about Eliza Bertram, before she changed her name to Gutzmer, she was born on April 9, 1612."

My mother's eyes widened.

"The combination number is her birthday."

"Wow," she said.

"We typed in her birthday and a link came up on a Godfrey National Museum on Maberly Street."

"Maberly Street! That's outside of Belle Isle," said my mother in an alarmed tone.

"Mommy, we get that diary."

"No!" she said as she got up. "You're not going anywhere out of town to get some diary. I nearly lost you today. Just leave it alone, Analisa."

"NO!" I said.

My mother looked at me in shock.

"Mommy. We've been through this. I'm going, and you will not stop me," I said with a defiance.

"Excuse me!"

"Romaine is going to remain in that coma forever. It's been a month now Mommy and we have not heard Romaine's voice. The Ol'Hige can throw whatever she wants at us, but we're still breathing. We're going to stop her.."

My mother stood there, stared at me with her lip folded. I could tell she wanted to scold me.

"I will not stop until that parasite is in hell where she belongs. She's not going to hurt anyone else I love."

My mother saw the hurt and anger I was feeling. She said nothing else. She took up her purse and went to the door. She turned to me.

"I'm going to the doctor; then I'm gonna check on Dean and Hanna and get you guys something to eat."

"Okay," I said softly.

She opened the door and closed it behind her. I turned on my side and looked out the window, watching the raindrops pelt against the glass. I had so much on my mind that I didn't know how I kept my sanity in check. So much has happened and people have died around me, and I wondered if I was cursed. What if I was the reason Romaine got sick? If I never went to see Dr. Michaelson, he wouldn't have died, the bus driver, other babies, Priscilla. Dean and Hanna got dragged into this mess because of me, but they volunteered to be a part of it.

The door opened. I didn't bother to look around because if it was my mother, I just wanted her to think I was sleeping, so I closed my eyes. But I heard nothing — suddenly, I smelled something rotting, like day-old cabbage. The smell burnt my nostrils, and I was trembling in the bed. Outside got dark, just like at school…. then I had that bad feeling again.

I didn't want to cause an alarm or move too much without the risk of getting hurt. I felt cold, dry hands massaging my face. After laying there stiff and shaking, it stopped. I cracked my eyes without moving — then the hands pressed against my face, forcefully shoving my head into the pillow and a coarse voice whispered in my ear.

"You… will NOT escape me again. Your friends, your family, including your little brother, will suffer by my hand. When all this is over, child. You…. will…. DIEE!!!" The witch said menacingly.

I was shaking with fear. I didn't know what to do. She was breathing on me and cackling, then I shut my eyes and screamed as loud as I could. I opened my eyes minutes later and saw the doctor holding on to me. I looked over; the rain was still falling. I looked over, I saw my mother with two cups of pudding and two tuna sandwiches.

"Ana, what happen?" Dean asked.

I couldn't answer. I held on to my chest as it got tighter.

"Oh god, her asthma and I forgot her inhaler," my mother panicked.

The doctor listened to my chest and pressed his fingers against my body. He then shook his head.

"It's not asthma. She was having a panic attack. Panic attacks include sudden attacks of fear and nervousness, as well as physical symptoms such as sweating and a racing heart. Something is triggering these attacks and we need to find out what it is. Is there anything that I need to know?" The doctor asked.

My mother looked at me and Dean. They couldn't come up with an explanation.

"She's just tired Doctor," Dean said quickly, "Probably from the crash. I feel dizzy myself."

The Doctor looked at both of us and didn't seem convinced but nodded in agreement. "Alright fine, but I'm going to do some more tests. In the meantime, I urge you both to rest."

"Yes doctor," I said.

He walked out. I turned to the window and then I turned to Dean and my mother.

"You saw her again?"

I nodded slowly. My mother walked over, put the food on the table, and sat beside me.

"You sure? Nobody saw her?"

"I don't know how she's doing it, but if she doesn't want to be seen, she won't be," I said, shaking. "She gave me a message."

Dean walked up to the bed.

"What message?" he asked curiously.

"She said all of you, everybody that I love will suffer at her hand," I said with a trembling sound in my voice.

My mother caressed my face.

"That won't happen. Mama trying to contact somebody, I don't know who, but we are going to get somebody to help us, okay?"

I nodded. She took up the Jell-O and the sandwich and handed them to me.

"Eat," she said. "Dean, yours are right here. When you finish, you both can see Hanna."

I looked up at my mother.

"She's up?"

"She a little weak, but you can see her. I'm going to the doctor. I'll be back."

"Okay," I said.

She got up and left the room. I opened the wrapper with the tuna sandwich first and started eating. I tore into the sandwich like I hadn't eaten in weeks. Dean grabbed a chair and sat down. He pulled the Jell-O pack first and ate. Confusion was written all over his face.

"Seems like the Ol'Hige getting more violent, like she's determined to kill us."

"Something is in that diary she doesn't want us to see," I said.

"Every time we get closer to the truth, the more she comes after us. Maybe we should just stop Ana; it's getting too dangerous," said Dean.

For once, I thought about what Dean said, and I agreed. We almost lost our lives today — me twice in one day. The witch displayed powers I never thought were possible, making me think that the more we dug, the more unpredictable and dangerous she became.. Maybe there was something more about her we didn't know that my grandmother thought she knew. Part of me wanted to give up, but every time I thought of Romaine and him just lying there. It reminded me why I was doing this, why I would not allow the Witch to scare me or try to dissuade me from stopping her. I was doing it to save him.

Her actual life started when she was brought in by that woman, Constance Gutzmer. I bet she wrote everything in her diary along with other things she didn't want anyone to know.

While I munched away on the rest of my sandwich, I was contemplating on what we might find when we finally had it in our possession. It would change everything, give us a fighting chance, to find out more about Eliza Gutzmer and find out what her weaknesses were.

I finished eating the sandwich and placed the wrapper on the table.

I got up out of bed, put on my slippers, and opened the door. Dean followed behind.. We walked down the hallway and I covered my nose to mask the smell. The entire corridor smelled of death and misery. I turned to Dean.

"What room is she in?" I asked.

Dean pointed forward.

"Room 110 down there."

We walked further down the corridor and arrived at 110. We opened the door and walked in. Hanna was sitting up, smiling, while the nurse checked her pressure. She looked over at us and she was happy.. We walked over and hugged her tight.

"I'm glad you guys are okay."

"You too. We were afraid you would not wake up."

"Yeah… me too…. I heard the driver died," she said sadly.

"Yeah, he did. He didn't deserve it."

Hanna looked at me and then at Dean.

"Let's finish this," she said firmly.

"Really?" asked Dean shocked "After all that you still want to do this?"

"I want to be there when she burns and rots in the ground," she said with conviction.

I looked at Hanna. I was proud of her. Then I held on to her hand.

"Don't worry, she will get what's coming to her."

Later in the night, the doctor discharged us from the hospital, and we went home. I told my Mother I wanted Dean and Hanna to sleepover, and she agreed. Dean called his parents and told them, and Hanna did the same. They went home and came with their change of clothes. My mother started preparing dinner while we went into her room to check on Romaine. My grandmother was there standing over him, telling him stories of the old days.

Even though he wasn't responding, I know he could hear her.

She looked over at me and smiled. I went over and hugged her.

"I love you, Grandma."

She smiled at me and brushed back my hair.

"You look just like me when I was your age. I love you too, my child. Come, he hasn't seen you in a long time. He needs your voice now," she said.

My grandmother walked off hugging both Dean and Hanna; then she walked out and closed the door. I turned to Romaine; his little frame still hooked up to this — machine I wish I could rip off.

Dean and Hanna stood beside me, and both held on to my hands.

"Thanks guys," I said, looking over Romaine.

"Hey Romaine, it's your big sis. I miss you. Feels like I haven't seen you in a long time," I said, smiling, "We're going to save you; we're going to save everybody. I won't let you stay like this for long, I promise."

I touched him on his head. Then Dean did the same, then Hanna.

"We promise," Hanna said.

"We promise."

Next morning, we left for the road. We know we had school, but we all agreed that this was more important. We got off the bus and headed for Maberly Street. It was further away from the bakery where I went to get my mother's birthday cake.

We hadn't said a word to each other on the journey. Dean and Hanna sat directly behind me. I turned and looked at them. Their faces were long and melancholy, and I could only imagine why that was. What happened yesterday was like a wake-up call out of everything we have seen so far.

"Young Miss," the bus driver called out.

I got up and walked up to the front of the bus. He looked at me and pointed.

"That's where you want to go, right? Godfrey National Museum?" he asked.

As we turned into Maberly Street, it was crowded, filled with vendors and business people. I looked up and saw a tall brown building with the name **GODFREY NATIONAL MUSEUM** etched on the front.

"Yes, that's it," I said, "You can let us off here."

"Yeah, just give me a $120," he said as he pulled over.

I gave him $360 for the three of us and we stepped out of the bus. The bus drove off, and we walked up to the building. We pushed the door open and strolled inside.

The sight was breath-taking. Despite what we came here to do, the visual aesthetics of the place and amazing historical artefacts that we were seeing blew our minds. I knew it thrilled Dean as he was grinning his teeth from ear to ear as he walked in.

"You know they named this museum after Godfrey Boggart?"

I turned to him.

"Godfrey Boggart? The tailor?" I asked.

"Yes, seriously Ana, where are your history lessons going?"

"Obviously, I'm not that much of a nerd like you. I just didn't know that part of history, that's all," I said.

"Yeah, he used to be Marcus Garvey's tailor," he said proudly, "And once he tied himself to a tree in front of a university until the administration allowed his children entry into their school. They arrested him for disturbing the school grounds."

"Soooo… why was he famous?" Hanna asked.

"Because he believed in multicultural society and multicultural education. He didn't believe that people, no matter the colour, should be shunned because of how different they look or their social status in society."

"That's not the history I care about right now, Dean. I'm more focused on what we have here now," I said.

They both nodded in agreement. We walked further into the Museum and parents were walking around with their children showing pictures of Bob Marley's guitar. Teachers brought their students, giving them tours of the exhibitions like, the footstool from National Hero, George William Gordon, National Hero, Marcus Garvey's walking stick, and Jewellery making tools used by indentured East Indians. Musical instruments such as the Goombeh from the Maroons represented an important instrument used in religious ceremonies.

As we walked further, a young woman greeted us, very pleasant looking.

"Good morning, welcome to Godfrey National Museum. We are so glad you could join us today. My name is Elsie, one of the tour guides of the Museum. Are you travelling with parents or a class?" She asked.

We looked at each other.

"No, we came by ourselves, actually. We are from the Mount Techa High School and they gave us this assignment to do on the history of Eliza Gutzmer," I said, lying through my teeth.

The guide's smile faded instantly.

"Oh, I see… Eliza Gutzmer, that name has not floated around these parts for many years."

"So, you knew about her?"

She walked off, and we followed her.

"Bits and pieces, actually. I only know what I know from my father."

"Did Eliza ever come to this museum?" I asked.

The guide turned to me and looked around.

"Thing is, Eliza kept a diary. Anything that could tell us who she was and how she lived would be in there. Our teacher told us we needed to be as detailed as possible, so that's why we're here."

Elsie stared at us, then slowly leaned forward.

"There is something here that belongs to her, but I don't know what," she said gingerly. "According to my father, before she perished in the fire, it was said that she was looking for something important but couldn't find it, so it could be the diary."

"That's why she wants it so bad. She never knew where it was."

Elsie nodded.

"But that was a long time ago. I don't think anybody cares about that now. Everybody comes in here looking for fresh stuff, some leave excited, some leave disappointed. We just do our best to preserve history. Ahm! EXCUSE ME! Please don't touch that… thank you," she said in a nervous smile as one child was touching an Arawak artefact.

I turned back to her.

"Well, what we want to know is if it's possible that… the diary could be here," I said.

She looked at me strangely.

"You sure this is for a school project?" she asked suspiciously.

We all nodded.

"You're not lying to me, are you?"

"Let's just say, it has value to us," Dean said.

"It's for research. It's very important," answered Hanna quickly.

 Elsie sighed and shook her head.

"Fine… do you have the combination number?"

"Yes," I said taking out the piece of paper handing it to her.

She took the paper and looked at it. Then she turned and motioned us to follow her. We walked behind her away from the crowd down a narrow hollow path. At the end of the path was a metal door. It looked very heavy and concealed.

We approached the door and looked up. In the middle was an owl etched on it, with the wings sticking out. It also had a list of numbers in the middle of its stomach.

Dean looked at it and looked like he was ready to run.

"What an ugly owl," Dean said.

"I don't like it either. It creeps me out. Eliza was crazy about Owls, she loved them a lot," Elsie said proudly.

"We know," the three of us said.

Elsie's smile faded, and she turned and frowned at us. Then she looked at the paper and punched in the numbers. We stood there holding each other's hand waiting to see what was behind the door. We honestly did not know what to expect, but we were ready for whatever would happen.

Elsie finished punching the numbers, and the door crumbled. The Owl's feathers moved across each other, stopped, then moved downwards. Elsie held on to the feather, pulled it up and opened the door slowly.

As it opened, there was no room but a wall with a safe inside. There were no combination numbers, only a handle. Elsie opened it.… and there it was — sitting there, didn't look old or torn. It looked just as my grandmother described it. We froze for a moment — none of us took it up. We stared at it and smiled.

"This is what you wanted?" she asked, bewildered.

We didn't answer, we just kept looking. Elsie looked over at us and snapped her fingers. We jumped.

"Hello, I shouldn't even be around here. So please don't let me regret this. Take the book and go."

I took up the diary and caressed it. She had her name written on the front of it when I turned it over. I smiled, then turned to Dean and Hanna.

"We got it."

"We need to leave now," Hanna said.

I turned to Elsie.

"Thanks Elsie. I actually, thought it would have been hard to get."

"Why is that?" she asked curiously.

Realizing that I almost revealed why we were there in the first place, we thanked her again and rushed out before she could get another word in.

Hanna took the diary and hid it in her bag before we went back outside.

We stepped out of the hallway, dashing towards the front door. We walked out and stopped. Hanna took out the diary, and the three of us looked at it once more.

"You know what this means?" I asked.

"We might finally stop Eliza," Dean said proudly.

"Question is, are we going to like what we see?"

"It doesn't matter right now. Whatever happened in her past happened already. All we need to do now is to find out more about her and that — is why we have this," I said.

They nodded in agreement. We walked further down the street and stopped at the bus stop.

An hour later, I arrived home. I passed my mother in the living room with the TV on, but she was fast asleep, so I didn't bother to wake her and went straight into the kitchen to get something to eat.

Hanna and Dean came over later and their guardians didn't mind them staying with me. I told my mother we were staying in the room for the rest of the night because we had a lot of reading to do.

CHAPTER NINE
THE UNREST

Dean shut the door and threw his bag on the floor. Then he knelt beside it. Hanna climbed in bed beside me.

We all looked at each other nervously because we had the diary in our possession finally, the last remnants of Eliza Gutzmer's memory. The diary was very thick, so she had made hundreds or more entries over the years. We didn't know what to expect from reading, but we were about to find out. I opened the diary and her earlier entries started from way back as 1620 right up to 1634.

Each day, she made a different entry about how miserable her life was and how she hated her parents. We skimmed through most of her entries, and we almost felt sorry for her. They abused her viciously as a child. We could understand why she ran away. But we wanted to see if she made any entries about her time with Constance Gutzmer. I skipped pages rapidly until Dean stopped me.

"Wait…. right here, June 6, 1634," he said.

Hanna looked over.

"Starting over. Sound like it.".

"Alright, let's see," I said. "Who wants to read?"

"You read Ana."

We were about to read the thoughts of Eliza, and I was excited. I don't know why, but everything that we needed to know about Eliza's life, every secret that she had concealed about her running away and her meeting up with Constance, was right here at our fingertips.

June 6, 1634

"Starting Over,"

It was a chilly night I would never forget. Sleeping on the roadside, sharing bed spaces with the rats, was not something I wanted for myself at 16 years old, but I had to leave that retched house. That miserable existence that haunted me for many years was behind me. Until I met her, I was but a misfit, an outcast. Ridiculed by those who refused to understand me. She did. We smuggled on a boat and travelled to a distant country in the Caribbean. She took me to a home she had owned years ago in Plantations Grove. It was up a very steep hill in a small town known as Belle Isle. She gave me cookies and milk, and we ate some delicious goat water for dinner. This comprised of goat meat, carrots, and special spices. I did not understand the hospitalities she was showing me because I wasn't used to it, but I was appreciative. Her name is Constance Gutzmer, she is a farmer. Her name was exquisite, so innocent. She took me to her garden once. She had many plants, only two of them I could remember; the Gloriosa Daisy and the Pineapple Lily, but they were all beautiful. She asked me where I was from. Of course, I lied. However, she did not care where I came from, and I didn't want her to know. I could not go back to that filthy retch of a family. All they ever did was beat me and force me to steal again and again. I hated them and I wished they died.

She took me to the market today; it was my first experience going somewhere pleasant for a change. She let me pick up Mangoes, Oranges, Apples, Guavas, Tamarinds, Naseberries, and Star apples. She would show me how to peel them and eat them. I asked her if she had any other family because I didn't see a family portrait or anything. She told me she didn't have anyone; she was alone like me. She normally kept to herself and travelled a lot. Kept out of distance from people and just focused on building and living for herself. She was fascinating and I wish I had met her sooner. I felt safe, like I could tell her all my problems and she would not judge or criticize me. I cannot wait to see what tomorrow brings.

I turned the pages, and the rest were empty. I skipped and skipped to the very end, but nothing was there.

"That's it? Dean asked in shock as he snatched the book from out my hands shaking it up and down.

"You expecting the words to miraculously fall out?" I asked, looking at him hilariously shaking it.

He looked at me with a distinctive frown.

"This is what we almost got killed for?" Hanna asked in disgust. "There's nothing in here."

She got up and walked over to the window. She turned around with a puzzled look on her face.

"You guys knew about this Plantations Grove Eliza was talking about?"

Dean and I shook our heads. It was the first we were hearing of it.

"Is there anything else she has that we can use?" Dean asked.

I took up the book and scanned through quickly the first couple entries again. Nothing remotely talking about how she became who she was or her connection to Constance.

"This was a waste of time."

"Maybe not. There must be a reason. This can't be it," I theorized.

Dean and Hanna turned to me.

"What you mean?" Hanna asked. "Look Ana... the rest of the pages are empty,"

"Why would the witch or Mr. Francis try to kill us for a diary that had nothing in it? It doesn't make sense. Maybe the last couple of entries weren't meant for mortal eyes."

Dean chuckled, and I looked at him.

"You have any better theories, chuckles?"

He stopped laughing.

"Look, maybe Eliza never finished the diary. Maybe she died before she got to finish and is livid now that we're trying to dig up her secret."

"Rain's drizzling outside," Hanna said, looking out the window.

The rain started pouring heavier, pelting against the windowsill.

PLOP! PLOP!

I felt drips of water coming from above. I looked up and I could see a crease in the roof that was there for as long as I could remember.

"MOMMY! THE ROOF IS LEAKING AGAIN!" I shouted.

"Ana.... LOOK!" said Hanna, pointing at the diary. Dean's eyes widened as he looked at it, too. I looked down and I couldn't believe my eyes.... words. We could see letters forming out on the page. The more drips of water went on the page, the more words we saw, but overtime they disappeared.... and the pages were blank again.

"I'm not the only one who saw that, right?" Hanna asked, looking at both of us.

"No, you're not. I told you, there had to be more."

"But how's that possible?" Dean asked, puzzled.

"Seems like it was cloaked by magic. Only one way to find out right. Hanna, get me a bucket a water please, bucket in the bathroom. Just catch it in the shower."

"Okay," said Hanna, rushing to the bathroom.

She turned on the pipe, and we could hear the water filling up in the bucket. Afterwards, Dean went to help her carry the bucket, and he set it on the floor.

"Hanna, pass the small cup on the table."

Hanna picked up the cup and handed it to me.

"I think it's best we do this on the floor."

So, we sat down on the floor and looked at each other.

"Here goes," I said as I dipped the cup into the bucket of water and threw it onto the page.

We each moved back in case the water splashed on us, but it didn't. It only splashed on the pages.

The water seeped unto the pages and the words filled out on both sides.

"Wow!" Hanna said in astonishment.

"Looks like it needed a lot of water to be visible." "Let's read before it disappears," I said. "This one doesn't have a title, just the date she wrote it."

June 12

Today, I decided I was going to do it. My name was going to be changed. I craved the change. Constance was the guardian I always wanted, the guardian who listens to me, encourages me, not beat me, or calls me 'worthless' or 'stupid'. That's all I ever got from my pathetic excuse for parents. But I did not have to worry about that anymore. Constance taught me many things; she taught me how to sow for the first time, how to kill a chicken, boil it then skin it. The most disgusting thing I ever saw was when she had to clean out the chicken's insides. It was awful, smelled awful too. I wanted to vomit…. but overtime, as I watched her, it became easier, and I started doing it. I had gotten more and more comfortable around her. Constance was also a master pianist and a storyteller. After dinner, Constance sat me down and told me many folktales…

Stories of gods, fairies…. even magic. Her stories intrigued me, so I wanted more. At that point, I wondered if what she was telling me was true, because she had passion in her voice when she told them. There was one story that she told me I would never forget — these spirits called 'Jumbies'. Jumbies, she said, were mythical creatures from Caribbean folklore, spiritual demons, very nasty who roamed the earth seeking souls to inhabit so they could live in the human world. Each time she told me the story, I wouldn't think nothing of it. It frightened me a bit, but.... it was her expressions that terrified me most. She sounded serious, like she believed them. She said Jumbies had roamed the earth for many years, and no one ever knew. It was Constance who told me who she really was. We had developed that bond, the feeling that she could tell me anything and I would be okay with it. She told me when she was little, her mother locked her up in the basement whenever she misbehaved, left her there for days, even weeks.... most times without food or — The ink vanished, so I dipped the cup into the bucket with water again and threw it on the page. The words came back, and we continued to read.

Water. She said she was so miserable; she started to hallucinate and mumble words that made little sense. I didn't know whether to believe her or call her insane, but I saw the hurt in her eyes as she recounted the story. She told me her time in the basement gave her time to train herself, to meditate. I did not know what she meant at first, but as she spoke, something strange happened. I thought I was imagining things, but she kept telling the story, then suddenly her plates levitated in the air next to me, spinning in a circle.

I almost jumped out of my skin, but she looked at me and smiled.... she was a witch. She has been one for a very long time. Her grandmother was an obeah practitioner, and that's why her mother punished her, because of what she was practicing. To her mother, she was an abomination, a freak of nature. Constance told me that from the moment she saw me, she knew I was hurting inside; she knew I was being ill-treated and beaten, which is why she took me in. She thought I was special.

She told me she could teach me how to be strong, how to defend myself and be fearless, only if I was comfortable and ready. I hesitated, because I didn't know what she meant or how she would teach me. But then I remembered all the pain I endured. I closed my eyes and flinched at the times my parents brutally struck me, took advantage of me, and basically starved me. Most nights I went to bed having nightmares and Constance would come and console me. That very morning, I woke up and went to her garden where she was pulling up some fresh tomatoes; I told her I wanted her to teach me how to be strong, like her, not to be weak or be pushed around anymore. She was proud. That day, I denounced my last name. I didn't want to be associated with those filthy retches any longer. Eliza Bertram was weak, could not stand up for herself and who was afraid to speak her mind. Now.... my name is Eliza Gutzmer, strong, fearless, and powerful. I spoke it all into being and that night, my evolution began.

The ink disappeared again. So, I turned the page and dunked the cup into the bucket of water. Then I looked over at Hanna. She had a concerned look on her face. I placed the cup on the side table.

"Hanna, what's wrong?" I asked.

"She wasn't evil. She had a horrible childhood. All she ever wanted was to live a normal life and be a normal child, and all that wasn't possible all because her parents were rotten. She had parents and look how they treat her. I would give anything to have mine again…. anything."

Dean leaned over and consoled her. He too, looked concerned.

"Everything she went through was all because her parents mistreated her. Not excusing her for all the wrong she did, but…. it kind of made sense."

"Guys, I know you might feel sorry for her, but…. we can't ignore what she's doing now. Look, I feel bad about what happened to her too, but that innocent little girl died when she met Constance. Now we need to finish this."

Suddenly, we heard a loud commotion outside. People were shouting at the top of their voices.

We put the book down for a bit, got up, and opened the door. We walked out, and the shouting got even louder. My mother was standing outside the door with a herd of angry neighbours gathered at the front door.

"WE WANT TO SEE YOUR SON," bellowed one neighbour.

"WHY IS HE ALIVE AND OUR CHILDREN ARE DEAD?" shouted another.

My mother tried her best to get a word in, but the shouting towered over her. A neighbour tried to push past her, and my mother pushed him back and got very upset.

"No, no, let me tell you something now. Anybody thinks they are brave enough, try to push past me again. NOBODY IS COMING IN MY HOUSE UNLESS I INVITE THEM IN!" she shouted.

"Step aside Margaret, don't make this get any harder," said a familiar voice my mother knew very well.

"Ann Marie, you know better than to test me. You're not coming inside my house."

Ann Marie walked up to her slowly. "This will not end well if you stand in my way. There is something happening in the district, something strange and your family is right in the middle of it," she said seething.

"Yeah… something strange happening in the district, but it has nothing to do with me. My family is affected just as much as yours are. So, if you know what is good for you, get out of my face."

The shouting started again. Dean, Hanna, and I stood behind my mother.

I held on to her hand. She turned and looked at me. I wanted her to know that I was here for her, and I wouldn't let anybody take advantage of her.

"We need an explanation," Ann Marie said.

"I don't owe you anything."

"We have all been excellent parents, loving parents… we did nothing wrong. Your son was just as sick as ours, so why is he in a coma and ours are dead? We just want answers."

The crowd cheered in agreement.

"Why does he get to live?" A man asked, looking over Ann Marie's shoulder.

"Listen…. I'm sorry for what you all going through, okay, I am. I didn't ask for any of this. The night my son got sick, I panicked. He was laughing and being cheerful as he usual is, and then he just got sick, that's it. Romaine is in a coma and God knows if he's ever going to wake up," my mother said sadly, "Please don't think my son being in a coma means you're being punished. I'm sorry your children are dead, but coming at me won't bring them back."

The crowd shouted again and this time they got even angrier. I was getting upset, and I pushed past my mother.

"EVERYBODY SHUT UP!!!!" I bellowed.

Everyone got quiet. Ann-Marie stared at Analisa.

"Mind your place child, we're all grown folks here, learn manners."

"If you are so grown, then act like it," I said. "You marching up to our house like an angry mob and for what? You forget I was there when your babies died, and I cried for them. I still cry for my little brother because I want to hear his sweet voice. We still don't know why he survived, but all we want for him to wake up but we can't do that unless…."

I stopped talking. My mother shook her head and asked me not to say anything. I clenched my fist.

"What is it, child? Speak."

"The reason the babies were sick, the reason any of this happened, is because of a witch," I said.

My mother rolled her eyes and hung her head. The townsfolk murmured to themselves and looked at me as if I was crazy. Ann Marie laughed.

"A witch? Let me guess, the legendary Ol'Hige witch, right?" Ann Marie asked in a somewhat sarcastic tone. "Ya'll have some nerve, you know that. It's the same crap your grandmother been spewing for years. You remember right Margaret."

My mother looked as if she was about to pull a muscle. The veins in her neck pulsated and the look on her face was clear; she wanted to rip Ann-Marie's head off. I would accept no one disrespecting my grandmother, but I would end up in jail if someone disrespected my mother.

"You seem to forget when your brother died all those years ago, how your mother started spreading foolishness about Ol'Hige, this Ol'Hige, that. Ol'Hige killing children, when maybe she's the one who cursed her own son and killed off all those innocent babies."

Seconds later, without hesitation, my mother's hands were wrapped around Ann Marie's throat. We tried pulling her off, and the others tried pulling Ann Marie away.

"MOMMY STOP!" I said, trying to break her grip.

She finally let her go and she stepped back. Ann Marie held on to her throat and stared at my mother with intensity.

"You going regret that… just watch."

"Ann Marie, move away from my front door…. NOW!" she shouted.

Ann-Marie and the others stepped away.

As they walked away, they looked back at us with disdain. I had a bad feeling come over me, like something awful was going to happen, apart from the already obvious threat we were under. I closed the door and walked towards the living room. Dean and Hanna were with my mother, trying to comfort her. She sat in the chair and frowned.

"Mommy, you okay?" I asked.

She looked up at me.

"I'm okay, just…. fine. The nerve of Ann Marie blaming us for her baby's death."

"The entire district blaming us," I said.

"Well, it's not right. I need to go check on Romaine."

She got up and walked out of the living room and into her room.

"What is it going to take for them to see what is actually going on?" Hanna asked.

"We need to keep reading," Dean said.

I looked at them and nodded.

"Let's go finish that diary."

We returned to the room, turned off the light and got back to reading. I poured water over the page again and continued reading.

June 25

Nights came and passed, swift like the wind. Constance had me locked up for days, training me, teaching me how to channel the powers of the Jumbie. The first step I had to complete was the blood pact between a witch and an apprentice. It did not happen on the first try. She pushed me again and again until I got it right. She used a knife and made a huge gash in the middle of my hand. It was so painful, even now as I'm writing this. She then cut herself and joined our hands together and muttered a spell. The next step I had to perform was to drink chicken blood. I did not want to. At first, it was difficult. I had so many things on my mind that I couldn't concentrate, but I had to if I wanted to be powerful. Constance told me to banish all doubts, all things about my past from my mind. That I was no longer a Bertram. My name change was a testament to my transformation, and I needed to focus on that. For eight nights, she taught me the art of levitations, how to move things with my mind without straining my body. The first time was excruciating. I concentrated too hard until I had a horrible nose bleed. Constance was very hard on me the first couple of times, but later, she was a bit more lenient. I had resented her like I did my parents, but she told me she only did that because she wanted me to be stronger than even her. That people wouldn't understand people like us, understand our abilities. We were different.

I didn't want to disappoint her. I was ready. Night after night, I practiced on my own. I would take out different objects out in front of me and practice to levitate them. I wasn't there yet, but I could tell I was improving, so I continued until I got it right. There was one thing I wanted, but Constance told me it was out of bounds to me.

There was a book that she kept in her private study that contained dangerous magic. She kept it locked in a case protected by magic; I suppose. She told me I was never to touch it, but I was even more intrigued.

That was the end of that entry and the ink disappeared. So, I turned the page and stopped with a look of concern growing over my face. Dean and Hanna had it too.

"So, there's a black book?" Hanna asked. "What do you think that is?"

"Grandma told us that obeah practitioners used a book to conjure up spirits, remember? Maybe the jumbies are the spirits they conjured up from the book."

"Could be the black book of dark magic," Dean said with a straight face.

Hanna and I looked around at him.

"How you know that?"

"What else could it be? You ever heard a black book that had good stuff in it? I mean, she's basically training to become the most powerful witch in existence. This was her first stage of training. What are the chances that she found this black book and became the very thing we are trying to stop now? This book could have all sorts of evil spirits we don't know,"

The thought made us uneasy, but it made perfect sense.

"Let's keep reading," Hanna said.

"Right," I replied. "This one is June 30th."

My skills were improving. I was getting stronger, more confident. I've been using Constance's black book, and it was exhilarating. I don't think she knows I have been reading it and practicing with it, but I think she would be most pleased. She was always telling me about standing up for myself, Why did she keep this from me? It didn't matter either way; I was going to find it eventually no matter where she hid it. There was merit in being the daughter of thieves, after all. In the book, I found all kinds of things, real dark magic spells. As I read, I practiced, in secret at least, and I got stronger each minute. I perused through all the pages and in it had different monsters, spirits and demons and how to conjure them.

 I was changing. I was growing and becoming more aware of who I was or who I was about to become. I wanted more; I wanted it all, and I was going to do whatever it took to get it, even if Constance didn't like it. She started me on this journey and I was going to see it through.

 As I read through the fascinating black book, looking through different spells and reading about different creatures and spirits, I came upon one that caught my attention…. "POWER OF THE OL'HIGE SPIRIT" was what it was called. My eyes flared up with anticipation. The power of the Ol'Hige was an interesting read that I wanted to know more and it fascinated me so much that I couldn't put the book down, but I had to read in secret so that Constance didn't catch me reading it.

There was a very peculiar symbol beneath it, as if they carved it into it. I ran my finger across it and it felt very coarse. It was said to be the most powerful and deadliest of spirits known to humankind, and only a few witches were fortunate enough to wield its power. There were four steps needed to become one with the Ol'Hige spirit and the steps were quite brutal. One of the first steps was to first denounce your past and embrace the power you were about to receive. Everything that you were, everything that you loved, had to be cast away. Second step was to create blood binding spell and connect your energy with the Ol'Hige spirit with an incantation. The third and fourth steps were crucial. The book said that these last two steps were not for the faint of heart, only those who were worthy of the power of Ol'Hige could channel the spirit. You had to sacrifice the life of someone close to you. Once that is done, you take the blood of your victim with yours and recite the incantations, calling forth the Ol'Hige spirit. Right away, I knew who to sacrifice. If I was to succeed and become the most powerful witch in existence…. I had to get rid of Constance. My conscience weighed on me and I was having second thoughts, but I came this far to stop now. I loved Constance like a mother, but I had to do this…. and so it begins.

We read through the rest of the entries, and it was horrifying. Eliza had snuck into Constance's room. She looked over at her as she was sleeping peacefully. She cast a spell on her, causing her to choke herself. Constance awoke and saw Eliza standing over her. She stretched out her hands towards Eliza and then her hands became limp and fell on the bed. Constance was dead. Eliza stood over her body as she took her last breath. No remorse, and no inkling of regret.

We had to read it over countless times because it still amazed us at how Eliza could brutally murder her foster mother like that; granted that Constance was a witch herself.

I guess Constance had no idea that teaching Eliza the art of witchcraft would one day become the single most regrettable mistake she ever made.

If she could see into the future and know that Eliza would become the most dangerous person in all human history, she probably would not have taught her.

After killing Constance, Eliza packed her things and left with the black book.

She travelled far and wide, trying to find somewhere to live and lay low. She walked through various markets stealing fruits and vegetables without being seen and she was happy. More than happy, happier than she ever was in a long time.

Weeks after, she realized that her work was not yet done. She had already killed Constance, so she had everything she needed to call on the Ol'Hige spirit. But then she found out that her biological parents were in Belle Isle for a visit unbeknown to them that their only daughter was there. They were staying at a hotel and she wanted to visit them. She thought they would have been happy to see her, probably be proud to see how changed she was and how strong she had become. They didn't care; they were just the same when she left; they called her a disappointment, a gutless failure and how they wished they had never created her. Eliza broke down, but she wasn't sad. She became angry. Suddenly, the room shook, and the walls cracked.

Eliza's hands were outstretched, and her parents started grabbing their throats. She strolled over to them and smiled, then — she snapped their necks. Their lifeless bodies slumped over.

She stood there, brushing back her hair and looking at the bodies of her dead parents, she rummaged through the hotel looking for a jar. She took a knife and extracted blood from both her parents and then walked out.

Later that night, she travelled up the Belle Isle hill with her bag and found a secluded area with plenty of grass where she could complete the transformation. She sat down in the open space with tall trees surrounding her and crossed her legs. She opened the bag and took out the jar with her parents' blood, along with the book. She took out the book and turned to the page with the incantations of the Ol'Hige spirit. After closing her eyes, she spoke the words.

She read the words out loud. Suddenly, she heard strange noises in the distance, moaning noises, then she saw images swirling around in the sky.

Eliza opened the jar and stared at the symbol carved in the centre. She always wondered what it was for, then she realized what it was meant for and what she had to do.

She poured the blood from the jar into the symbol. It moved slowly, taking its shape.

Then she took a knife, cut the tip of her finger, and placed it over the symbol. Her blood completed the formation, and the symbol glowed. Suddenly, the swirling entities plunged deep into Eliza's body. Eliza said she felt a massive rush of electricity come over her. She felt power like she's never experienced before. Her transformation into the Ol'Hige was complete, but before we could read anything else…. the ink disappeared again.

Dean, Hanna, and I were at a loss for words. Now we knew how Eliza became the Ol'Hige, but it still didn't tell us how to stop her. She killed the one person who took her in and loved her, then she killed the very people who ill-treated her. We still felt like we were missing something. Suddenly, we heard a glass window break. We all jumped at the sound. Then we heard it again.

"What was that?" I asked.

I closed the book and put it down. I went to open the door and looked out. My mother opened her door as well. We walked towards the living room and noticed two enormous stones in the middle of the room.

"Jesus Christ," my mother exclaimed.

She walked over to the window to see what was going on, but before she got close, another rock came sailing through the window, striking my mother right in the head, sending her crashing to the ground.

"MOMMY!" I shouted.

I ran over to her, and I kept my head down. Dean and Hanna came out, and I told them to look after my brother. Then ran towards my mother's room. I looked at my mother and I could see she had a deep cut on her forehead.

The shouting came from outside. I turned towards the window, and I was very careful. I saw a massive crowd lead by non-other than Ann Marie. She apparently came back with a vengeance and my mother was now knocked out because of a stone. My whole body shook, and it brought me to tears. I got up enraged and flung open the door. I stormed out and walked out in front of my yard.

Ann Marie and the others stood by the gate. Some came with torches and pitchforks. I stood there panting, with tears flowing down my face.

"We have nothing against you, Analisa, just bring us the child," Ann Marie said.

"You going to get through me, because you not COMING in here."

"Don't make this any more difficult than it already is. This can go either one or two ways: you either bring the child to us, or we come in by force."

"I SAID YOU'RE NOT COMING IN HERE!" I shouted "Somebody throw a stone inside my house and the stone hit my mother in her head and now she bleeding. I want to know who?"

They all looked around at each other, not saying a word. I became impatient and walked further out.

"Think about what you doing, child," Ann Marie said.

"OH, SHUT UP! YOUR BABY DEAD GET OVER IT!" I bellowed, without thinking straight.

Ann Marie's eyes widened, and she bit her bottom lip and looked around her. The others murmured in shock. I instantly regretted what I said.

"Listen, Ann…."

"You hear that? Analisa Kelly showing her true colours. You are Mabel's granddaughter. I knew you never cared about our children.

"You didn't even come to visit us; it just shows that this family is the disease that has corrupted this district for years and it's going to stop."

"You and whose army?" said a familiar voice.

I turned around and my grandmother came up behind me.

"Grandma, where…."

"Hush Analisa, I'm here now." She said confidently, "Now, I want to know which one of you bright and stupid enough to throw a stone in my daughter's house?"

"Does it matter?" Ann Marie asked.

"IT MATTERS TO ME," my grandmother shouted. "THAT IS MY CHILD!"

"All we care about is the baby. Bring him to us. We're not asking."

My grandmother walked out in front of me as Ann Marie and the crowd walked further into the yard.

"Ann Marie, you ugly ol goat, if you think you bad, make one more step in here. You will see how mad I am!" snapped my grandmother.

They continued to move forward, but then we heard something crack. Ann Marie and the others stopped in their tracks; we all heard it too. We looked up and noticed that a tree shook. It was shaking and then the tree collapsed. Ann-Marie and the crowd had jumped out of the way and it landed outside of our gate. I looked on and I didn't understand what was going on. My grandmother smiled and blinked as I looked up at her. I was confused.

Ann Marie and the others tried to get up but couldn't, as if they were stuck to the ground.

"What is this?" she asked, looking at my grandmother.

"Next time you come and threaten my family again, this will be the least of what I will do to you."

Suddenly, out of nowhere, roaring flames circled us.

"If you know what's good for you, Ann-Marie, you get off my daughter's lawn before things get real ugly, real fast."

Ann-Marie stared at my grandmother with immense hatred.

"We deserve justice for our children," she said.

"We're not the ones who killed your children. How dumb are you, Ann Marie? How much time must I tell all of you that this is the work of the Ol'Hige witch?"

"WHAT WITCH? WHERE IS SHE?" Ann Marie asked in frustration.

"You keep making up these stories about witches and duppy, when clearly weird things only happen around you. For all I know, you could be the witch.

I walked out from behind my grandmother.

"Please leave."

The crowd gave us mean look. They, slowly turned around and walked out of the gate. Ann-Marie stood there looking at us, then she too turned and left. I didn't move until they were clearly out of sight. Then I turned and hugged my grandmother.

"There, there, child, it's okay, you safe now," she said lovingly.

The flames then died down. I turned and looked around, still confused. I looked up at her.

"Grandma, where did that fire come from?" I asked.

"Come inside. We have lots to talk about," she said as she turned to walk inside.

I followed behind her. I walked in and shut the door. As I entered the living room, I saw a strange-looking woman with a shawl over her head and a very peculiar necklace with the symbol of a Raven around her neck. She bent down with her hands outstretched over my mother and her eyes closed, muttering in a strange language.

My instincts kicked in and I was about to go push her off, but my grandmother held me back.

"It's okay Analisa, relax," she said.

"Grandma, who is that?" I asked.

"I brought her here. Her name is Madame Bruge…. an obeah woman."

CHAPTER TEN
OBEAH WOMAN'S WARNING

I stared at the woman chanting over my mother. I didn't know what she was doing, and I didn't care to know. I just wanted to know my mother was okay. My grandmother was still holding on to me as I turned back to her.

"Grandma, she needs a hospital. We have to get her up."

"Madame Bruge knows what she is doing. Let her work," she said. "We don't have time for hospitals."

Madama Bruge placed her hands over my mother's head wound and chanted some more. My mother convulsed like she was going into shock. I didn't enjoy seeing her like this. I broke my grandmother's grip and ran to my mother's side, trying to stop Madame whatever her name was from possibly killing her.

"Stop, you're hurting her," I said hysterically.

"Your mother is fine. Keep disturbing me and she won't be," Madam Bruge said calmly.

After a couple more chants, she removed her hand from my mother's head…. the wounds were gone, like they were never there. I looked on in shock, but I was glad. My mother's eyes started to open. I hugged her before she could even get up.

Madame Bruge smiled and nodded in approval. She got up, brushed off her dress, and then went over to the couch to set her bags down. I looked over at Madame Bruge as she stood. She was a tiny, petite woman who walked with a limp. I helped my mother up, and she looked all around her, touching her head, realizing the wound had disappeared. She looked confused.

"Wa… what just happened?"

"They hurt you Mommy," I said.

"This woman here saved you," Hanna said walking over to help my mother to the couch.

Dean walked into the living room with a glass of water for my mother. She sat and drank in satisfaction. I could tell she was feeling a little better.

My grandmother bent over to kiss my mother on the forehead.

"I'm glad you are okay, daughter," she said lovingly.

My mother looked up at her and smiled.

"Thanks Mama."

She turned to Madame Bruge, who was looking around the house muttering to herself.

"Thank you, miss," she said, trying to figure out who the woman was.

Madame Bruge turned to her and smiled.

"You're most welcome Margaret."

My mother was shocked.

"How do you know my name?"

"I've known you since you were a child, dear. I was there the night your brother died."

My mother's expression was now blank. She didn't know what to say after this or how to process it. She looked over at my grandmother, then Madame Bruge looked at her as well, feeling as if she had told a tremendous secret.

"You didn't tell her Mabel?" Madame Bruge asked.

"Didn't think it was the right time."

"You could have said something, Mama!" my mother said. "Let me know she was coming."

"Well, you know she's here now, end of discussion.".

"Mama, I'm not a child anymore. You can't keep these things from me. How does she know me?" my mother demanded.

No one said anything. The living room was as silent as the grave. Madame Bruge finally sat and made herself comfortable.

"1990 was the year it happened, as you well know Mabel. It was a tough time; many people had lost their jobs; pregnancy rate was high. In that time, the Ol'Hige was at the height of her powers. She could sense the essence of all the children that were living in Belle Isle and I could feel her too. I tried to prevent her from taking anyone else by casting various protective spells around the district. I didn't want anyone to know I was here, much less practicing, because witchcraft was forbidden, so I had to fight her in secret. I cast a spell to protect Marcel, but it wasn't strong enough. The sickness had already gotten to him and then it was too late."

"How do you know when a child's life force is drained?" Dean asked.

"Weather patterns, a change in the atmosphere. Children are pure, innocent. They make the world brighter and easier to live in. When a child's essence is being corrupted or taken by an evil force, the atmosphere changes, so does the child's innocence," she said gravely.

"Did you find her?"

"Yes, I did. I fought her, but it wasn't an easy fight. She was powerful, and it's a miracle I made it out alive. But I wished I had gotten to her sooner, put an end to her. If I knew then what I know now, those poor children would still be alive, including your uncle, Analisa."

"What do you know?" Hanna asked.

"The witch is afraid of fire, but that's not all. The power of the Ol'Hige is very rare. For centuries, the Ol'Hige spirit has taken many forms. When they find a host, it can shed its skin and transform into any creature at will or they just take one natural form. But it is through the witch's essence that the Ol'Hige takes the form of whatever the host held dear in his or her life."

"The Owl," I answered. Dean and Hanna nodded in agreement.

Hearing this was like music to my ears. We were finally getting some insights about what could destroy the witch. We should have guessed it from the very beginning. I figured the witch was afraid of fire. Eliza was burnt in her cottage. We already knew the Ol' Hige shed its skin. My grandmother told us this earlier, so that bit of information wasn't new to us.

"What's the point of shedding the skin? Why do they do it?" Dean asked.

"The shedding of the skin is their rebirth. It also enables them to steal the essence of a child. It gives them more power, more durability and when they're ready; they revert to their original form even stronger, more powerful."

"How many times do they shed their skin?" I asked.

"They shed when they are ready to feed."

Dean, Hanna, and I looked at each other gravely. If we were to count the number of children, the Ol'Hige has fed on between then and now, she would be immensely unstoppable. I wanted to ask Madame Bruge more questions, but I was interrupted by a ---

CAW!

I saw the two crows with blue eyes perched on the windowsill, looking in. We all jumped and backed away, but not Madame Bruge. She opened the window and began petting them. All of us looked at her strangely. My grandmother didn't seem the least bit surprised. She then turned to us and smiled.

"Don't be afraid. They won't hurt you," she said. "I believe you already met them, Analisa,"

"These are YOURS?"

"Who do you think has been protecting you… and Romaine all this time?"

"I don't understand."

"The witch has been trying to get to you from the day you were born. Your grandmother told me what was happening, and I protected you. These are powerful crows, old but powerful. They have been my eyes and ears for many years and they have always looked out for you."

"That's why the witch couldn't touch you.. The reason your brother is not dead is because I placed a protective spell around him. It would not prevent the witch from draining his essence, but it was enough to keep him alive. But the protective spell can only last for so long, and she is still trying to kill him."

"You said the witch couldn't touch me. But she has. I could literally feel her cold hands grabbing me. How do you explain that?

Madam Bruge's brow furrowed.

"Her powers are growing. We cannot underestimate her."

"Why didn't you end it when you had the chance? Why you make us go through all of this if you had the power to stop her in the first place?" Dean asked in frustration.

"You're all stronger than you think. You survived everything the Ol'Hige has thrown at you, you could have died, yet here you are. If you have that kind of will, you can destroy her without magic."

"I have a question," Hanna said, raising her hand. "If she is so hell bent on taking Romaine's life, why hasn't she done so? What is she waiting for? She's basically toying with us."

"She's buying time."

"Buying time for what?" my mother asked.

Madame Bruge continued to pet her crows, then she answered, "The full moon."

Our mouths fell open. "The full moon," I repeated. "The full moon…. there was a man who came into the bakery I went to when I was buying Mommy a cake. He told me something."

"Beware the child… beware the owl," Madame Bruge said.

I looked at her, amazed and in disbelief.

"It was you…. wasn't it? You possessed the old man?"

"More like channeling his body to speak to you without the witch knowing where I was," she admitted.

"There was another message, too. When the moon rises, her true face is revealed. What does all of it mean?" I asked.

"She is in hiding until it is right or until she feels fit to feed again; but make no mistake, she's going to come for your brother again, so you best be ready."

"Yes, but what does it mean?" Hanna asked.

Madame Bruge looked towards my grandmother, who was still standing in the doorway.

"Just tell them," she said.

Madame Bruge leaned over and whispered something to the crows, then they flew off.

"The coming of the moon will enhance her powers and when it does…. she won't need to be near a child to take their essence anymore — she can take them by will."

We all stared at her.

"What you mean, take them by will?" I asked.

"Meaning that she can steal their essence from anywhere."

"So, she can take hundreds or even a thousand more babies if she wants," said Hanna in disbelief.

"Which is why it's very important we stop her before that happens."

My brain was scrambled. Everything was becoming clearer now but it made it all the more alarming.. I couldn't process any of it. When we thought we had the advantage, she always was ten steps ahead of us. Now she could channel the moon's power to become even more powerful than she already was.

"We still don't understand the first message — beware the owl, beware the child."

"When the Ol'Hige sheds her skin, she turns into an unstoppable creature. I've seen this transformation before and it's the most frightening thing I have ever seen. Don't take it lightly, the Ol'Hige has evolved over the years, killing adults, commanding an army of birds and taking the shape of other humans is a whole new level of different."

"If she can do all that, imagine when the full moon hits," said Hanna worryingly.

"Which is why we can't waste any time. The full moon will be here in a couple of weeks' time."

"Now we know fire kills her. How do we get close to her?" I asked. "It's not like she's going to stand still and let us burn her."

"When she leaves her skin, that's when she's most vulnerable. You can kill the witch by destroying her animal form with fire, or you can burn the skin with salt and then throw fire on to it. The animal form can be destroyed this way as well."

Now we were getting somewhere. But in order to do that, we would need to get close to her and so far, she has always had the advantage over us.

"First things first. We need to protect your brother. The spell is wearing off. I need to put up another charm so that when the witch comes, she can't easily get to him," she said. "I need to get to his room."

I opened the door to my mother's room after she took up her bag. She walked in and looked around. She paced the room twice before she stopped in the middle. She closed her eyes and started muttering in a strange language, then… her eyes shot open and they turned blue.

She opened her bag and took out a bible, placed it on the ground in front of her, then chanted while shaking the bible up and down. A wave of blue light sparkled around the house, then it formed a circle around Romaine.

Then, she pulled a bag containing a white substance, poured a little in her hand and sprinkled it around Romaine. She stopped chanting.

"It's done…. he is protected…. for now. The Witch won't be able to get to him,"

Suddenly…. the room started to tremble, then we realized it was the entire house that was shaking. We lost our balance. My mother ran over to Romaine to protect him and Dean, Hanna, my grandmother, and I held on to each other. Madame Bruge stood by the window to prevent herself from falling. The walls began to crack and even the pictures fell and broke. Then we heard a loud rumbling. It started slow and guttural, like a deep thundering voice.

CHAPTER ELEVEN
THE GIANT OWL

The house trembled something fierce and we couldn't hold our balance much longer. Dean and Hanna lost their grip and rolled over to my mother's bed, hitting their heads. Then we heard screeches outside the window. Madame Bruge crept up to the window and looked out, then she turned to us.

"CROWS!" she shouted. "SHE KNOWS I'M HERE!"

We heard the loud flapping of wings, and then the crows sped past our window like little black rockets.

"WHAT ARE THEY DOING?" Hanna shouted, "WHY ARE THEY JUST FLYING PAST THE HOUSE?"

"They're not just flying by, they're surrounding the house," Madame Bruge said.

A loud, rumbling bang came soon after, sort of like a loud, raspy, thunderous voice.

"SO, YOU THINK YOU CAN HIDE FROM ME? THERE IS NOWHERE YOU CAN GO THAT I WON'T FIND YOU! I WILL KILL THE LITTLE ONE, THEN I WILL KILL ALL OF YOU! AND SOON THE ENTIRE DISTRICT."

"JUST LEAVE US ALONE!" I shouted. "YOU"RE NOT GETTING MY BROTHER!"

"STUPID CHILD!!!" thundered the witch. Lightning struck another tree outside and fell right in front of our house.

While the crows continuously surrounded the house, Madame Bruge sat on the ground, her legs crossed. Her eyes flashed blue again, and she started muttering under her breath.

Blue and red lights flashed outside. I went over to the window, almost falling over to see what was happening. Two of Madame Bruges' crows were fighting off the swarm of crows. How did she expect just two crows to fight so many? While I was worried that the two crows wouldn't be able to beat them, they were handling themselves well as flashing blue lights spewed from their beaks, knocking out birds out of the sky. The rest of the birds surrounding the house dispersed and soared high into the sky to join in. My eyes widened. I turned to Madame Bruge.

"Her crows are going to kill them."

"I know," she whispered. "But they won't perish without taking a few with them."

As the rest of the crows went up, the only thing that was left was a cloud of darkness. We heard loud shrieks…. then all the birds disappeared in a puff of smoke. Suddenly, the house stopped shaking, and I breathed a sigh of relief. I ran over to Dean and Hanna and hugged them both, then I went over to my mother, who was hugging on to Romaine the whole time. She lifted herself off him and looked at him as he continued to sleep peacefully, unaware of what was happening.

My grandmother, the strongest woman I know, held on to whatever she could hold on to.

I strolled over to Madame Bruge, still seated on the floor, but she looked like she was about to pass out. I kneeled in front of her, held her face up. Her nose bled. She was sweaty and her breath was rapid. She then slumped over.

"Grandma."

My grandmother came over and looked at her closely.

"Get her on the couch outside," she said.

Dean and I lifted her and carried her to the couch in the living room. We placed her down gently and just watched her.

I looked around and saw that the living room was in chaos, all the picture frames shattered and most of the furniture shifted, out of place.

"My god, look at this mess," I said with a heavy heart.

Hanna held on to my hand. I turned to her. She smiled.

"It's going to be okay."

I smiled back at her, feeling comfortable and thankful I had her by my side. We turned to Madam Bruge.

"What you think happened?" Hanna asked.

I bent down and placed my hand on her chest.

"She's still breathing, but slowly," I said.

"How are we going to stop her?" Dean asked, "The witch is too powerful, even for her."

I pondered this question as well. Eliza was toying with us, and she enjoyed doing it. We had all the answers on how to stop her, but the Ol'Hige never ever kept in one place for too long and it seemed like she always had the upper hand. She kept popping up and disappearing whenever she felt like.

"Hanna, get some water, please," my grandmother said.

"Okay," said Hanna, rushing to the kitchen.

My grandmother sat in the chair next to Madam Bruge, held on to her hand and watched her. Madame Bruge moaned and twitched, then suddenly she rose, gasping like she was choking and in a trance. The lights started blinking. Hanna walked in just in time with the water and handed it to my grandmother.

"Thank you, Hanna," she said, turning to Madame Bruge, who was stiff as a board. "Here Madame Bruge, drink this."

My grandmother placed the glass up to her lips and drank. Madame Bruge broke out of her trance and grabbed the glass, gulping down every drop of water.

We all stood there watching her as if she hadn't had a glass of water in years.

After she finished, she gave the glass to my grandmother and breathed in slowly, then the lights stopped blinking. She looked up at me, and all I could see was the troubled look in her eyes.

"What's wrong?" I asked.

"I saw it."

"What do you mean? Saw what?" Dean asked.

"The end!"

Nervousness crept in all of us like never before. What did she mean by that? Did she see something that made her breath sound so heavy?

"What you talking about, Bruge?" my grandmother asked.

Madame Bruge turned to her, her eyes widened with fear, then she grabbed my grandmother by the arm.

"Mabel…. this is not the same witch I fought before," she said in a panicked tone.

"Bruge, you tired. Maybe you need some more water," my grandmother said, picking up the glass and handing it to Hanna.

"NO!" Madame Bruge shouted, slapping away the glass, breaking it. "Mabel…. you don't understand. She is not who she seems. I saw it…. the full moon, the terrible things that have happened. I was wrong… this witch is way too powerful. She wiped out the entire community,"

"Wait…. you mean you actually saw her doing that?" I asked curiously.

She turned to me and barely nodded.

We all looked at each other, wondering what this all meant. Was she getting stronger? Earlier, she told us what we needed to do to kill the witch. Now she got some vision, and she looked as if she almost wet herself.

My mother walked out of the room. I turned to her, and she had a grave expression all over her face.

"Romaine's breathing is getting slower," she said sadly.

"What?" I asked. "What does that mean?"

"I don't know baby…. I don't know."

I turned to Madame Bruge."Madame Bruge, tell me, please. Can we beat her?" I asked.

"I don't think we can," she said gravely.

Madame Bruge's expression was uncertain.. That confident streak she had in her earlier when I first met her was no longer there.

It's as if the visions she saw clouded her abilities and her own power.

"You said that the witch is not what she seems, what you mean by that?" Hanna asked.

"It's rare for an Ol' Hige spirit to be defeated, very rare. Some of the most powerful obeah practitioners in the world who dedicated their lives to fight evil have often died at the hands of an Ol'Hige spirit, worse if they inhabited the body of a witch. Eliza Gutzmer was a powerful witch, and she died a most horrible death. I thought — I thought she was the witch I faced when I was trying to protect those babes so long ago," she said, gazing into space.

"Bruge, what you saying?" my grandmother asked.

Madame Bruge glanced at all of us.. She was pale and her hands were fidgety.

I was worrying because she seemed genuinely afraid.

"When Eliza Gutzmer perished in that cottage fire, she remained dead. As you recalled me telling you, the Ol'Hige's weakness is fire."

Dean and Hanna looked confused more than ever. So did my mother and grandmother. We already speculated how dangerous the witch was based on the things we had gone through, frankly — we were lucky to even be alive, but to have an obeah practitioner with us, who seemed powerful in her own right, reduced to fear, was bad, terrible even.

"So, the witch you fought off at the abandoned house years ago…. that wasn't Eliza?" my grandmother asked.

"Apparently not," she said.

"So, you mean we suspected Eliza Gutzmer for nothing?" asked Dean, disappointed.

"That's ridiculous, it has to be Eliza. She had every motive to want to destroy Belle Isle and the people in it."

My grandmother had a direct, intimate bond with Eliza. She knew her. spoke to her and befriended her before she was betrayed. My grandmother paced up and down the living room with a sense of confusion building up in her.

"The only thing Eliza loved more than anything was Constance. She loved me once upon a time, so I understand the frustration, even after my son was taken from me. So, you're telling me, it's not Eliza?" she asked Madame Bruge.

"You and I both know spirits don't need motive to terrorize a community or innocent people. But this one…. is full of hate towards your family. It—"

Madame Bruge gagged; her eyes rolled over in the back of her head.

She slumped over in the chair, her body jerked back and forth. My grandmother went over her using both hands trying to subdue her, but Madame Bruge's arm swung over and slammed hard against my grandmother's face, sending her flying across the room, breaking the mirror on the wall. I ran over to help her up; she was bleeding from her forehead.

As I helped her up, we looked over, and Madame Bruge's body stopped shaking. Then she sat up stiffly and turned to us. Her eyes flashed open and was red. She spoke, but not in her usual tone; her voice became harsh and raspy — as if the witch possessed her body. .

"Your district will not survive the night. Each baby that is born, each man or woman that has ever lived will bathe in their own blood and BURN!!" the witch thundered..

We all watched on in horror as Madam Bruge's face grew crooked and sunken. Her features were becoming more and more frightening as the witch transformed her from within. Suddenly, we felt a chill in the air. The lights started flickering and her voice grew much louder and colder.

"NOW COMES THE HOUR WHEN YOU SHALL WITNESS THE END. YOU HAVE SEALED THE FATE OF THIS DISTRICT AND EVERYONE IN IT. THIS WILL BE YOUR UNDOING AND TO PROVE MY POWER, I SHALL START WITH THIS ONE!"

Madam Bruge's body deteriorated as if her life energy was being drained, reducing her to skin and bone. Then…. her pale body slumped over on the couch. The lights stopped flickering and the instant chill had disappeared.

We all stood there looking at the lifeless body of Madam Bruge, and we couldn't do anything. We just stood there and watched it happen. But what could we have done against an insanely powerful witch? My grandmother was transfixed.

She trudged to Madam Bruge's body and dropped to her knees, sobbing severely. I have never ever seen my grandmother cry, not this much. My mother walked over and knelt behind her mother and leaned on her shoulder.

There was nothing I could say that would make my grandmother feel any better. The pain she felt was like losing a best friend. I observed Dean and Hanna, and they were speechless. We all shared a moment of tense silence. The mood was very grim.

An hour passed, and our house swarmed with police officers and EMTs. The officers were dumbfounded when they asked us what had happened, and we didn't know how to explain without sounded utterly mad.. We couldn't exactly say that there was this mad, powerful old witch killing babies and terrorizing the town. So, my grandmother came up with a plausible, logical explanation that it shocked even me how she remained so calm, even after just losing a friend. She told them that Madam Bruge had been very sick for a long time, and she was trying to self-medicate.

She told them she hated doctors and always fooled around with special remedies and unorthodox ingredients. The police officers searched the bag she carried and found the strange contents inside, and they looked up at us suspiciously. The officer started taking notes.

"Is there anything else we need to know about this…. Madam Bruge and why your house looks like a hurricane hit it?" the officer asked.

"No sir, I've told you everything — nothing else."

The officers seemed to think that she was hiding something. But if I was being honest, it was best they knew nothing. The second officer closed his notepad and stuffed it into his pocket.

"We're very sorry for your loss. If you remember anything else, please call," he said.

He took out a card and handed it to me.

"Oh, I have a number for a man who works in construction. I can have him come and fix up your house."

My grandmother took the card and looked up at him.

"That's kind of you, sir, but we wouldn't have the money to pay anything," she said with a heavy heart.

"No problem, it's on me. It's the least I can do, besides he owes me a favour."

The EMT's had finished processing everything in the house and left, then the officers finally stepped out. I watched as they walked to their vehicles and drove off.

Early the next morning, it was 3:00 am; I got a little sleep, and the rain flopped against the roof. I stayed up staring blankly at the ceiling, wondering how my grandmother was doing. How would we be able to erase this from our memory? We all felt so helpless. Madam Bruge was murdered in front of us and we just stood there.

I was frustrated, so I got up. I opened the door and headed towards the living room. I looked around and the TV was on, and my grandmother was fast asleep in the very chair Madam Bruge died in. Dean and Hanna were across from my grandmother, sleeping like little babies. I didn't want to disturb them, so I left them alone and moved to the kitchen. I was glad they were keeping her company.

Hours later, I was almost finished with breakfast. Ackee & Saltfish, Callaloo, plantain with fried breadfruit. With everything that was happening, I thought we all needed some good food to keep our minds at ease. Little by little, Dean, Hanna, and my mother walked into the kitchen. Of course, Dean was always first because he was drawn to food like a magnet, yet somehow, he still could not put on weight. The only person I didn't see was my grandmother.

My mother said she wasn't inside, and she didn't know where she went.

We started eating, and it was quieter than usual. We often said a word or two around the table, but this time it was quiet. I didn't like us not talking, so I broke the ice. My appetite was already long gone, but I was still hungry and had to eat.

"I wonder if we're still going to do that community service thing," I said randomly.

Dean looked at me, raising his eyebrow.

"THAT'S what you are concerned about?" he asked, surprised.

"Well yeah, I'm still wondering, and no one is talking."

"You have missed school for quite a while now. I think you all should go, get back to your normal life," my mother said.

"I don't think that's possible anymore, Mommy. I doubt Belle Isle will ever be normal again."

"We're losing too many people and I don't think she's going to stop," said Hanna, twirling her fork mindlessly into the food.

"Madam Bruge didn't die in vain," Dean said firmly. "Maybe she knew it was her time. Maybe she knew it wasn't long before the witch found her, and maybe she knew she wasn't strong enough. So, she told us how to kill her."

Hanna and I agreed with him. My mother shook her head in disagreement.

"Even so… how would you even get close to a witch this powerful? You think she won't hesitate to kill you because she will."

My mother got up from the table, pushed it under and stood behind the chair.

"She playing with us and scaring us until either our hearts give out, or she rips it out of our chest," my mother said. "Teenagers are supposed to have fun, to go to class, parties, go on a school project. Not to hunt down centuries old witch spirit whatever."

"Mommy, you know we don't have a choic—"

"Yes, you do," she interrupted. "Why you think it needs to be you? Why you?"

"I don't know…. I just feel it," I said confidently, "Maybe I'm stupid and with everything that has been happening and our brush with the witch more than once, we should already be dead. But somebody must do it Mommy."

My mother still didn't agree with our plan, but she decided not to argue anymore. The witch was fixated on our family, and it was personal.

"Alright, I have to realize I can't baby you anymore. Any decision you make is yours and yours only. I don't have to like it…. but your heart is in the right place. It always was," she said, smiling at me.

I smiled back. She cleared up the plates and pots in the sink. I walked over to her and told her to go rest, and that Dean, Hanna, and I would clean. She took off a piece of paper towel, wiped her hands and mouth with it, then walked out of the kitchen.

Dean, Hanna, and I cleaned the kitchen, and we were taking out our sweet time. Dean started packing up dirty plates in one part of the sink. Hanna cleared the table, and I was wiping off the counter from the spilled grease.

"You think it's true?" asked Dean, packing up the last of the dirty plates. "What Madam Bruge said about the witch not being Eliza?"

"Maybe she was being delirious," Hanna said. "Maybe it was her mind playing tricks on her."

Dean and I looked at each other and we weren't the slightest convinced that she was making it up.

"Guys, come on; you actually believe that? We spoke to Dr. Michaelson; my grandmother told us the tale of how she met Eliza and we even read her diary."

"Yeah, maybe she was, but what if it isn't her," said Dean. "Ana, the three of us, saw how frightened she looked, like she had seen the end of days or something. Yeah, we know she was evil, she did many bad things…. but she loved, and she had a heart. It's not her fault that she had a crappy childhood."

Dean started washing the plates while I stood there thinking about the possibilities that he might have been right, that we might have gotten this all wrong from the beginning.

But everything we had done to get to this moment, all the bad things that have happened to us was because we went in search of Eliza's diary. How could it not be her? Maybe Madam Bruge was hallucinating, or the witch tricked her, showed her false images of what will happen on the full moon. We didn't know what to think, but we literally had a couple weeks left for the full moon to appear, and if what Madam Bruge said was true and the full moon comes, something worse was about to come our way, worse than what she was already doing. She could steal children's essence at will and wipe out the entire district.

After Dean and Hanna finished cleaning, they told me they were going to go home because they hadn't seen their families in a long time. I really didn't want them to go, but I understood. Holding them back would have been selfish of me because I knew their families missed them.

Later in the night, no dinner was prepared, because I was immensely tired, so my mother ordered pizza. She looked exhausted and melancholy.. I could tell by the way she looked around the house, probably wondering how she could pay to fix it. I told her that one of the police officers my grandmother spoke with said that he knew someone who could fix up the house for us for free. At first, she thought it was some sort of hoax, but I told her that the construction guy called the house earlier and said he would be here in the next two days. Her facial expressions changed and now she was happy to hear that, and it eased her nerves.

I retreated to my room the rest of the night, not before kissing my baby brother, counting down to when I could finally hear his voice again. I sat on my bed and started reading Eliza's diary one more time, reading it from the very first page.

Reading her diary, I honestly questioned which side I was fighting for. If Eliza's parents weren't so horrible towards her, she might have turned out to be a good woman. I mean, she loved her child and would have loved to see her child grow, but they ripped her child from her, then she died, which led to her taking revenge on the district. She didn't trouble anyone; she was ill-treated and forced to run away. But someone loved her, nurtured her and taught her how to be strong and how to use magic — which turned out to be a huge mistake.

I read the rest of the entries and it was simply heart-breaking, so I closed it and put it away in my drawer. My grandmother said she was silent, but she poured out her most inner thoughts into her diary. She never tried to seek help, or try to get some counselling, well…. that probably would have made it worse. But if she had gotten help, her mind wouldn't have been so twisted into seeking revenge on the district when it wouldn't have brought her daughter back.

How did someone who was so thoughtful and caring of others and the simple things in life turn out to be a cold-blooded, frightening thing? I already knew the answer, but I still couldn't comprehend the lengths someone would go through just for revenge.

I kept thinking and pondering until my eyes got heavy, so I just let myself go and drifted into a deep sleep.

I woke up hours later, and it was still dark. I picked up the phone off the table and looked at the time; it was 2:30 am. I got up and went to the bathroom to wash my face thoroughly. I opened the door and headed towards my mother's room door. As I opened it, I froze instantly. My jaw fell open, and I rubbed my eyes rigourously, wondering if I was seeing correctly. Over my brother, suspended in the air, was a massive, sharply hooked beak, black owl. I tried to tiptoe over to my mother, who was fast asleep and not aware of what was happening. Suddenly, the gigantic bird turned its head to me slowly. Its devilish red eyes pierced the very core of my soul. When I looked at it closer…. it was an owl — a giant owl. This must have been the creature the witch turned into, and it made sense now. Madam Bruge told us that when Ol'Hige spirits inhabit a body, it takes the form of something that the host held dear, and Eliza had a love for owls.

I got to the bed still eyeing the Owl and stretched my arm out to touch my mother, trying to wake her. She kept fanning me off and slapping my hand away. I finally turned to her.

"Mommy!" I breathed

She grumbled and woke out of her sleep, she looked up and saw the giant owl towering over Romaine. She jumped up and almost screamed until I pressed my hand against her lips.

"Mommy…. don't move…. don't say anything," I whispered to her.

The giant owl continued to stare down at us with its wings flapping heavily. Every little move I made; it followed with its gaze fixated on me. I felt trapped.

Suddenly, the owl widened its eyes and opened its beak, letting out a deafening shriek. My mother and I covered our ears, grimacing in pain. The owl stopped shrieking and turned towards Romaine. It lowered its head, opened its beak and a red streak of light escaped it. I tried to move, but the pain from the shriek left me dizzy.

As I reached out to him, I whispered. "Ro… Romaine."

My mother also couldn't move. I felt helpless again. My brother would die if I didn't help him. The owl tried taking Romaine's essence, but nothing happened. The Owl turned to us and frowned, obviously upset because Madame Bruge set the protective charm. I gleamed at the owl, delighting in her defeat.

"What's wrong? Lost your appetite? You can't hurt him anymore. We're going to stop you, everyone you ever hurt, every baby you've ever killed — you're going to pay for their deaths," I retorted. "YOU HEAR ME ELIZA!"

The owl stared deep into my eyes and then it gave a vile smirk.

It stretched its head so long that I heard a loud cracking sound. It pushed its head towards me.

"How are you going to stop me when you can't even help your own family?" "You're helpless, you're weak. Honestly, I expected the daughter of Angus Kelly to be more formidable than he was. Do you miss your Daddy Analisa? Do you miss the good man that he was? If only you knew the horrible things he did."

I tried talking, but words failed to come out. Either the witch was playing mind games with me, or she believed what she was saying.

My whole body trembled, and I could feel an intense adrenaline pumping through my body. My eyes filled with tears.

"You're a sick woman Eliza and I will be glad when you burn in hell!!" I said, enraged.

"Who says I am Eliza? Ha ha ha," she cackled.

My mouth flung open in shock and my eyes widened. Madame Bruge was right, it wasn't Eliza. Then who was it?

As the owl raised its talons, the door flung open in time and there stood my grandmother. She flung her arm forward and something flew out, a white substance swam through the air towards the owl.

It screeched in pain and scowled at my grandmother. She then turned into a cloud of smoke and disappeared under the windowsill. I got up and ran towards the window and opened it, looking to see if she was still out there.

"Everybody alright?" my grandmother asked, attending to my mother. "Analisa, you alright?"

"Grandma, it wasn't her," I said, panting.

She looked at me, confused.

"What? What you talking about?" she asked.

"She said it. Madame Bruge was right, it wasn't Eliza."

I opened the front door and ran out into the road, darting my eyes all around me.. I looked up into the trees, wondering where she went. The breeze was swaying calmly, and the street was silent. The witch was out there, but it's not who we thought it was, and now we had a distinct problem. She knew who my father was.

CHAPTER TWELVE
LIFE OF ANGUS KELLY

A week later, the house was undergoing repair, as the Police officer promised. It took more muscle to move the large tree in front of our house, but the Fire department heaved it out the way. My mother had suggested that we move, because it was becoming too dangerous to stay here with the witch constantly trying to kill Romaine. Even though the charm protected him, it was becoming extremely difficult, trying to watch him when she was going to find all ways to get to him.

Apart from finding out that Eliza Gutzmer was not the witch that was after us all along left us in a bind. All the clues that we had, everything that we had searched and the people we spoke with led us to Eliza, so now we were left at a crossroads, not knowing which direction to take. Also, that she spoke my father's name as if she knew him was also unsettling.

Not once since the school term started, have I really thought about my father. I was so focused on Romaine and my mother and trying to keep this family together that I didn't even take the time to really mourn my father's death. There were still some unanswered questions about how he died. My mother still couldn't understand it herself, but she seemed to have made peace with the fact that he was no longer here with us. However, because of what the witch said, I wondered, and my mind starting racing.

Doctor Michaelson's and Madame Bruge's deaths all weighed heavily on my conscience. I could barely keep track of what has been happening, and all started with crows and the witch, finding out who she was, getting information from various sources, finding out Mr. Francis was in league with her, and I still intended to find out how and why. No one knew where he was, and the principal said that he left without saying a word. He just vanished.

Hanna and Dean hadn't been over since that night Madam Bruge died and I honestly didn't blame them. No one in their right frame of mind would want to stick around a house where bad things kept happening. I called Dean and Hanna to find out if they were okay. They both answered in the same monotonous tone, told me they were fine, but I knew deep down they weren't. I could hear it and part of me wanted to keep them out of this, keep them out of harm's way as I have tried many times, but they were so insistent on being there, wherever I go, and I truly loved them for that.

My mother was cutting up vegetables when I walked into the kitchen. She turned to me and she smiled.

"Well, you're up early."

I said nothing, but I was building up the courage to ask her, even though I knew she didn't enjoy talking about it.

"Mommy."

"Hmm," she answered, cutting up Cabbage.

"The box with Daddy's things. You know where they are?"

Suddenly she stopped cutting and looked up, her expression changed.

"Why you ask?" she asked dryly.

"Just some things I want to look for."

"I put the box somewhere, don't remember where. Haven't looked in that thing in years."

She continued cutting the Cabbage.

"Mommy, you can't pretend like you didn't hear," I said.

"Hear what, Analisa?"

"What the witch said. She called Daddy's name, like she knew him."

"She said he did bad things. I know I shouldn't believe anything she says, but you can't tell me you don't find that strange Mommy?"

"I made peace with your father's death long ago, even though I talk about him. I try to keep his memory. The witch is a liar. She's twisting your thoughts with her cursed tongue. Do not allow her to tarnish your father's good name, no matter what he may have done."

My mother was behaving strange. She barely looked at me. I walked up to her slowly and each time I got close, she would turn away.

"Mommy… you know something."

She moved from the sink and walked over to the fridge, opened it and took out tomatoes and headed back towards the sink. I held on to her hands and looked into her eyes. I could tell that something was on her mind, something she didn't want to talk about, which involved my father.

"Mommy, what are you not telling me?"

She let out a deep sigh, held her head down, then turned to me.

"Look in the closet in my room, up at the top. There is a box in there with some of your father's things."

"Mommy, you had a box here all this time and you never told me," I said in disbelief.

"I didn't want to tell you because it will bring up painful memories."

"I would believe you if that was the only thing you're not telling me," I replied.

Before she had time to say something else, there was a knock on the door.

I walked towards the door and opened it. It was the mailman. He handed me two bills, the light and water bill, and walked off without saying a word. I closed the door and walked to the kitchen, handing the mails to my mother. She finished cutting the vegetables and placed them in a bowl. She wiped her hands on the kitchen cloth, took a knife, and tore open the light bill first. I stood there and watched her as she scanned through the bill, then she was low-spirited. I could only imagine what she was looking at.

"How much is it Mommy?" I asked softly.

She didn't answer; she was doleful. Her mind was absent from me as she kept looking at the bill. She then folded it, putting in back in the envelope paper it came in. She looked at me.

"Go on now, the box is in the room. I'm going to freshen up."

She walked past me and left the kitchen. I took up the bill and opened it. I got wide-eyed when I saw the amount owed at the bottom. It came up to $80,000, and she hadn't even opened the other bill. I didn't know we had owed that much and how she was going to pay for it. If we didn't pay our bill in time in this district, the companies would not hesitate in taking action, they didn't care about your situation. If you owed, you had to pay.

I volunteered for this program they had at school, and the principal compensated me handsomely. Most of the money I made helped my mother around the house, to buy groceries, paying off some bills owed and basically sending myself to school.

I put down the bill and left the kitchen. I headed straight for my mother's room. I opened the closet door and pulled it. Maybe the box was behind the two bags I looked up at. I grabbed the chair and stood on it, trying to keep my balance and not fall. I moved the bags and threw them on the ground. There was a big brown box after I threw the last bag on the floor.

I took it down and set it on the floor. It was really dusty, and this has been up here God knows how long. I brushed it off with the cloth that was hanging on the window. On the top it marked "Kelly's Belongings".

I opened the box, and it was filled with all my father's stuff from his childhood to adulthood. As I took out each item, I sat on the floor and smiled. There was a very dirty old cricket ball, I turned it around it marked 'AK'. He loved to sign things that were his, so people knew not to touch it. Next thing I took out was his old construction hat. He used to love wearing it even before he went to the site. He said it made him feel important, like he was worth something to the world.

Going through his stuff made me forget what it felt like to have a father. It was a long time since I had that feeling. It had been two years now since we lost him, and it felt like a lifetime. I was 15 years old, and we still had not come to grips with how he died. He was a healthy man who never ever got sick; he had never gone to a doctor in his entire life, then suddenly, we heard they diagnosed him with cancer. It was all too sudden, and we didn't understand it.

I dug deeper and I found a couple of pictures my mother took with all of us. Romaine wasn't born yet. There was a picture that I found with me and my father. I was about six or seven years old, and we were at the beach. I remembered that day like it was yesterday. He was lifting me high into the air, and I was laughing away. My mother took the picture, and I could remember her giggling because she said I was kicking and screaming while he was throwing me up in the air.

There were other pictures as well, some I didn't even remember that we took. We were such a happy family. My mother was chirpy. She smiled a lot more back then because of my father, but his death took a toll on all of us, especially her. She often told me that when she looked at me, she saw him and that gave her some sense of comfort and closure.

But it still didn't feel that way because each time I brought him up, she would close up, or change the subject entirely.

I put the pictures back into the box, but I had hit something, something hard. I shuffled the rest of the stuff out of the way and took out a necklace. I stared at it for a while and noticed something familiar about it. It was a round pendant with a raven attached to it, the same necklace Madam Bruge wore.

My mind raced with a million questions piling up. Why did my father have this same necklace? When Madam Bruge died, she still had hers around her neck, so it couldn't have been hers. I set the necklace down and, packed the box up and placed it back in the closet. I looked at it again. There were so many unanswered questions that I needed to solve.

I headed out of the room and went to the living room. My mother was tidying up. I stood there watching her, then I held it up. She turned to me and she froze.

"Mommy, why was this in the box?" I asked.

She didn't speak. She just stood there staring at me like I had done something wrong, or I had stolen something.

"I was hoping you didn't find that."

"Why? What does it mean?" I asked.

"I didn't know anything about it, but I know your father used to wear it a lot. It was his. Whenever he came home from work in the evenings, I would watch him, seriously watch him and ask why he had to wear that ugly thing around his neck. He would turn to me and say, it protects me, Margaret, it protects this family."

My mother sat down in the chair and stared out of space.

"But that didn't protect him, did it? He was a very stubborn man, always adamant on doing things his way."

I sat beside her on the couch.

"Mommy, what was Daddy a part of?"

"He was a part of some group. I don't know what it was. He never told me. But one thing I know, he was serious about it, said he was helping people. But I knew…．

I knew it was something that would have put him in harm's way. She said, breathing deeply and trying to keep calm. He came home very upset, told me he had to leave. I asked him why? He told me that if he stayed, he would have put the family in danger — put you in danger."

"Me?" I asked, puzzled.

She nodded slowly.

"Romaine was kicking away in my belly. Your father, he did things…. things he wasn't proud of and it hurt him deeply. He tried to get out of it, but he couldn't."

"Why not?"

She got up and walked out of the living room. I sat there and watched her, wondering if I was asking too many questions because she seemed uncomfortable. I peered at the necklace again, caressing the Raven carving in the centre. Then I looked up and my mother walked in with a rectangular looking box. She sat down beside me and looked at it.

"I wish it didn't have to come to this, but your father wanted me to give you this when you were older." She said, handing it to me. "I tried my best to keep whatever was happening away from you and hoped that nothing was going to come of it. But what happened to Romaine, and everybody else, just confirms that this won't end until the witch is dead."

I took the box from her and opened it. Inside it, neatly outlined, was a horseshoe. Just a plain old regular horseshoe.

I hoped this was a practical joke my mother was playing on me. Looked for a sort of smile or something to lighten the mood, but she just stared at me with her bleak eyes.

"Are you serious Mommy?" I asked, taking up the horseshoe.

"As serious as cancer," she replied.

"How is a horseshoe going to help me?"

"Analisa, I don't know. Before your father left here that night, he went into your room and kissed you on the cheek. I stood by the door and watched him. I could see the pain in his eyes, knowing what he had to do, to make up for what he had done."

The heartbreak in my mother's voice was vivid. She recounted the story to me from memory. She told me he had given my mother the box from his drawer and told her to give it to me when it was the right time.

"He said the horseshoe brought him great luck. It passed down to him from his father, your grandfather, for protection. He also said that you were to use it, to call on someone, I don't know who, but you were to go up to the Raven's Peak, about 5 miles from here, use the horseshoe, speak into it and utter these words."

My mother took the box, opened the bottom and took out a folded piece of paper. She opened it and handed it to me.

"*Reveal thy space, oh noble faction*," I said confused. "What does that mean?"

"I don't know. I told your father he was a fool, an idiot, a stubborn old jackass for leaving me like that. He knew he would not come back," my mother broke down.

I leaned over and hugged her tight.

What was he chasing that got him killed? I eased up and looked at her. I wiped her tears and kissed her on her cheek.

"It's okay Mommy. I don't know what Daddy was into, but I'm guessing if he didn't, we probably wouldn't be here. I'm going to see where this leads."

"Analisa —"

"Mommy, you can't protect me forever. Trust me."

My mother's expression changed. She closed her eyes and smiled.

"So, what am I supposed to do when I find this Raven's Peak?" I asked.

"When you get there, you will a follow a yellow path," she said, sounding even more confused. "And only those who are worthy will see it. When the trail ends, you will see a Raven's beak pointing…. I don't know what the hell that means but… that's all you father told me." my mother said.

"And you remembered that all these years?" I asked.

"I loved you father very much. There was nothing I wouldn't have done for that man. It was important to him — so… yes, I remembered."

"Well, I won't waste any time then. I need to go there now."

"Why now?" She asked.

"I'm tired of this witch messing with my family and destroying others. I'm going to put a stop to her once and for all."

"Aren't you going to call Dean and Hanna?" she asked.

"No, when I need them, I will call them. I need to do this on my own. Need to find out what this necklace means."

"Okay…. but Analisa… please be careful," she said.

I leaned over and kissed her.

"I will," I said lovingly.

I didn't know what I was getting myself into, but one thing was certain: I was my father's daughter and this witch messed with the wrong family.

CHAPTER THIRTEEN
ELIZA'S SWANSONG

took out my phone and was about to call Dean and Hanna, but I thought they needed to rest from all this mess with the Ol'Hige and focus on just living normal lives. It felt selfish of me not to tell them I didn't want them to be a part of this anymore because it wouldn't be fair to them. But then I knew how that conversation would have ended, that they put themselves in danger and I didn't force them.

The full moon was just a week away, and that's when bad things were going to happen. The witch almost killed us more times than I cared to remember. And now because she confirmed that she wasn't Eliza, it really set us back because we were up against an entity we didn't know that would kill a lot more babies and lay waste to the entire district.

I got dressed and prepared to leave out. I was thinking of carrying a bag with me, but I didn't want to add so much weight. The plan was to get to Raven's Peak before nightfall. I walked out of the room and past the living room. I stopped and stepped back; my mother was speaking with the hospital nurse. She turned and waved at me; I waved back.

Halfway trough the day, I looked up and noticed the clouds were bleak, so I had to hurry. I stood by the bus stop, waiting as I had always done. Practically for two hours and still no bus. Night was coming fast.

The droopy feeling in my eyes was setting in. They became so heavy that it made my head jerk forward. I held my head down for just a second when I heard an extremely loud…...

HONK! HONK!

I jumped up instantly.. There was a bus right in front of me. I didn't even see it pull up. It wasn't an old bus either; it was semi new, spotless, small, glass tinted slightly. I got up and stepped back a little. Suddenly, the window came down. There was a dreadlocked man in shades behind the wheel. He turned to me and lowered his shades to the tip of his nose.

"So, you coming or what?" he asked coarsely.

I looked at him, my brows knitted together.

"Excuse me!"

"Hurry man, I don't have the whole day. Dangerous times now," he said, sticking his head outside the window. "Clouds darker than usual, come little girl, come in."

I moved but kept hesitating, thinking about whether to go with this man, because I had never seen him before.. He slid the shades back on his face.

"He's expecting you, so if you want to stay out here and make rain catch you, be my guest. Your choice," he said with serious conviction.

I looked around and noticed the district was quiet, lonely. No one in the viewing distance was out. I opened the bus door and stepped in. As I sat down, the driver turned to me.

"I would advise you to put on your seat-belt. The driving will not be pretty."

Without hesitation, I strapped on the seat-belt and grabbed on to the seat for dear life. Then suddenly, I felt a powerful jerk and the seat I was in thrusted forward. Having the seat-belt on was useless if the seat was going to do that.

I didn't even feel the bus move at all, like it was virtually driving through a different time with no one seeing it.

It felt as if my soul had drifted from my body in a split second and I wasn't conscious of it. The mere moments I was in the bus for made me shut my eyes the entire drive, then suddenly — it stopped. I opened my eyes slowly only to see the driver staring down at me.

"You reach," he said.

I looked on both sides of the road, and I saw nothing but vegetation, trees, and plants. It was a forest.

"Where is this?" I asked.

"Where you wanted to go, obviously," he said smugly.

"Okay then," I said, opening my purse to hand him the money. He refused.

"Not accepting that."

I glared at him.

"Why?"

"Because I'm not that type of driver, I don't take cash. Go down that path there, it will guide you, and him will find you. Remember…. follow the path." he said, pointing to the right side of the forest.

"Who's he?"

He didn't answer; flinch or look at me, so I didn't bother to ask him anything else and came out of the bus. The bus then drove off into fog and disappeared as it cleared. I took a deep breath and prayed to God that I made it out of here today…. alive.

The beautiful scenery captured my gaze as I sauntered through the forest. How I never knew about this place was beyond me. There was nothing out here, no wildlife, no birds, no noise except for the steady trickling streams of water flowing. It was getting dark real soon, and I didn't know if I should continue or turn back. I even forgot to carry a flashlight because I was so eager to come out here. I really hadn't thought about this all the way through.

While I was mulling this over and over in my head, I paused. The sound of twigs cracking was loud through the deafening silence.

I hid behind a tree, took my phone from out my pocket and turned it off. The wind howled, and it got rather chilly. Something was out there, I didn't know what, but it seemed like it was following me. My chest tightened. I covered my mouth, closed my eyes and tried to breathe in and out slowly without making a sound. It sounded like footsteps coming towards me. Was it the witch? Did she know I was out here? I didn't want to wait around to find out; I had to do something. Then…. it stopped — There was silence. I opened my eyes and slowly peeped around the corner; nothing was there. I turned around, and I looked down… yellow lines became visible on the ground and they began a pattern, leading somewhere. So, I followed it. The lines started zigzagging across the landscape, making it very hard to keep up, but I kept going.

As I reached to the end of the trail, the lines stopped in the middle. I looked up, and I saw a pole with a Raven perched on top of it. It leaned forward with its beak pointing at something.

"When the trail ends, you will see a Raven's beak pointing," I said, reiterating what my mother told me.

Then I took out the box from my pocket and opened it. I took out the horseshoe and looked out into the empty forest. I held it up and then…. I started laughing.

"This is retarded. I'm out here with a dirty old horseshoe," I mused, "Well…. here's to looking like an idiot."

The horseshoe was close to my lips.

"Here goes. *Reveal thy space, oh noble faction,"* I whispered.

The horseshoe glowed with bright, infinite colours, and the ground rumbled. I looked around me and noticed that I wasn't losing my balance or falling over.

Then — something appeared before me, shimmering blue lights emitting from it and then I saw it, another old house, in the middle of nowhere. It looked as if it had been here for ages and nobody knew about it. The door opened slowly. Inside was very dark. I sauntered slowly towards the door and looked around, making sure no one followed me. As I entered, the door slammed shut behind me. I turned swiftly, trying to pry the door open, but it wouldn't budge.

The eternal darkness consumed me, and I could barely feel where I was, so I didn't move a muscle. Then, without warning, the house lit up, but they weren't lights. They were candles, lined off around the wall, lit one by one. My nose twitched at the potent scent of incense and something else, a burning smell that I couldn't quite pick up, but it was irritating..

The contents of the living room were fascinating, at least what I assumed to be the living room. Faded wallpaper peeled off the walls, revealing layers of history and nostalgia. The creaky wooden floorboards sang beneath footsteps, possessing an almost musical quality. Photos and newspaper articles about the recent baby killings were plastered all over the wall, then a photo in the middle showed a group of people posing together. I pressed my fingers against it, and I could tell it was old, judging by its outdated colour and stiffness. Then, out of nowhere, I heard something, a strange hissing sound, but very faint, and it was coming from behind me. I felt about a thousand bolts of electricity course through my body. The hissing got closer and closer now. As I turned, there was a very large black snake with green eyes, hissing wildly and slithering sneakily towards me. I froze. I couldn't move if I wanted to because if I did, I would have died for sure. The snake got closer, then it stood upright. Its bulging eyes pierced into the very depths of my soul, and I could feel it ready to attack me.

"*Tedal Na*!" came a strange, raspy voice.

The snake stiffened, drew back into a hand, that pushed out behind the wall. The snake wiggled and transformed into a long staff. That was outstanding, yet terrifying. Suddenly, I saw a man walking out in long robes, slowly. I glared at him as he became visible in the candle lit lights. He was tall, short hair, his pupils were snow white, bald with a short black beard.

He entered with the staff in a godlike fashion and stood in front of me, staring. "Are you alright child?" he asked calmly.

I nodded without uttering a word.

"Forgive my friend. He gets very protective. Cannot trust anyone in these times," he said, walking towards the wall and standing in front of it, looking at the picture.

"You mean your snake?"

He turned and smiled. "Yes, my snake. He's an excellent friend, ally, protector. He's friendly when needs be, but very protective when he feels I'm threatened."

"Well, you didn't seem threatened just now. Why didn't you let him kill me?"

"Because I know who you are," he said. He turned to me. "You are Analisa Kelly," he said.

My mouth fell open instantly. "How did you—"

He walked towards me. "I knew your father. I trained him, and he was very strong. He showed promise, even in the time of his death, his courage and loyalty will always remain with me."

There were so many things wrong with that sentence. Trained? I stared at him, tried to study him, who he was, how he knew my father and what my father did for him. I was wondering if anything in my life was normal.

"Who are you?" I asked.

"My name is Obadiah Griffiths. I don't believe you've ever heard of me."

I shook my head.

"I wouldn't expect that. You came here to ask me a question."

He somehow knew that I had the necklace in my pocket and the reason I came here. I took it out and showed it to him. He approached me and held on to it. He massaged it and closed his eyes as if he was trying to channel some sort of memory, then he handed it back to me.

"Do you know what this is?"

"No, I know nothing about it. That's why I came here."

"That raven is the symbol of the Factions," he said.

"What is that?"

"In the old days, witchcraft was a forbidden practice. If you performed magic, you would be hanged or burnt. So, we practiced in secret, brought order to the chaos of the supernatural."

He opened his hand and fire ignited, balanced the fire using both hands as if he was holding a small cricket ball. Then he closed both hands, opened them and the fire disappeared. I imagined that if my father knew him and learnt magic from him, he also knew Madam Bruge, then he must have been the good one. At least, I hoped he was.

"You still haven't told me who the Factions were."

"The Factions were a group of Obeah practitioners who banded together to stop evil magic from plaguing the district," he said.

"Did it work?" I asked.

A crestfallen look came upon his face. His eyes seemed displeased, as if all the memories came flooding back. "I lost many friends. Those of us who fought the witch many years ago perished. We did not know she was this powerful to beat. She wiped out many of us."

"But you seem powerful enough. Couldn't you have stopped her?" I asked.

"Madam Bruge and I could have stopped her, kept her at bay, but the Ol'Hige had dark magic at her disposal. She was too powerful. There were some of us, in the obeah faction, that thought magic was great pride, great honour, to be used to rule, to be worshipped. They betrayed us and our position, so we banished them for using dark magic to release the Jumbies."

"Wait, are you saying, there were other things released from the book?"

"Yes, there are things far worse than even an Ol'Hige spirit," Obadiah said.

This was very troubling. As if things weren't bad enough. "So the Factions were a group, and some members turned?"

"There are so many things you do not know. Things your father should have told you, but I suppose he wanted to protect you. This is no burden to bear for someone so young."

"I can handle myself," I said firmly.

He smiled. "Well then, it's time you know everything," he said, walking over to his table. "Come this way."

I followed him into another room. He placed his hands over a book and it opened by itself, flipping over pages. It then stopped at a page and at the top, there was a word; "Coven". On the page, there was a squiggly circle and what appeared to be faces intertwined.

"Coven," I said, confused.

"You know what covens are?" Obadiah asked.

"Ah… no."

"A coven is a group or gathering of witches. When witches band together as one, their powers are limitless. Just like us, the Faction. We were strong individually, but powerful as a group. Madam Bruge and I led the first Faction, but she wiped them out forcing Madam Bruge and I into hiding. Your grandfather was a part of our Faction. Then, I recruited your father — he created the new Faction," he said.

I placed my hands on the page, running my fingers across the symbol. I looked up at him. "Did the witch kill my father?" I asked in a soft voice.

He looked down at me and touched my shoulder. "She ordered the hit. But another killed him, by a person you know as…. Mr. Francis,"

My mouth fell open, and I was dumbstruck. I felt as if my head was about to explode upon hearing this news. I leaned over the book and breathed in slowly. I turned and walked away.

"All this time…. all this time," I repeated. "Is he a witch too?"

"His real name is Quilon, and he was a part of our group. an obeah man," Obadiah said.

I turned to him, enraged. "So, you knew all of this, you felt it, you saw it, and you did nothing," I spat. "You said you and Madam Bruge were the most powerful out of all the obeah practitioners, yet you cowered and hid."

"Careful of the next words you say, child," he said firmly.

"Or what, you going to strike me down?" I spat back.

As we locked gazes, our eyes bore into one another with an intensity that could not be broken. Neither of us spoke, but the silence between us was loaded with emotion., Then he walked off into the other room. I followed him.

"You could have saved him. You could have saved my father. Just because you're afraid of the witch doesn't mean you couldn't have tried."

He turned to me. "I FEAR NOTHING!" he shouted.

"Me and my friends faced this witch time and time again. Almost getting killed, each time worse than the next, and we were lucky, but at least we faced her."

His jaws clenched, and his muscles tensed. He was angry, but I didn't care. He was a coward; he hid while innocent people, babies had died. He did nothing to save them.

He and Madam Bruge protected themselves, thought about their own safety when they both had the power to stop the witch. We could have had help. We could have saved so many lives.

"There are many things you don't understand, child, so many things. We had the black book in our possession. We kept it from reaching into enemy hands, but then we realized the enemies were in our backyard. When I found out your father had trusted Quilon, I wished I had saved him. I did, but I would risk exposing myself to the witch, exposing my location. The witch and her minions killed the new faction, all except your father. The things they made him do," he said, staring off into space.

"What did he do?"

His eyes were downcast, his eyelids drooped over, and I could see the slight pulling down of his lip corners.

"He killed people. He didn't have a choice. The witch told him if he didn't, she would have killed your mother and you," he said.

"I don't believe you," I said in disbelief.

"He had to do it, to protect you, but he found something. He found out who the witch was. He was planning to go public with what he knew. So, I communicated with him and told him to see me first."

"What did he find?"

Obadiah moved to his desk and opened a drawer. He took out a thick envelope and walked back over to me.

"Before he died, he left this for me to give to you, hoping that one day you would find me."

"I just want to know something," I said, "Is Eliza Gutzmer the Ol' Hige terrorizing the district?"

Obadiah looked at me and judging by eyes, I could tell he knew I had found out, but I wanted confirmation.

"No, it's not her. This one, is far worst. More reason not to take this one lightly."

"Okay, fine… but we need to stop her before the full moon or she's going to kill everyone in the district," I said.

"What do you know about the full moon?" Obadiah asked.

"Only that it enhances the witch's power, so she can steal essence and kill at will from anywhere."

"Yes…. but you don't know the full story," he said.

What was he talking about now? I honestly didn't know if I could take anymore revelations about something else coming.

"The Black book helps not only the moon increase a witch's power. It also helps resurrect dead witches from the past…. a coven."

I swallowed my tongue when he said that.

"You mean to tell me—"

"She's going to resurrect all the witches that have fallen by our hand. Hence why she needs the black book to do so. Which is why you should be the one to end it."

He handed me the envelope, and as I was about to open it, a strange whooshing sound came from outside. I looked up at Obadiah. His eyes closed. He inhaled softly. Then his eyes shot back open.

"She found me," he said.

"What? How?" I asked panicked.

"I knew I sensed one of them out there. It was only a matter of time. He trudged towards the window and I followed him. I peered through the window and I could barely make out the images. But then, I could see faint silhouettes of five men, one of whom I recognized all too well…. Mr. Francis, or should I say Quilon. They were muttering something and then I saw blue sparks flying around and something opening, like a portal. Apparently, the charm that was protecting the house was being broken."

Obadiah left from the window and moved over to the wall to grab his staff. As he touched it, his eyes glowed white. He then tapped the floor two times, and it shook. I looked outside and the men all tumbled over.

"It's time for you to go. Hold on to that envelope. I will get you out of here safely."

"OBADIAH!! YOU CAN'T HIDE IN THERE FOREVER!" bellowed Mr. Francis.

The barrier had broken further. Was this how it was all going to end? Obadiah put his hand on my shoulder and smiled.

"You might need to put on the necklace," he said.

I searched my pockets, took out the necklace, and threw it around my neck.

The barrier broke, and the men ran through. Obadiah opened the door and threw his staff in the air. Suddenly, the staff transformed into the snake. Its green eyes piercing the night sky. Obadiah then directed the snake towards the men. It unhinged its jaw and sank its teeth into each of them. Mr. Francis' eyes and mine met. Obadiah told me to run because I would have been no match for him. I ran as fast as I could, tucking the envelope under my arms. I kept looking back and I could see green and blue sparks flying everywhere. I didn't see where I was going and tripped on a rock.

Obadiah took on five men on his own.

His powers were amazing. He swatted them away like flies. But then, more appeared from opposite directions.

The numbers were growing. I couldn't help him. I turned my head to the side and saw one of them glancing in my direction. He stared at me and then grinned a devilish grin. I got up instantly and ran. He started chasing and almost caught up to me. Each time I pushed through, I bruised my skin by brushing past bushes and twigs. I didn't look back because it would have only slowed me down and I didn't care how bruised I was; I had to get out of there.

Up ahead. I saw a clearing, then suddenly, the same bus appeared before me. I looked back, the man was already close behind. He jumped and attempted to grab me. I put my hands up to block his advances — but then I felt a surge, like an electric pulse surging through me. The man flew backwards when I moved my hands. The window came down and the man with the shades glanced at me. I looked down at the pendant and noticed it glowing. I breathed a sigh of relief and turned to the bus.

"Good work. I see you met Obadiah," he said.

"We need to help him. He's in trouble," I said, gasping for air.

"Don't worry, old man can take care of himself," he said, taking out a cigarette to smoke.

"Did you hear what I said a while ago? I said—"

"And I said…. the old man can take care of himself. I've known him longer than you, so trust me. Get in."

I wondered if Obadiah was okay. Was he dead? Did he make it? Part of me wanted to go back and help him, but I would not be any good to him dead. What was in this envelope was going to prove who the witch really was.

I got in the bus and closed the door. The bus then drove off at full speed, disappearing around the corner.

An hour later, I arrived home and pushed through the door, grimy, with cuts on my arms.

I entered the living room and saw everyone sitting. Dean and Hanna were there.

Everyone looked at me like they just saw a ghost.

"Jesus Analisa, what happened to you?" my mother asked.

"Ana, you okay?" Hanna asked.

They all started talking at once. I couldn't get a word in edge wise.

"Hey, I'm fine."

"Where'd you go and why didn't you call us?" asked Dean angrily.

"I chose not to call you," I answered back hotly.

"We're in this together. That's what we agreed on, or you forgot all of that?"

"Listen, I was thinking about you and wanted to keep you guys safe."

"Analisa, where did you go?" my grandmother asked.

"I went to Raven's Peak."

"Where is that?"

"It doesn't matter…. look, I met this man named Obadiah Griffiths. He's an obeah man, a powerful one, and he and Madam Bruge were a part of some group called the Factions."

"Obadiah Griffiths," my grandmother repeated. "I've often heard that name, heard stories about him. Thought he was a myth."

"He's very real," I said.

"So how we just hearing about them now?" Dean asked.

"Because if the witch knew they were still alive, she would kill them. Madam Bruge came out of hiding and the witch killed her, and now…. I'm hoping he's not dead. They were the ones keeping the order in the district away from evil magic. That book, the black book, it exists."

"Everything started because of that book. Daddy was a part of it too," I said, looking at my mother. "Obadiah said that he had recruited him and trained him forming the new Faction. "

They all tried to process the information, but I didn't think it was sinking in straight.

"Did the witch kill him?" Hanna asked.

"No…. it was Francis," I said, seething with anger.

A nerve had struck Dean because I could see the fury boiling in his eyes.

"Francis? As in Mr. Francis?"

"His real name is Quilon. He is an Obeah man too, but from the Old Faction. Obadiah found out that Daddy had trusted him, but it was too late. He was already dead."

My grandmother could barely fathom what she was hearing, and my mother barely spoke, but I hadn't yet gotten to the worse news.

"Guys…. that's not all. Obadiah also showed me something in his book, a symbol like… a spiraled circle of faces intertwined. He called it the Coven."

"Group of witches," my grandmother said.

I tried my best to explain it in a way that didn't sound horrifying, but there was no way of doing that.

"By the time the full moon comes, the witch won't just be channeling the moon to wipe out the district — she's resurrecting witches."

A deafening silence echoed throughout the room. The state of shock was clear on everyone's faces. I swung the envelope in my hand, forgetting that I had it. I looked down at it.

"Ana, what's that?" my mother asked.

"It's an envelope Obadiah gave me. He said Daddy gave it to him after he found out who the witch was. That's what got him killed."

"Well…. open it," Hanna said anxiously.

I pulled it open and reached inside to take it out…. it was a picture frame. I was sorely disappointed.

"Seriously!" I bellowed angrily. "This is it?"

It was a picture of a mother and her baby. I looked at the baby and noticed something familiar. The second time the Ol'Hige showed up, she was holding a portrait of a baby and the baby in this picture looked exactly like her.

"Grandma, look at this… is this who I think it is?"

My grandmother walked over and took the picture from me. She looked at it and her eyes widened.

"That's Eliza, and that's Constance," she said. "They must have digitized the picture. Haven't seen this in ages."

I took back the picture, and I paced around the room, looking at it.

"I was told that Eliza wasn't the witch, so why…."

I looked deeper. Constance, the baby, had a strange mark on her forearm.

"This mark looks so familiar," I said.

"What mark?" Dean asked, walking up to me staring at the picture.

I started muttering to myself, wondering where I had seen that mark before, in the same spot. Everybody stared at me like I was crazy, but something was oddly familiar about that mark. Then — it hit me, and I shuddered to even think about it, but it made perfect sense.

"Oh… my… god."

"Ana, you scaring me. What is it?" Hanna asked.

"After Romaine got sick, I got called into her office. She asked me a bunch of questions, wanting to know if he was okay, telling me stories about her life growing up. But…. how, how is she? Oh, my god!".

"Child, what is wrong with you?" My grandmother asked impatient,

I turned slowly to all of them.

"She's been here this whole time…. she never died…. it's her, not Eliza."

They all exchanged glances.

"Analisa, SPIT IT OUT!" shouted my mother.

"This mark on Constance's hand, Grandma. did you ever notice this mark before?" I asked.

"Can't recall. It was a long time ago and I've only seen her once or twice," she replied.

"Well, I did, and I have been seeing her for the past five years now."

"Who?" Hanna asked.

"Miss Wynters! Or should I call her by her actual name — Constance Johnson. She's alive…. she was the Ol' Hige witch…. all this time."

"Child, you speaking nonsense," said my grandmother. "Constance died years ago."

"You sure?" Dean asked, looking directly at me.

"Yes, it all makes sense. You all know me. I'm very visual. I remember things as clear as they come, and they stick with me. That is the same mark on Miss Wynter's forearm. Grandma, you said Constance died. Did they ever find her body?"

'Come to think of it. I don't they ever did," my grandmother theorized.

The revelation came as much as a shock to me as much as everybody else. All this time we had thought Eliza was behind all these attacks, coming back for revenge when it was her daughter, who we thought was dead, living all these years, teaching at our school. It made me sick to my stomach.

"If this is Constance, you know what that means?" I asked, looking at everybody.

"What?" my grandmother asked.

"We now know Miss Wynters is the witch. That she caused all these attacks. Madam Bruge and Obadiah were the only ones who could stop her, so she had to get them out of the way. She's waiting until the full moon, and she has the black book. Who wants to bet that she's not just stopping at raising any old witches? But one particular one."

They got into deep thought for a second and then, like a light bulb, it finally hit them.

"She's going to resurrect her mother. She's going to bring back Eliza," my grandmother said.

CHAPTER FOURTEEN
OL HIGE & THE FULL MOON

It was much worse than we thought. Constance and Eliza, both powerful witches at the height of their power, wreaking havoc on Belle Isle, was not good. My grandmother and my mother sat in the chair, pondering. This was something we weren't expecting at all.

"It was Miss Wynters the whole time," said Hanna still reeling from the shock. "That's impossible."

For five years, I had her as a teacher. All those years she was always kept a close eye on me. I always wondered why. To monitor me, know my every move. Finding out that someone who you admired and looked up to your entire life was the one creating havoc and trying to kill countless people, bored a deep hole in my heart. I felt betrayed, and I honestly wished I hadn't known. I was running out of people to trust.

I called up one of my friends from school, Trisha Stanford, who apparently thought I fell off the face of the earth. I asked her if she had seen Miss Wynters lately and how she was doing. Trisha told me she hadn't seen Miss Wynters in weeks and thought that she was sick. Even the principal hadn't seen her, which confirmed to me even more that she was Constance.

"So how we find her?" Dean asked.

Everyone looked at me. I didn't have the answer, even though it was obvious. Find her and burn her or burn her skin if we could get that close enough. But I didn't think it was going to be that easy. She knew we were unto her, and it was going to be a matter of time before she made her last move.

"The full moon is next week; we can't wait until that time comes," I said.

"How is she going to resurrect the witches?" Hanna asked.

"With the black book. That book caused everything that is happening, and we do not know where it is."

"Sooooo, if we find it, can we destroy it?"

I looked over at Dean, wondering the same thing.

"Maybe, but with a book that powerful, it has to be protected by dark magic, so simply burning it would be pointless."

"It has to be nearby. Miss Wynters office, maybe we should try there," Dean said.

"We can't go in there. It's a teacher's office."

Dean and I looked at Hanna very straight faced.

"A teacher we trusted; we just found out she is the Ol'Hige witch. There is no point in continuing to treat her like one.".

"Exactly, so we will go tomorrow evening, search her office, then leave."

The three of us agreed, but my grandmother became sceptical of everything. She had said nothing until now.

"It's very dangerous out there. I think you ought to sit this one out," my grandmother said in a very concerned tone.

"Grandma, I expected this from Mommy. I thought you more than anyone else would understand."

"If this is Constance, as you said, she has more hate in her heart for our family than we realized. Complete resentment for killing her mother. She has nothing to lose, which makes her even more dangerous and harder to defeat. I knew what Eliza was capable of, but Constance could be ten times worse."

I walked up to my grandmother and held her hand.

"You don't have to worry about us grandma, we're going to stop her once and for all," I said confidently. "But…. I think it's best that we are not in contact with each other."

"What is that supposed to mean?" my mother asked.

"It means Dean, Hanna and I are going to find somewhere secluded to stay, plan our attack so that we can end this, but not while we're here."

"Where are you going to stay? What you going to do for food? I don't want you out there like that," my mother said.

My mother was not happy about this plan. My grandmother was sad as well, but she gave a faint smile. She understood and caressed my cheek.

"Your mother has a right to feel scared. No parent wants to see their child take on something they don't understand. I am scared too, but you do what you must do to stop her. The fate of the district right now rests with you three. Your mother and I will look after Romaine," she said.

"Thank you, grandma," I said, wrapping my arms around her.

I let her go and turned to Dean and Hanna, telling them to go home and pack some things and to bring some extra cash. They agreed and left right away. I went into my room and started packing away some clothes in my bag and other essentials that I needed.

I didn't know where we were going or what we were going to do, but it was now or never. Taking the fight to the witch was now the only priority we had in our minds now.

Later that night, Dean and Hanna came back with full bags of clothes. I had already finished packing mine, and I made us a couple sandwiches to keep us until we were hungry again.

I headed out to the kitchen. Dean and Hanna were sitting, waiting for me. My grandmother and my mother were there too, not entirely happy to see us off, especially my mother. I hugged my grandmother and told her I loved her. She looked at me, caressed my cheek and kissed me on the forehead, as she had always done when I was little. My mother,barely kept eye contact with me. I walked over to her and turned her face towards me. She had the saddest eyes I had ever seen.

"Mommy, we will be fine," I said.

Her lips moved, but she could barely get the words out. She was speechless, trying her best to find something that would keep us in the house instead of going out to endanger myself, Dean, and Hanna.

"I don't know what else to say to you. I thought I could accept you risking your life, your schoolwork, your education to go fight some evil, but…. it's too much and I don't think I will ever accept it," she said firmly.

She smiled. She held on to my hand and kissed it. "I know you miss hearing you brother, God knows I miss hearing him too. Please…. please be careful. Make sure you have you phone with you because I'm going to be calling you and checking up on you. You hear me?"

"Yes, Mommy," I said, giving her a big hug.

She looked over at Dean and Hanna, calling them over for a hug as well.

"Please look after my little girl," my mother said.

"Yes ma'am," said Dean.

"We will."

She let them go and we took our bags and headed straight for the door. We closed it behind us and started walking until we reached the front of the road. It was chilly out, and we felt it. The breeze made this very eerie moaning sound that had us unsettled.

"Are we sure we're ready for this?" Hanna asked, looking rather unsettled.

"Nobody would be ready for this," Dean chimed in.

"We would be fools not to be, but there's no turning back now. We can't let Madame Bruges' vision come through."

Dean and Hanna agreed. I was playing the unflinching hero, but deep down I was way in over my head — but someone had to be brave. Further up the road, we walked. We looked back to see if a bus was coming, but it was way too dark to see anything. We would normally see a blaring light coming across the corner, but nothing came, so we thought it was best to just walk the way and see where the journey was going to lead us.

As we walked, we were tired. We passed Mr. Murray's shop and the town hall, which all looked deserted. The district was practically a ghost town. No one was out.

"This is creepy. It's like everybody's locked up in their houses and it's not even that late," Hanna said, looking all around her.

"I think they finally figured out what's happening around here," Dean said.

"I think so too. We need to get a bus; we can't keep walking like this. Hope we can find a shop."

Suddenly, we heard a loud engine. We turned but saw nothing. Then it got it even louder towards us. We backed away, but we still saw nothing.

Then a familiar sight appeared, and I was both shocked and relieved. The driver who drove me to meet Obadiah. The window came down and he stuck his neck out as usual, with his shades on. He pulled it down and glared at us, then he looked directly at me. He loved those shades.

"You seem to love walking the streets."

Dean and Hanna clammed up. The bus magically appearing in front of them had them in bewilderment. They wondered how I was so calm.

"Guys, it's a long story, will tell you about it once we get off the road."

"So, where are you headed?" The driver asked.

"Ahm, well thing is we don't know, we kinda just improvising," I said.

The driver stared at me like I spilled something on his shirt, or I told him something offensive.

"You just improvising? What kind of stupidness that you telling me? You know what is lurking in these streets at night, and you just improvising?"

Dean leaned over to me.

"Does he know about the W.I.T.C. H?" Dean asked.

The driver frowned at him.

"You know I can spell, right?".

"And you know he can hear you," I said to Dean, smacking him on the back of the head. "Yes, he knows. He's the one that took me to Obadiah. Speaking of which…. is he?"

The driver said nothing except give me a sombre look. I didn't know how to respond to that. Was he okay, was he dead, or was he not allowed to say anything?

"Look, we just need somewhere to crash for the time being undetected. We plan on taking down the witch before the full moon."

"Really now? So, you have it all figured out, eh?" he asked.

"No, but it's better than doing nothing."

"Fair enough, well get in. We have little time," he ordered.

The door flung open by itself, and I motioned to Dean and Hanna to get in. They were hesitant but had no choice but to trust me. Dean went in first, then Hanna second. I looked around me; the trees swayed silently, yet very eerily. I had a feeling she was out there lurking, watching us. I got in and the door closed itself. The driver then drove off.

Hanna and I turned to look at Dean. Mesmerized by the bus's interior, Dean touched everything from the seat to the handles and he kept sliding up and down like he was in some magical land.

"Dean…. seriously, what's wrong with you?" I asked, concerned.

"This bus…. it feels and looks big from the inside. It's a small bus but big on the inside. Wow!" he said.

The bus driver looked over for a moment, giving Dean the stink eye for putting his hands all over the leather.

"HEY! ARE YOUR HANDS CLEAN?" he snapped.

"Yes, my hands are clean," Dean responded hotly.

"Miss, tell your friend stop touching up my seats, please."

I reached over and slapped Dean on his hands. He shot me a nasty look and sank into the seat, folding his arms.

Hanna sat in between us laughing. She laughed out loud, then the three of us started laughing all the way.

I looked through the mirror and I could see that the driver's impatience. His brow furrowed. But deep down, I know he enjoyed our company. Half an hour later, we had completely left Belle Isle and went deep into the hills, where there were barely any lights on. The driver turned to where it was mostly bush, and he stopped. We looked around us and all we could hear were flickering sounds, and they got louder. Dean, Hanna, and I held hands. We didn't know what was happening and the driver just sat there, not saying a word.

"What's happening?" I asked.

"Just relax…. and wait," he said calmly.

Just then, brief flickers of light sprinkled around the bush and they lit up. The bush cleared and gave way, revealing an endless stretch of road. The fireflies were many, and they positioned themselves along the stretch to provide light. The driver turned to us.

"I told you not to worry. He's expecting you."

"Who?" I asked curiously.

The driver drove in further, following the fireflies as they lined off the road to give direction to wherever it is we were going. There was so much ugliness in the world of magic that we didn't realize the beauty in it as well.

As we neared to some sort of end, we noticed the fireflies flew off and dispersed into the air. It was so beautiful, but they revealed a small house.

"This is where you come off," the driver said.

I grabbed my bag and came out, then Dean and Hanna followed right out after. We looked up at the house. It was still dark, but the fireflies provided much needed light. The door closed, and I looked at the driver.

"Aren't you coming with us?"

He looked at me, smiled and broadened his shoulders.

"I belong on the road, child. I'm called when I'm needed," he said in a brave tone.

"Wait, how did you know when to come for us?" Dean asked.

The driver said nothing, and the window rolled up. He backed up and vanished in the dark. We stood there looking up at the house, the fireflies still hovering above us.

"Well, we're here, wherever here is," I said.

We walked up to the house and up the steps. I raised my hands to knock on the door, but the door slowly opened by itself. None of us wanted to go in, but then we heard a small hissing voice.

"*Come in.... don't be frightened,*" hissed the voice.

"Too late for that," said Dean shivering.

"Why should we?"

"Because it is bad manners to not accept a humble invitation," came a familiar voice.

Out of the darkness came a man whose face I was happy to see. It was Obadiah. He walked out, smiling at me. I ran up to hug him.

"Obadiah," I rejoiced.

"So, these are your friends?"

"Yes, that's Dean and Hanna."

"H… hi," Dean said stuttering.

"Nice to meet you," Hanna replied.

Obadiah stopped smiling and looked down at me.

"It's not safe to be out here, everyone come in," he said.

"Don't need to tell me twice," said Dean as he zipped past us into the house.

We stepped in and the door closed. The house was very dark that I could barely see where I was going. Then I heard a stool and a couple glasses being shattered followed by a loud, "OW!" and I knew all too well who that was. Suddenly, the candle lights flicked on, and the room became dazzling. The house was not what I expected. More like something dreary looking, old, with lots of mould; but the house looked very new.

Obadiah motioned us to sit. Dean and Hanna sat down and looked around the house. There was a painting above a small table. It was a group portrait at the very top; I recognized Obadiah standing with some other people, possibly the old Faction that he kept talking about, but then I saw a man, a man whose face I didn't need no reassurance about. Obadiah came behind me.

"Your father…. brave man he was," he said. "You should be proud."

"I am," I turned to him.

"I thought you were dead."

"It almost came to that, but I was lucky. I'm not so helpless, you know," he said smiling. "But I sense something is on your mind."

Looking at the picture of my father. He was youthful and happy.

"I know who the witch is," I said.

There was silence. Obadiah's expression was as normal as they come.

"You knew…. didn't you?" I asked.

"Yes…. I knew."

"Why didn't you just tell me?"

"It was my intention before I gave you that package, but we had company, if you recall," he said.

"How did you escape?" I asked. "Last time I saw you, Mr. Francis and his guys almost came down on you."

"I told you before, my snake always protects me. He bit your teacher and paralyzed him. We have him here locked up."

"He's here!" interrupted Dean as he jumped up.

Dean went into a full panic attack and there was no calming him down.

"Dean…. stop making a fool of yourself. He can't hurt us."

"You don't know that," he muttered.

"I want to see him," I said firmly.

"Are you sure about this?" Obadiah asked.

I nodded without hesitation.

"Very well, follow me."

I followed him out of the living room. Hanna grabbed Dean by the shirt collar and they tagged along.. Obadiah took the candle off the shelf, and we walked with him to a dark back room.

There was a symbol engraved on the floor, the same Raven symbol. Obadiah stretched his arm over it and muttered some words in a strange language.. The Raven glowed and made a hissing sound.

Its wings moved upright, and then the floor parted ways, revealing a spiral stairway. Dean, Hanna, and I looked on in amazement.

"Wow!" Hanna said.

"Follow closely and watch your step."

He stepped down first, and I followed closely behind with Dean and Hanna. The floor then closed above us and we continued on until we entered a very spacious room, like a meeting hall. The light flickered. It wasn't bright, but we could see that there was a round table centred in the middle of the room and books that could fill an entire library. Obadiah placed the candle on the shelf and turned to us.

"Welcome to the Faction's meeting room. Protected from unholy and unwanted magic."

The fascination of books already engulfed Dean. This was no surprise. Hanna was enthralled by the room itself.

"So, where is he? Where's Francis?" asked Dean.

Obadiah raised his arm above his head. We heard muffled screams coming from above. We looked up and saw a man plummeting towards the table below him. Suspended in mid-air. Obadiah held Mr. Francis still as he hovered; tied up and gagged. He looked up at me and suddenly, I could see the fury in his eyes. Apparently, he thought I was dead. I approached him slowly.

"Analisa, what you doing?" Dean asked.

I removed the gag from his mouth, and I stood there, staring at him.

"You're brave or stupid to come here, Miss Kelly," he snapped. "You and your pathetic friends. You have no idea what's coming."

He smiled.

"Cut the crap. We know the Ol'Hige is Miss Wynters and we know her real name."

His smile faded.

"We know her real name is Constance Johnson, and that she is planning to use the full moon to wipe out the entire district, bring back Eliza and the coven of witches. Am I close enough, or you just want to keep pretending we don't know anything?"

He struggled, trying to break free of Obadiah's hold on him, but he couldn't.

"You're not as dumb as you look after all, Miss Kelly. Certainly smarter than your father ever was."

My heart rate increased. My jaws clenched as soon as he mentioned my father. I had forgotten about it, but then the rage came rushing out like a thunderous flood.

"You killed my father," I whispered. "All because he knew her secret and you just couldn't allow him to go public, right?"

He snickered. "He deserved it. It was foolish of him to trust me," he said, grinning away. "Always loyal to the noble factions."

Suddenly, there was a hissing sound in my head. I couldn't hear anything else except that voice. It called to me. It felt my rage and I could hear it saying something to me. I was angry, too angry. I wanted to hurt him.

"Do it. He murdered your father; he doesn't deserve to live," hissed the voice.

I held on to my head and then covered my ears to drown out the voice.

"You know what you must do," the voice hissed again. *"It's over there in the corner. Pick it up."*

There was a knife on the shelf. I rushed over and grabbed it. I positioned the sharp knife at Mr. Francis' throat. He looked at me wide eyed and afraid.

"Ana DON'T!" shouted Hanna.

Dean pulled me back from going any further. This time, the hissing voice became clearer, more audible, like it was in the room with us. I turned around slowly and saw the snake…. Obadiah's snake, its piercing green eyes slithering towards us. Dean and Hanna froze in terror. I couldn't move even if I wanted to. I was more afraid of the snake than of wanting to kill Mr. Francis. The snake came up to my ears and started hissing.

"Do it, end his life. He causes your misery, your pain. He left you without a father. Put him out of his pathetic existence," the snake hissed.

I gripped the knife firmly and pressed it against his neck. I could see drips of blood oozing from his neck.

"Aren't you going to stop her?" Hanna asked, turning to Obadiah.

"Only Analisa can decide his fate. Let her choose."

"This is stupid. I'm stopping her," said Dean stepping off.

Obadiah grabbed him by his collar.

"If you make another step, you will never walk again. Let her be," he said, shoving Dean into the corner.

My hands trembled. I wanted to hurt him, make him pay for killing my father. The snake's taunting gnawed at me, clawing at my emotions.

"Do it.... DO IT NOW!!" snapped the snake.

The knife continued to shake in my hand and then I just dropped it.

"TEDAL NAH!" shouted Obadiah.

The snake froze and flew directly into Obadiah's hand, transforming itself back into a staff. I turned to him, furious.

"You were going to make me kill him?" I snapped.

"I would not make you do anything. That choice falls to you." .

Mr. Francis breathed a sigh of relief. I looked at him and then I just punched him hard in the face. Blood spewed from his lips, and he turned to me and only smiled.

"Didn't know you had it in you, Miss Kelly. You're more like you father than I realized."

"Where's Miss Wynters?"

Mr. Francis looked over at Obadiah and then looked back at me.

"It was very hard all these years trying not to kill you. Miss Wynters wanted so much to end you and your family, but she became drawn to you. She admires you."

"I don't want her to admire me. I want her to suffer."

"How is she alive? Not talking about Miss Wynters, her actual name. How is Constance alive?"

He twisted and turned, trying again to break free. I looked over at Obadiah, his hands still outstretched.

"Magic is a hell of a thing. The things you can do that no mere man can explain. It was hard to keep her hidden, but I knew I had to do it. I had to protect her.... didn't want to lose her. She was the only thing I had left.... after your grandmother killed her mother."

I could see the hatred in his eyes, the way he spoke about my grandmother, as if he knew her personally. Something wasn't right. Then Hanna walked up to me.

"Ana, what's wrong?" She asked.

"Who are you?" ignoring Hanna and looking directly at Mr. Francis.

He grinned, then his face widened and morphed into something ugly. He groaned as his face changed in front of us and he held his head down. Even Obadiah looked shocked. Mr. Francis cried out and shook his head all over the place.

"What's happening to him?" Dean asked.

Then — he was calm. He lifted his head up slowly, sweat dripping heavily from his face. But he was now different. I didn't recognize him.

"Who is this now?" Hanna asked.

I looked at him, and I couldn't picture him. I didn't know who he was. I turned to Obadiah and his eyes widened, his mouth agape.

"It's not possible."

Mr. Francis turned to him, smiling. "Like I said…. magic is a hell of a thing.".

"Obadiah, who is this?" I asked.

"Victor Johnson."

"Constance's father!" Hanna said, shockingly.

"Surprised," he smiled.

"One of the oldest council members in Belle Isle practiced Obeah?" I asked, astonished, "How are you still alive?"

"You'll be amazed at what aging spells can do," he snickered. "At the full moon, my daughter will be at the peak of her power, resurrect her sweet mother, and destroy Belle Isle. With that said, bye bye."

Suddenly, a loud crack. Then, a lightning bolt came crashing down, burst through the ceiling and zapped Mr. Francis, releasing him from Obadiah's grip, and he threw all of us across the room. Then he disappeared. Suddenly, there was a loud bang upstairs. The house then collapsed, and the walls crumbled. There was debris and smoke everywhere.

My ears rung, and the pain was excruciating.

I got up slowly and tried to clear my vision through the thick smoke. I could hear faint coughing and voices calling my name. It was Dean and Hanna. I was happy they were okay.

"Dean! Hanna! Obadiah! Everybody okay?" I shouted out.

Cough! *Cough!* "Ana- we're here. Where are you?" Hanna called out.

"I'm next to the window," I said.

I looked over, but there was no more window. The lightning had completely obliterated a section of the house, leaving an enormous gaping hole. I climbed on the rubble searching for Dean and I could hear him moaning over by the corner, with Obadiah slumped over beside him. I helped Dean up and went over to Obadiah.

"Is he?" Dean asked.

I felt his hand jerk, and he grabbed on to mine. He looked up at me. He was weak. There was a piece of board lodged deep into his chest. My eyes widened at the sight, and I turned to Dean with a grim look.

"I don't think he's going to make it," I said gravely.

"We have to help him.".

Obadiah pulled on me further and tried to talk.

"M… my… stick… get my stick."

"Look for his staff," I said to Hanna.

Hanna looked around for the stick.

She brushed aside little rubbles of stone and gasped at what she saw. I turned to her, and I could tell by her expression it wasn't anything good. She took up a broken piece of Obadiah's staff — pieces, to be exact.

"Oh, no," I said.

I didn't have to say anything to Obadiah for him to realize what had happened to his staff. He was weak but torn. He must have had that staff for a long time, and now it was just a shattered piece of wood. I felt terrible for him. He then grabbed my hand, and I thought he wanted to get up, so I tried pulling him, but he instead drew me closer and whispered something to me. I listened attentively and nodded. As I moved away and looked at him, he took his last breath and expired right before me. I closed his eyes, got up and walked past Dean and Hanna towards the kitchen. They followed me.

"Analisa, what did he say to you?" Dean asked.

I was way too angry to answer. Dean called to me two more times, but I didn't listen.

"ANA!" Hanna shouted.

"WHAT!" I shouted back, shaking with anger.

Hanna and Dean stared at me, concerned.

"How many more have to die because of me?" I asked.

"Stop blaming yourself. None of this is your fault."

"Even if you knew nothing about the Ol'Hige, she would have still come after you, after all of us," Dean chimed in.

I walked up to the cupboard, opened it, and I saw another compartment inside.

There was a pack with a white substance in it and a small blade. I took them out and showed them to Dean and Hanna.

"He told me to take these. Slaves who practiced obeah crafted this blade."

"How does a blade stop evil?" Dean asked.

"It was coated with the blood of a pure-hearted. Anything it touches instantly burns them but doesn't kill them."

"So, we can use that on Constance," said Hanna.

"Yes, but we need to be careful."

We hid Obadiah's body in a safe place and gave him a proper burial. After leaving the house, we took precautions. We had to find somewhere else to stay.

Dean, Hanna, and I wandered out to the front, and the bus driver came out to us. The look on his face was very grave, and he felt that Obadiah's essence was no longer there. We told him we had to find somewhere else to stay. We had four more days left until the full moon was upon us and we hadn't a clue where Constance was going to be or where she was going to carry out her plans.

The driver told us that there was nowhere else he could take us, that the witch couldn't find us and if she wanted to find us, she would. With that said, he drove off and didn't stop even after we protested.

"What are we going to do now?" Hanna asked.

"I don't know," I said gravely.

We turned and walked back up to the house.

There was no door to shut ourselves in, so we had to go back down into the room. We searched and searched through the rubble for anything else that could help us, but so far, we found nothing except books and skulls that were now crushed.

"Everything's destroyed. There's nothing here," Dean said.

I picked up a rock and threw it through a broken glass, breaking it further.

"I'm done…. can't take it," I said.

"You're giving up?".

"Dean…. look around. Everywhere we go, everything we touch is destroyed. Maybe Mommy and grandma were right. We're just children fighting a war we have no business in. Going up against a witch we're no match for. We want to be heroes so bad; we didn't stop to consider she might actually kill us this time."

Hanna strolled over to me. She put her hands on my shoulder.

"Analisa, we're alive because of you. We're not the bravest set in the group, but it's because of you why we survived. We couldn't do this without you and if you give up, what hope do the both of us have?"

Dean walked over as well.

"You're the reason we're here. If you give up now, if you want to put all this behind you, we'll give up with you — but if you want to fight, we'll fight to the last breath beside you," Dean said, holding on to my hands. "The district needs us. Your brother needs us."

I smiled at them. "Thanks guys."

Suddenly, we heard a noise outside, crackling sounds.

"What was that?" Hanna asked.

We got up instantly and headed towards the entrance, grabbing the blade and gripping it firmly.

It would have been smarter to stay put whenever you heard a strange sound rather than play hero, but we weren't safe anywhere. So, we were prepared to fight to the end. It was a much better option than being scared.

"Stay close to me, guys," I said.

Dean and Hanna stuck close to me, as I had the blade ready.

We walked out; we saw nothing, but we noticed we could see our reflection. We looked up into the sky and to our shock — there it was, the full moon. The moon wasn't supposed to show until a couple days time. Was it wrong? Did we get the date wrong? Were we tricked?

Then, something huge blocked out the light. A large, dark figure rose from over the roof, hovering above us like a looming cloud with wings extended. It was her — the witch, in owl form, and this time…. a lot bigger. The giant owl loomed over us with its frightening red eyes and brandished a devilish smile.

"Now that I have you all together, I can finally get rid of you," sneered the Owl.

 Dean and Hanna grabbed on to me. I turned to them and they were deeply frightened. They looked to me for guidance, to protect them. I couldn't let them down, so I gripped the blade and turned, looking at the owl directly.

"Come get us, you ugly sack of filth!" I shouted.

The Owl's face contorted something ugly. It didn't like that. The owl shrieked and jumped off with its talons cracking the roof as it soared directly towards us. Dean and Hanna ran off immediately, but I stood there, waiting. Dean and Hanna turned and told me to run, but I didn't move. The Owl's sharp talons extended as it came closer. I jumped out of the way, just enough time to swing the blade. It sizzled as it grazed the left wing. The Owl screeched in pain, crashing into the ground. Its head spun, fixating its gaze on me.

"YOU WILL PAY DEARLY FOR THAT," snapped the owl.

"ANALISA COME ON!" Shouted Dean.

I joined Dean and Hanna as we ran out onto the road and didn't look back. There were no cars or anything in sight, so we continued to run until we got as far away from the witch as possible. Hanna kept turning her head, and then she stopped. We stopped and turned to her.

"Hanna, what you doing? Come on," I shouted.

"You hear that?" She asked.

We walked up to her, wondering what she was talking about.

"Hear what?"

We heard loud flapping and then, a massive wind developed like a hurricane. The trees started swaying violently, and we were being lifted off our feet, unable to maintain balance. I looked up; it was the Owl flapping its giant wings, which flung Dean and I backwards, while Hanna stood in front, trying to cover herself.

"HANNA!" I shouted.

I shouted as loudly as I could, but because of the heavy wind generated from the owl's wings, I couldn't hear myself, nor could Hanna hear me. We couldn't keep our balance much longer and we flew backwards, landing on our backs. The pain was unbearable, but nothing was as unbearable as hearing Hanna screaming. I got up instantly and looked out. Hanna was no longer there.

"AHHHHH!!!" Hanna screamed.

This time, the scream came from behind me. I turned around and saw the Owl soaring through the sky with Hanna clutched in its talons.

"HANNA!!!"

Dean got up and his mouth fell open. He wheezed. "Oh, no! No no no," he repeated as he paced up and down. "She's going to kill her! She's going to kill her!"

I slapped him across the face. He looked at me, holding on to his face.

"Get a grip. We're no good to Hanna if we panic."

"THE OWL JUST TOOK HANNA, THERE IS TIME TO PANIC!" snapped Dean.

Dean was angry. I could feel it, like he wanted to punch something. I felt it too. The full moon was here a bit earlier than we expected and soon, Constance was going to unleash hell in the district. Dean turned to me.

"You have the salt?" he asked.

I dug into my pocket and felt it, then I nodded. We saw a bright light shining on us down the road. A bus drove towards us and stopped. It was Obadiah's bus driver. We opened the door and hopped in. The driver turned to us.

"You guys okay?" he asked.

"Now you care? Just drive," I spat.

He pressed the gas and drove on.

"Had to leave, knew she was coming back, so now I know where she is going," he said as kept swerving and driving like a madman.

"Where?" I asked.

"Where everything started."

Dean and I looked at each other.

"What you mean?" Dean asked.

"The cottage — up on the hill in Belle Isle where her mother was burnt alive. It is where she is going."

"That's impossible. That cottage was destroyed," I said.

"It did, but before she died, Eliza performed a spell, a spell so powerful that it practically drained her. She latched a part of her soul onto the very living thing that was there with her, the Owl. In case anything happened to her, the Owl was protected."

"I don't get it. Why protect the Owl?" Dean asked, "What's the point?"

"No one knew. Maybe she thought someone would avenge her death, bring her back to life or something."

"But how did the cottage come back?" I asked.

The driver was silent. Either he didn't want to tell us, or he really didn't know himself.

Hours later, we made it back to Belle Isle. We hopped out of the bus and looked up the very steep hill with the full moon, big and bright, shining right over it. The moon looked so beautiful, but it was a pity it was going to be used to bring about the destruction of the district. We turned to the driver, and he looked at us as if he was sorry to see us go.

"Obadiah told me that whatever happens, I was to bring you back here. You would know what to do. He spoke a lot about you. I never see what he saw in you. I mean — you're just a child. But now…. you're a lot braver than I ever was and I think you can finally put an end to that witch," he said, smiling.

He extended his arms, and I looked down. I shook his hand and smiled back at him. He took up his shades from off the dash and slid them on. Then he drove off and disappeared.

Dean and I looked at each other.

"Maybe we should tell our folks that we're back," Dean said.

"No… not yet. We don't want them to panic anymore. We don't need them asking why Hanna isn't with us," I said.

I grabbed the blade from out of my pockets and took out two bags filled with salt.

"You brought two?" Dean asked, astonished.

"Yeah, in case we miss the first time."

"I hope Hanna is okay," Dean said sadly.

I put the salt bags back into my pocket and held on to the knife.

"She is… now let's bring her back."

We stood there looking up at the hill. It was going to be a long night. A showdown between us and the witch and there was no turning back now.

CHAPTER FIFTEEN
THE TRAP

We started walking, and I just remembered that we hadn't eaten anything. I turned to Dean and he looked famished. Should we have stopped to get something to eat before we continued? The thought had crossed my mind to go back, but Hanna was in danger, so we had to put our hunger aside until this was all over.

There was so much of school we had missed this past month. We didn't know if school was still in session with everything that was going on. The community service project that the principal wanted us to take part in seemed like a lost cause.

We were halfway up the hill and I wondered to myself as my grandmother was telling us the story, how she ever climbed without getting tired. It was so steep and rocky and there were bushes everywhere and monstrous mosquitoes who acted like they didn't feed in years. It was a beautiful sight, very majestic at night, peaceful. The stars twinkled brightly in the sky and I smiled. Then, through the clear opening above the tall trees, I could see the full moon shining brightly.

"Imagine, something so beautiful is going to be used to bring so much pain," Dean said.

"Try not to think about that. We're going to save Hanna and stop her."

It seemed like a never-ending climb up this hill and our feet hurt. I heard Dean mumble behind me. I turned around, and he had stopped to sit on a rock.

"Dean, come on. We can't stop."

"Ana, I'm tired. Let us at least rest before we continue. Hey, you brought food with you, right?" He asked.

I had completely forgotten that I did, in fact, pack food for us. But I left the bag at the house when we were running away from the Owl. I sat beside Dean, very upset.

We hadn't eaten since the time we left and now we were weak from hunger. Then I looked up, and I saw a tree filled with mangoes.

"Hey, you want to get us some mangoes?".

"Where?" He asked.

I pointed to the tree above us and he sprang up instantly, went over to the tree, and started climbing. He was very agile, especially with mangoes. He loved them. He grabbed four and brought them over. We devoured the mangoes in one go. They were so delicious; they were more than enough to sustain us throughout the night.

After finishing the mangoes, we got up and walked further to find water. We found a little stream up ahead. We stopped to wash our hands and our faces to keep us alert and ready. I looked over at Dean, who looked energized as well.

"You ready?" I asked.

"Very much," he said confidently.

I smiled at him, then we moved again. Suddenly, we heard moaning in the distance. It was all around us. We looked up and saw strange images swirling around above.

"What is that?" Dean asked.

"Looks like she's starting. Look!" I said, pointing forward.

There was a strange green light ahead. Then we heard a loud blood-curdling scream.

Dean and I looked at each other and we knew who that was.

"Hanna," we said together.

We climbed faster up the hill, and I pulled the blade from my pocket. We heard more screams, but they weren't coming from above. They were now coming from below us, from the district. My mouth fell in horror as I feared what was happening.

"She's doing it! People are being killed down there by her. The book must be in her possession," I said.

"But why does she need Hanna?" Dean asked.

I thought, then it came to me.

"She needs a host," I said with a frightened thought.

"For what?"

"For the one person she wants back in her life."

Dean's eyes widened.

"Eliza," he said.

"Constance has been toying with us the whole time. She wanted to separate us, catch us off guard so she could take one of us to complete her plan."

We saw fire hovering above us. It looked like a fireball. Then we saw more fireballs heading towards the district. It spread rapidly, destroying houses.

"NOOOO!" I shouted.

I turned and looked up into the direction of the green light. I couldn't grip the knife anymore because of the level of anger I felt rising within me. I climbed further, and Dean followed behind me. We almost reached to the top, but we didn't want to be seen. So, we looked for another path and hid behind a bush.

Hanna was tied up with twigs on a stone table. She struggled and tried to break free, but she couldn't. She was crying. There must have been some way to free her without the witch seeing us. We didn't see Constance anywhere. Then something happened. We saw a blurry image appear before us and then suddenly, a cottage came into view, and from looking at it, it looked just like the Cottage my grandmother spoke about in her story; it was still intact. The door swung open, and we saw her, the moonlight glistening off her skin — Miss Wynters, The Ol'Hige, the witch herself. She had something in her hand. I was still in disbelief.

"Look!" I whispered to Dean, "The black book."

"We have to get it away from her," Dean said.

Hanna squirmed, trying to wiggle her way free.

"Why are you doing this, Miss Wynters? I thought you loved us."

Constance stretched her hand out and muttered a spell. Twigs grew from out of the ground, forming a stand. She placed the book on top and opened it, skipping through a bunch of pages. She then took out a large knife and looked at Hanna. She smiled. She stroked Hanna's face and Hanna shrugged her off.

"My dear, sweet Hanna, you should never have been involved in this. I've always admired you, but you're not to blame. It's the cost of being at the wrong place at the wrong time. You know, you really ought to have better friends. But after tonight, it won't matter."

"You can't keep punishing the district for what happened to your mother," Hanna said.

Constance's face flushed red with anger.

"You know nothing about this district. This district treated my mother like an outcast, like she didn't have a right to live or have a family. She was just minding her own business until they killed her. Now, Belle Isle will know what it feels like to burn in fire."

"Who told you that?" Hanna asked. "Miss Mable said---"

"DON'T…. EVER MENTION THAT NAME TO ME!" she snapped.

Constance's eyes flashed red, then faded.

"I should have killed that old woman the moment I laid eyes on her. She was the main reason my mother is dead."

"But she loved you. She said you were the sweetest and most beautiful thing she ever saw. You were just a baby; you couldn't have known anything."

Constance grabbed Hanna by the jaw and Hanna clamped up.

"You've always been the chatty one, even in class you just…. wouldn't…. stop…. talking. And yes, I was just a baby when all that happened. But my father told me everything. He told me how they tortured her and threw her in the fire," Constance said, "And for that, she and this district will perish."

She turned the page in the book and looked up. Her eyes turned bloodshot red, and she chanted.

"EVIC UL TUC SAVIR CAN TUL, EVIC UL TUC SAVIR CAN TUL."

Something was happening. I could feel it. Dean and I saw streams of white light flowing through the air towards Constance. She was stealing essences, the very thing we were afraid of. The light swam through the air swiftly, all-around Constance until it went straight through her. She smiled and exhaled happily. She looked down at Hanna, who was beyond terrified.

"Now, little one, you will witness the power of Constance Johnson, daughter of Eliza Gutzmer. Once I resurrect my mother, she will be weak. She will need a young, vibrant host," said Constance in a distorted voice.

Hanna's eyes widened at the revelation.

"Nobody is possessing this girl, you're mad Miss Wynters, please let me go, please. I promise I won't tell anyone," Hanna pleaded.

"SILENCE," Constance thundered. "You don't have a choice. Your district could have saved her. Instead, they watched her burn. And now they shall know what genuine pain is."

I listened, and I was horrid at the lie that Constance was told. Her father lied to her and twisted her into thinking that they killed her mother. Eliza had stepped into that fire and killed herself. Dean and I were getting uncomfortable, so we thought of moving, but then we heard a twig snap behind us. Then we felt ourselves being grabbed and shoved out into the open. Hanna and Constance looked over. Hanna's eyes widened with joy when she saw us.

"Ana, Dean… you shouldn't have come."

"We would not leave you here Hanna," Dean said.

Mr. Francis was holding us when I turned around. I looked over at Constance. and I still felt the betrayal, knowing that this face who taught me for years, the woman I looked up to, was a cold-blooded, psychotic witch. Constance walked up to me and Dean.

"I know how you must feel, Analisa," she said.

"Don't talk to me," I snapped. "You have no idea how I feel. So, everything you told me about your parents. All of it was a lie."

Constance grinned.

"It wasn't all a lie. I had to let you in. Feed your vulnerability. Believe it or not, I sympathize with you. I do. But the very people you fight for are the same people who murdered my mother."

Mr. Francis gripped us harder. I did my best not to let him see the knife. I slid the knife into my back pocket.

"My father was the one who took care of me. My siblings loved me. I had them. But my mother was gone, thanks to your grandmother."

"Did your father even tell you about their relationship? Did he even tell you how they met?" I asked.

"What does it matter? She had her killed."

"WRONG!" I shouted. "Your mother went on a rampage. Do you know why? She was killing everything and everybody, because she thought you were dead."

Constance's expression suddenly changed, as if she was hearing this for the first time. I observed her and I realized, based on her expression, it was obvious she never knew.

"You didn't know? Your father never told you, did he?" I asked, looking up at Mr. Francis.

He became livid and roughed me up more.

"SHUT UP!" he snapped. "Darling, let's just kill them now."

"Quiet Father," she said, "What you mean she thought I was dead?"

"My grandmother told us everything. Eliza was told that you had died when they took you. That sent her over the edge. They had to stop her. But her death was her own doing. She stepped into that fire. The flames got bigger, and the house collapsed along with her."

Constance paced, looking confused.

"Obadiah, the man you killed, told me before he died, that your father lied to you, to keep you from her, so he could twist your thoughts and train you for his own purposes."

"I said shut up."

Mr. Francis said, throwing us to the ground. He took out a knife from his back pocket and moved towards us, but then…. he couldn't move. He looked up. Constance's hands were outstretched, controlling him.

"Constance… what are you doing?" he asked.

"Is she telling the truth? Did you have people tell my mother that I was dead?" Constance asked.

"You're letting these children warp your mind child, KILL THEM!"

"I am not a child anymore. You need to answer me," she said shakily.

Mr. Francis looked away and then turned back to her.

"Yes…. yes, I did for your protection."

Constance was livid, almost brought to tears.

"Your mother was becoming unstable. I had to take you away from her," he tried to explain.

"She was unstable because you told her I was DEAD!!!" she bellowed.

Suddenly, Mr. Francis choked. His eyes bulged out, and he was floating in the air. He pulled and pulled at this throat, trying to breathe. Constance's eyes flared. Mr. Francis reached out to her, but it would not save him. Then, he shrank. His entire body became sunken until the only thing left were bones, then his corpse fell.

Constance exhaled slowly and looked over at us.

"This changes nothing. I still want you dead," she said.

She looked up at the moon, then she groaned and grabbed her stomach. Her skin started to shed.. Her features changed, then her skin fell to the ground. What stood in her place was over 50 feet tall, covered in feathers. She turned into the owl, but now it was much bigger, its beak extended, and the eye sockets got thinner. Her pupils remained sharp red. She looked at us and smiled.

"Time to die," the owl snarled.

Hanna screamed. The Owl looked towards Hanna, then to us, allowing us to run. The owl shrieked loudly, and we could tell she was angry.

There was a giant flapping of wings and trees being knocked down. We hurried.

"We left Hanna," Dean said.

We stopped behind a large bush and kept our heads down.

"Hanna will be fine. I'm going back to get her. She shed her skin. Now it's our chance."

"How are we going to get past her? She's too fast," said Dean.

Before I could answer, loud footsteps trampled throughout the hill. The giant owl sprinted, looking for us, sniffing.

"You can't hide from me children. You will not leave this hill alive," the owl threatened.

Dean and I tried to keep our composure. We had to be quiet. Dean wheezed, and I had to cover his mouth. I looked around; the Owl stopped and turned quickly, coming over in our direction. It sniffed again, then chuckled.

"Clever children, you are the only ones who have ever lasted this long against my onslaught. I was too careless. I grew too fond of you three that I let my mission falter. No matter, that will not happen again because I will feast on your bones.".

Its beak came close to us. It was terrifyingly close. Suddenly, we heard crickets and the Owl quickly got distracted and scampered away. We breathed a sigh of relief and I reached into my pocket, taking out one of the two bags and handed them to Dean. He looked down and tried to give them back to me.

"Why are you giving me this? You do it," Dean said.

"She will suspect one of us to do it. Just trust me. When the time is right, you will throw the salt to me and then I will finish it," I said.

Dean nodded, but it was clear he didn't agree with the plan. I slowly got up.

"HEY! Over here! You ugly old bird," I shouted.

The Owl's head jerked. Its red eyes glared at me.

"Analisa!!" It hissed.

It flew towards me instantly, and I started running for my life. In the back of my mind, I was worried that Dean could not come through, but I trusted him.. I made it to the front where Hanna was, but then I tripped in front of the skin. It was disgusting to look at. The owl was coming. I quickly got up, took the matches from out of my pocket. I looked over, and I saw Dean sprinting from the other side and as he attempted to throw the bags, the Owl got to him before he could throw them and crushed the bags with its talons.

"NOOO!" shouted Hanna.

 Dean tried getting up, but the Owl rested its giant talons on his head. Dean screamed in agony.

"LET HIM GO!" I shouted.

The owl cackled. "Was this your plan? To trick me into chasing you so that you can use salt against me? I thought you were smarter than this Analisa."

The Owl increased the pressure on Dean's head more and Dean looked as if he was about to pass out. I held my head down.

"You have lost Analisa," the owl said, "I'm far more powerful than my mother ever was. I was going to resurrect her and other witches, but why bother. I can reach all babies at will now without being near them, and there is nothing you can do to stop me from killing them, and you."

I laughed, then I held my head up.

"I've already done it. You were so busy boasting about how powerful you are, you didn't think anybody could defeat you. Your pride is what will get you killed," I said as I lit the match.

"You have no salt," the Owl said. "Fire alone won't kill me."

"You thought you got rid of the salt? That bag you crushed wasn't salt, it was flour," I said, "When I fell, I did that on purpose to do this," I said, pointing to the skin.

The owl's beak fell open, and it took its talons off Dean's head. Dean got up instantly. The owl stared at the skin and saw little sprinkles of white substance.

"No… no no!" screamed the Owl.

"You have messed with my family for the last time. Burn in hell," I shouted.

"NOOO!!!!" shrieked the owl"

As she attempted to fly towards me, I threw the match on the skin, and it went up in flames. Suddenly the Owl's wings flamed up and it screeched in agony. Her wings flapped all over like a raging bull, flinging itself against the trees. The fire slowly spread all over its body. Its screams were awful and then…. it went up in smoke, leaving nothing but ash — the witch was dead.

Dean and I stood and watched as the witch's ashes floated and vanished.

"Ahm…. Hello," Hanna said.

I ran over to her, untied and helped her off the stone rock. I looked up and the cottage itself imploded, sucking itself into non-existence. Hanna turned to me and smiled.

"You saved me," she said.

"You're my friend. I wouldn't leave you like that," I said, winking at her.

Hanna hugged me tightly. Thank you, Analisa, you're a great friend.".

I hugged her back, then I felt Dean coming behind me and flung his arms in..

"Let's get out of here. I'm starving," I said.

"For real, those mangoes are going to go real fast," Dean said.

Then he let out a very loud belch.

Hanna and I looked at him in disgust and smacked him across the head.

Then we laughed, like really laughed. We were happy again, happier than we had ever been these past months.

"Wait!" Hanna jumped up.

"What, what, is it, Constance again?" Dean exclaimed, looking all around him.

"No, no, the book…. it's gone," she said. "Was it destroyed?" Hanna asked in a panic.

"I don't think so, but I hope we don't have to see it ever again. Let's go," I said.

The three of us walked down the hill, and we headed straight for home.

CHAPTER SIXTEEN
REWARD

My mother and grandmother gleamed with joy when they saw us. But nothing could fill my heart with warmth when I saw a tiny thing cuddled up in my mother's arms, thrilled to see me—cheerful and laughing. Tears flowed down my cheeks when I saw him.

"Romaine," I said emotionally.

I ran towards him, and I hugged and kissed him. He laughed out so loud and drooled on me. He grabbed on to my hair and I just stood there admiring him.

"I missed you so, so much. I'm so happy you're awake."

My mother touched me on my shoulder. I looked over at her and she was happy.

"You did it…. you did it," she said as she hugged me. My grandmother, Dean and Hanna all came in and we all hugged each other.

"We heard a sound coming from your mother's room. Opened the door and saw Romaine, talking up a storm," my grandmother said.

We all laughed.

"I'm proud of you, Analisa."

"Thanks grandma."

Two weeks later, the mayor wanted us to come to the town hall. They were having a general meeting to discuss clean-up efforts for the district and how to move forward, especially with the houses that were destroyed. On the day, my mother and I, my grandmother and Romaine sat in front. Dean and Hanna sat behind me. I looked around and the town hall was much crowded now, even Ann-Marie was there. The council members were on stage murmuring amongst themselves, then they looked out and addressed us.

"During these past months, there have been a series of unexplained deaths. Now, we in the Belle Isle district have always been a proud people, with proud values that believe in the human spirit, human nature. Even though we believe in God and the devil, good and evil, we never yet focused on the thought that there might be supernatural events happening around us. We have lived in denial, and it cost us dearly. What I am glad to announce is that the babies who developed the sickness again two weeks ago have all miraculously gotten better. Also, there are some things that we thought were best kept secret to prevent any panic amongst its citizens. We realize now, this was a colossal blunder on our part. With that said, on behalf of myself and members of the Belle Isle board, we like to apologize."

Romaine looked at me and started playing with my face, and smiled at me. I kissed him up a lot and smiled back. I held on to his fingers and he grabbed onto mine.

"Now that we know that these attacks on our children and the district were caused by the supernatural, we want to thank three brave, wonderful young people and we would like to ask them to come up on stage," he said. "I would like to call Analisa Margaret Kelly, Dean Walters, and Hanna Greenwood."

The entire town's hall clapped us. My grandmother took Romaine from me and the three of us strolled up to the stage and stood next to each other. The mayor placed a medal over each of us and then he shook our hands.

"I would like to thank you three for showing us great courage and great loyalty, where the people would not listen to reason. You three were braver than all of us combined, and you saved us all and for that, I present to you these medals."

The crowd clapped and cheered again. Dean, Hanna, and I exchanged glances and smiled, looking at our medals. Mayor Burton took up a paper and ordered the crowd to settle down.

"Also, since you had to sacrifice your education, sacrifice your lives to take upon your shoulders the problems that had befallen this town. I present to you three a cheque for $900,000 dollars as it will help you with tuition to continue your education and to help your families with bills or anything outstanding. You deserve it."

The mayor, his board members, and everyone in the hall got up and clapped for us.

I was overwhelmed. I thought nothing like this would ever happen to me, but we did it, for my family, for my friends, and for my district.

Later in the week, based on the conversation I had with the principal before, I wanted to do something with the community project and I used most of the cheque money that we got, to help the families who lost their children, to help them cope again. Those whose houses were burnt by the fire, we wanted to help them out. So, we had many treats for each of them. The boys from the home also came and helped with the day's activities. Dean and Hanna were busy making the children happy and helping them to paint. There were so many fun activities there; horseback riding, go cart games, and many other games. Everybody had fun. I stood behind the table and looked at what I had accomplished and what I made possible.

My mother came up to me and hugged me. She held on to my cheeks and smiled. "I'm so proud of you."

"Thank you, Mommy."

"You are getting mature," my mother said.

"Why are you surprised?"

She shook her head and chuckled.

"I have strong family support," I said.

"Yes, I'm sure your father is proud of you."

I held on to my necklace and smiled. "Yes, I think he is, too."

The emotions were overwhelming. I looked up. The clouds were moving, and the sky grumbled. It's as if my father was speaking to me.

"I miss you, Daddy. I wish you were here," I said, tears running down my cheeks.

My mother and I walked off together. Everything was good, everyone was happy and there were no more problems. However, one thing still bothered me…. the black book was still missing. That same night, something even more peculiar happened. I was in bed and I felt cold, like I was sitting on a block of ice. Suddenly, I heard a sharp scream and broken plates.

My eyes flung open quickly, and I felt strange and light. I turned and saw my mother with her hands clasped over her mouth. But I was looking down at her. It was then I realized…. I was levitating.

THE END

THE AUTHOR

Born and raised in Jamaica to Guy and Dian McCallum, Maurice McCallum is an avid reader of fictional and non-fictional stories. A graduate of the Edna Manley School of Drama and the University of the West Indies, Maurice has a flair for the dramatic and enjoys using his imagination to craft the most vivid and interesting stories. Maurice is a teacher of English and Drama and often lends his writing skills in the classroom when the need calls for it. Maurice's passion for writing garnered the attention of international actress, producer and author, Jacinth Headlam. Impressed with his writing ability, Jacinth gave Maurice an opportunity to pen her personal projects, and quickly rose as her main writer. He was also tapped as writer for her short film and current feature holiday film, Love After, based on her autobiography of the same name, which has won multiple awards and gained international acclaim.

Maurice's passion for writing has grown into him now becoming a published author and earning him several writing jobs in Film production and TV; such as his new YouTube web series, "I'm A Good Wife" by actress Shari Ellis. When he's not writing, Maurice loves to mentor young children and adolescents into being a better version of themselves as future generation of artists and masters of their craft. Like his late father, Maurice loves to impart knowledge and hopes to make a difference in people's lives, as his father did.

THIS BOOK IS DEDICATED IN LOVING
MEMORY OF MY FATHER,
GUY RUDOLPH MCCALLUM.